MW00945123

Advance Praise for
Pangu's Shadow

"Since *Dove Arising*, I have been waiting with bated breath for Bao's next SF—and *Pangu's Shadow* totally delivers! This stellar outer-space murder mystery is action-packed and beautifully nuanced. The writing is evocative, the science is fascinating, the characters are as brilliant as they are endearing, and the dual POV narration is heartbreakingly intimate."

—Romina Garber, *New York Times* and international bestselling author of *Zodiac* and *Lobizona*

"This technology-infused whodunnit combines an insider's perspective on STEM culture with truly creative, exploratory worldbuilding that teases the boundaries of what science fiction can do as a genre—and the results are an awful lot of fun."

—Andrea Tang, author of *Rebelwing*

"Full of humanity and heart, *Pangu's Shadow* will rivet readers with an out-of-this-world murder mystery and capture their hearts with an enthralling rivals-to-lovers romance. A unique, timely, and iconic addition to the young adult mystery canon!"

—Katie Zhao, author of *How We Fall Apart*

"*Pangu's Shadow* is a pitch-perfect murder mystery wrapped up in a scientific bow. A searing indictment of a system that discriminates against and 'others' so many of us, this book breathes life into our souls, shines brilliantly in its honesty, and ultimately sparks hope for us all. The disability rep and found family made my heart dance. Who knew science could make me feel so much?"

—Cody Roecker, Naperville Public Library

Pangu's Shadow

Karen Bao

carolrhoda LAB
MINNEAPOLIS

Carolrhoda Lab®
An imprint of Lerner Publishing Group, Inc.
241 First Avenue North
Minneapolis, MN 55401 USA

For reading levels and more information, look up this title at
www.lernerbooks.com.

Design elements: Nick Northern/EyeEm/Getty Images; Anton Eine/EyeEm/
Getty Images.

Main body text set in Janson Text LT Std.
Typeface provided by Adobe Systems.

Library of Congress Cataloging-in-Publication Data

Names: Bao, Karen, author.
Title: Pangu's shadow / Karen Bao.
Description: Minneapolis, MN : Carolrhoda Lab, [2024] | Audience: Ages 12–18. |
    Audience: Grades 10–12. | Summary: When Ver and Aryl, rival apprentices at
    the biology lab in the Pangu Star System, become the prime suspects in their
    teacher's murder, they reluctantly team up to find the real culprit, running up
    against system-wide inequalities and conspiracies along the way.
Identifiers: LCCN 2023004850 (print) | LCCN 2023004851 (ebook) |
    ISBN 9781728477510 (hardcover) | ISBN 9798765611807 (epub)
Subjects: CYAC: Murder—Fiction. | Equality—Fiction. | Science fiction. |
    Mystery and detective stories. | BISAC: YOUNG ADULT FICTION /
    Mysteries & Detective Stories | LCGFT: Detective and mystery fiction. |
    Science fiction. | Novels.
Classification: LCC PZ7.B229478 Pan 2024 (print) | LCC PZ7.B229478 (ebook)
    | DDC [Fic]—dc23

LC record available at https://lccn.loc.gov/2023004850
LC ebook record available at https://lccn.loc.gov/2023004851

Manufactured in the United States of America
1-52420-50736-6/7/2023

For the girls who've been told
their dreams are too big—
I'm glad you didn't listen.

Nothing in life is to be feared, it is only to be understood.
Now is the time to understand more, so that we may fear less.

—Marie Curie

CHAPTER 1

Aryl

I expected to be alone in lab tonight. Everyone says the place is creepy in the dark, when the supercomputers cluck and purr as if they're talking to one another, but I don't mind. Machines are only as scary as the people using them.

"Good to see you, Aryl," my boss calls over his shoulder, his transparent bioplastic arm twisting behind his back to wave at me. "I was worrying you forgot you worked here."

Cal's voice is softer than usual. Threatening, like the faraway white streak in the sky before a meteor impact. My delts and traps contract as I brace for a lecture.

"You should've started taking data for your project last week," Cal says, "but I guess 0:30 at night is as good a time as any. Since you're finally here, you're welcome to wipe the benches clean when you're done."

I roll my eyes at Cal's back, knowing that his hand can see me. A literal third eye, the camera lens is wired to his brain's visual cortex via a series of long, branching neurons grown from his own stem cells. He got into an accident as a teenager, and instead of opting for surgery that could've fixed the damaged muscles, bones, and nerves, he replaced his whole hand with a machine.

1

I straighten my neck so that the bones are stacked like building blocks and tilt up my chin. "Didn't know the custodians needed help," I say, referring to the wheeled bots that tidy up the lab space in the early hours of the morning. Cal knows they'll do the cleaning for us. He's ordering me around as punishment, like giving a time-out to a five-year-old.

To be fair, he has a right to lecture me. I haven't put in a full day's work all week, and I don't regret it. My schedule's been packed with dance team practice, parties, and afternoon naps when our star, Pangu, burns hottest in the sky. You know, *fun* stuff. But tonight, Dad messaged. *How're experiments, sweetgum? Can we send you some taro buns?* A sudden rush of responsibility made me tell my friends I was hungover and come into lab. I can't keep coasting, knowing that my parents are cheering me on from afar, so proud that I've won this place as a research apprentice at the Institute for Natural Exploration.

Maybe I should be working more. Though I wonder: How much is enough? We research apprentices may be among the nerdiest kids on the three Gui Moons, but like anyone else, we need to let off steam. Most investigators at the Institute encourage their apprentices to play sports and have hobbies so they don't lose themselves to the work. Not Investigator Cal Eppi, though. Cal *is* the work, and the work is Cal.

"I'll leave you alone," he tells me now. "But only if you stay at that bench. I'll be watching." Smirking, he flashes the back of his hand again to make sure I get the message. The lens catches a stray beam of light from a computer, seeming to wink at me. Eugh.

I toss my bag down in the entryway and gown up, keeping one eye on Cal. He's hunched over the thrumming DNA sequencer, his nose nearly brushing the readout screen. The experiment he's obsessing over at this time of night? A complete mystery.

When I applied to the Institute more than two years ago, I ranked Cal's lab as my first choice among the biology labs. And when my application got accepted, I was thrilled to land a spot as his apprentice.

At first I thought he was a harmless nerd. Young for an investigator, and cute, with his stubbled round face, messy yellow hair, and overlapping front teeth. He dresses in baggy black clothes, a casual look that belies his intensity. My friends on dance team tease me about working for him. Their bosses are over half a century old, with hands that can barely work a pipette. But the teasing's all in good fun. They know Cal's not my type.

They also know I can't stand him now.

Within weeks of starting work, I learned that Cal spends every day and night in lab, breathing down his apprentices' necks. When I called my mom to complain, she said my description of him reminded her of the overseers at the farm collective where she once worked on G-Moon Two—the place she and my father escaped before I was born.

If I don't succeed here, I won't just be a disappointment. I'll have wasted my parents' lives. If I were a better person, I'd ask myself more often: How do I make their sacrifices worth it?

Well, not by quitting my job.

Not even to audition for every dance company on this moon?

Nope, even though I think about it every other night. I could sustain a career-ending injury in a few months or years and have nothing to fall back on. Then I'd depend on my parents instead of being the one to lift them up.

As I enter the cluttered lab space, the inner door to the

clean room swings open and Ver Yun emerges. Great, my other favorite person. My new lab mate's been backstage this whole time—probably spying—waiting to make her entrance.

One of Ver's mint-green pant legs is rolled up, and her pink carbonglass cane taps on the spotless floor, marking a steady beat. If we weren't in lab, I'd give in to my dancing instinct, unfold my arms and extend my legs.

"Hey, Ver," I mumble, slumping into my seat. If she's here working late, then *I* have no excuse for not getting scrap done.

"Hello, Aryl," she says to a spot on the wall behind my head, her voice breathy and high-pitched. In her offworld accent, my name comes out sounding like "arrow." Ver's sixteen, one year younger than me, but her small body and floaty white shirt make her look about twelve. Her black hair is hacked at irregular angles, like she cut it herself, and her skin is olive with gray undertones, probably from living indoors on her home moon.

She joins Cal at the sequencer and deposits a tube in the machine. They'll get a genomic readout immediately. I watch them for a moment, the girl with the cane and the man with the transparent hand, their heads almost touching.

Ver's never told us what happened to her—unlike Cal, who's described his rock-climbing accident in gory detail and gushes over his replacement hand, with its constant software updates, as if it's a cool toy. Maybe Ver had a rough childhood, like giga numbers of other people from G-Moon Three, but you couldn't pay me to pry. During her first week here, I absentmindedly asked her to grab me a heavy tube-shaker on a bottom shelf. Ver was silent for five seconds or so, then rapped her cane on the floor and said, "I wouldn't follow your orders even if I could."

Her reaction made me feel like such an awful, ableist human

errorcode that I was too embarrassed to even speak to her again until the next lab meeting. Now I watch what I say to her. I can't afford to gas off Cal's new favorite even more.

Keeping one eye on Ver, I sit at the microtome and slice fifty-nanometer-thick mouse brain tissue sections. Later, I'll blast the tissues with gravitational waves, electromagnetic waves, and chronowaves on the dinky wave generator. Then I'll watch how the cells age with a diffraction device. It's mind-numbingly repetitive, but the results will tell us something new about the way the universe works. Supposedly.

As I work, my flexitab lights up green with messages from my friends. The device is as thin as a layer of skin, and the rectangular screen is the size of my hand. I can stick it onto most surfaces, though usually I wear it as a bracelet. If you slap the flat surface on your wrist, it'll curl around and show the moving colors or designs you've programmed as your resting screen. Mine's shimmering gold, eye-catching but classy.

We're climbing the poles, Rhea's typed. *You'd crush every-body here.*

People are full of ethanol already. I should be there, joining in the drunken good time. I can shimmy up the metal struts that support the Institute gym higher and faster than anyone, but I also get in the most trouble with security.

Cal raises his arm and waggles the fingers of his bionic hand at me. Scrap, he's watching. I turn off my flexitab. But I'm still distracted by Cal and Ver, hunched together over the sequencer. Ver's babbling about something she sees, and Cal's head bobs up and down.

They work symbiotically during normal hours too. Jaha, our lab manager and Cal's wife, raises an eyebrow at them from time to time, but she's never said anything. Even the two older research apprentices have noticed how Ver's sucked our boss into her orbit. She's the only one who seems to escape his criticism.

"What are you two doing?" I say, trying to keep the irritation out of my voice.

"A side project," Ver says flatly, keeping her eyes on her work.

"One of her *many* side projects," Cal adds. As if one wasn't enough.

I can't suppress another eye-roll. Thankfully, Cal's bionic hand is busy, so the camera on the back can't see. He can record from it at will, like he did during my latest fumbling presentation at lab meeting.

Ever since Ver started here six months ago, nothing I do has been enough for Cal. She's better than me. Even though I made it to this lab against all odds, her journey dwarfs mine. I haven't had an easy life, but I didn't cross two moons and battle some awful health problem. Nor did I get immaculate data within weeks.

There's nothing left to do but try. Again. I place the sliced tissue in the path of the wave generator. Squat down to observe, my lab notebook at the ready. I try a chronowave—a wave that moves through the time dimension, intersecting with the space continuum. The machine lets out a squeal as it boots up—

The squeal dies.

Everything goes silent and dark.

So dark I can't see my hand in front of my face. Not even Lucent City's glittering lights can filter in through the blackout shades covering the windows.

Before any of us can speak, an alarm rips through the air.

CHAPTER 2
Ver

If a chemical reaction is stalling, add a catalyst. It will nudge the molecules to cooperate without itself undergoing a permanent change. The reaction will run faster.

I wish there was a catalyst to make my body run faster. Or run at all.

This is why I hate emergencies. Why I panic and cry and sometimes wet my pants. Because I cannot run, and when the people around me do—*bump thump*, I am hurt. That is how it has been since the pain started. How it will always be.

There were plenty of emergencies back home. But I thought that by coming here, to G-Moon One, I would find safety. Aiyo, I hate being wrong.

When the alarm tunnels into my ears, I drop the chemically treated bone marrow sample I am holding. The tissue pops out of the dish. *Splat!* Onto the floor.

No! My head is exploding with alarm like a sealed bottle in an autoclave. That was the only sample I had prepared. Weeks of work that someday could have helped someone like me—lost!

The yellow emergency lights flick on with a hum. I cannot process what Cal is saying, but I can identify his expression as shock. After a moment, the face I love turns away from me. His hands cover it up.

"Sorry! Sorry!" I say, stooping down to clean up the mess. Have to save what I can.

Cal trudges off toward his office, wringing his hands over our lost work. He must need to deal with the frustration alone. I know he is not angry at me. He understands that my physical limitations can make me clumsy. He has never treated me like I am inferior to anyone else.

The alarm is still screaming. I look up from the mess to apologize again . . . but Cal is lying on the floor, folded in the fetal position. His face is hidden.

I blink, and he is still there.

Even as I inch toward him, panic rising in my chest, a blur flashes by me. Aryl Fielding. Running across the lab, throwing her sliced tissue back in the freezer, and grabbing me around the waist. My lower back squeezes, seizes, as she hustles me toward the exit, her curls bouncing in front of my face.

I did not ask to be manhandled! Why did she show up to lab tonight, of all nights? "Put me down!" Seething, I thwack her arm with my cane. "I cannot leave that experiment!" Or Cal.

"You think I want to leave mine?" Aryl shouts over the alarm. Normally her voice is lazy and low. But now it is angry, like the violet lightning on the churning, gassy surface of our moons' planet, Gui.

Aryl wrenches open the heavy lab door with her free hand. Its motion sensor is not working. Nothing in the dark hallway indicates that anything is wrong. No fires, no sparks, no explosions. No people.

With rage still singeing my insides, I whack Aryl's arm again. Hard as I can.

"Ow!" she cries. "Lay off the stick!"

"*What about Cal?*" I shout. "He is still in there!"

"Cal can take care of himself."

"No! I saw him—he collapsed, just after the alarm went off. He must have passed out!"

Aryl's body stiffens. "For Pangu's sake," she mutters and plunks me back on my feet. "I'll go back and get him. You get out of the building."

I shake my head. "With this alarm, the elevators will be stopped. You will need to help me down the stairs. I should not go alone. Fourteen stories. At eighteen steps per story, that is two hundred fifty-two steps. If the probability of my falling on any given step is—"

Aryl throws up her hands. "I get it, genius. You'll end up faceplanting. Wait for me here, then."

She dashes back into the lab, leaving me to bump behind her as fast as I can. My cane clatters against random objects in the blackness.

"Cal! Cal!" I cry. The air is empty. I search with every sense, desperate for a sign of him. Maybe he left through a secret exit. Maybe he is safe.

The alarm dies and the lights blaze back to life, burning my eyes. I sway on the spot, waiting for my vision to return.

And I hear Aryl screaming.

CHAPTER 3
Aryl

Cal's lying face down, completely still.

When I stop screaming long enough to catch my breath, I lift his head off the floor. My hands are shaking. My chest is heaving. I can barely see.

Blood dribbles out of a gash on his forehead. He's gone limp, reminding me of the lab mice I've sacked. I slip my arms under his side. Bending my knees at a right angle, I suck air into my belly, dig my heels into the floor, and heave to roll him over. Proper hip-hinging, just like Dad taught me.

Cal's body easily flips. His head lolls 180 degrees, loose curls flopping, and I recoil.

Deep breaths: In, out. In, out.

Kneeling down, I lay my hand over Cal's heart. No pulse. I pump on his chest, almost pushing it into the floor.

A minute passes this way, according to the digital clock on the wall. He doesn't move.

Ver clatters over to me, a pastel-colored mess of snot and tears.

"It's not working," I whisper. My party makeup has left sparkling green streaks on Cal's white lab coat.

"We should try adrenaline." Ver lurches over to the

controlled-substances cabinet. She fills a syringe with clear solution, an amount presumably proportional to Cal's mass, and stumbles back to us. Refusing my offer of help, she uses a desk to lower herself onto the floor. Her hands are trembling more than usual, but she manages to jam the syringe tip into Cal's neck and push the clear adrenaline solution into his artery.

I'm almost expecting his heart to jump-start beneath my hands. Cal's always called me too optimistic. *It's nice to want things, Aryl.* He'd say it now, if he weren't unconscious.

Unconscious. He's got to be. I can't consider the alternative.

Images flash through my mind: Cal's droning criticisms of my work, the times I tuned him out by fantasizing about dancing out of lab meeting. Like last month, when he tossed six weeks of my data because I'd failed to control the tissues' growing conditions before experimenting on them. I can't say I didn't snicker into my hand when he nicked himself with a surgical blade during a dissection later that day. But I never wanted Cal *dead*.

If he dies, what'll happen to me? This lab's my escape from my past. It's my present and future and hope. It reassures my parents that they raised me right. And it lets me access the Institute dance team, which feels more real than my actual apprenticeship.

The empty syringe clatters from Ver's hand onto the floor. She's kneeling beside me, weeping. Is the science prodigy really out of ideas?

"Stop crying!" I urge. "Try again. Doesn't Cal mean anything to you?"

Ver's black eyes narrow, her glare sharp as a laser-cutter beam. "You will never understand what he means to me."

I glare back. Frankly, I don't want to know.

Without breaking eye contact, I take the flexitab off my wrist, unroll the screen, and call the authorities.

CHAPTER 4
Ver

What is physical pain? Electricity. A current of ions flowing through pore-like channels on our neuronal membranes, long axons like wires conducting the signal up to our brains.

Tonight, it takes only words to shock my body. The Lucent City Police examine Cal and tell us, "He's gone."

Gone! I am free-floating through space, without gravity to anchor me to this world or the next.

Still, amid the emptiness, I hope.

Clinical death is the cessation of a heartbeat and respiration, but brain activity may continue until the organ's oxygen supply runs out. Does Cal know I am here? My palm cradles his cold cheek, and I imagine transferring every oxygen molecule in my blood to him. I would gladly give all I have.

His blue eyes—which often changed unpredictably from sunny to stormy, as if they had their own climate controls—are now blank, staring. A blond eyelash has drifted into his eyeball. I consider grabbing forceps from my bench and fishing it out, to blow it away and make a wish on it.

A stout female officer peels me off the floor and away from Cal. Two male officers hustle Aryl and me into the hallway. They tell us to return to lab—to the scene of the crime—at 9:00

tomorrow morning. And that if we try to run, they will know.

"Young scientists don't drop dead for no reason," says the green-haired female officer. "From the unencrypted vitals records on his artificial hand, we know that he didn't have a heart attack or a stroke. His blood composition is . . . off. After we determine the cause of death, we'll need you both for questioning."

Gou! Not only did I lose Cal—they think I may have murdered him! It hurts my heart worse than my disease ever has. Worse than not knowing how I will manage to keep asking the questions I must ask—alone.

The police look at me, at Aryl, as if we are no better than the back-alley killers who plague the rougher neighborhoods of Lucent City. Many lawbreakers are homegrown, but some come from my moon. Others come from Aryl's. And those are the ones who make the news. With two offworlders in front of them, the police probably will not investigate anyone else. How do I prove that they are only right about one of us?

If Cal was murdered, the killer must be Aryl. She was the only other person in lab tonight. I know little about her, except that she loathes Cal. Most of their conversations devolve into hisses and, in some cases, shouting. Once, when he criticized her faulty methods, she listened with her fists curled at her side, then returned to her experiment and—probably intentionally—heated an untempered glass beaker till it shattered, while Cal was only a benchtop away.

I manage to stay calm—keep face, as Three-ers would say—in the officers' presence. Even on the fourteen-story elevator ride to ground level.

Aryl leaves without a word, takes off at a sprint toward the second-year dorms. I watch her, burning with envy. She has no idea how lucky she is to feel air rushing past her face, her lungs expanding with effort, the satisfying thud of her feet on the ground.

Cal fell down before Aryl dragged me out of the lab. Maybe he tripped. Maybe not. When Aryl ran back into the lab without me, she had nearly a minute to stop his heart. I am certain that she killed him. That she took Cal away from me.

I must confront her. But not tonight. I will not follow her, and not only because I would never be able to catch her. I need to be alone. My heart is singed and blackened from conducting so much electric pain.

Back home, on G-Moon Three, people I had known for much longer died all the time, of disease or violence or poison. These people fell like meteors. They made impact and buried themselves in the dust, digging their own graves. But Cal is different. He was a One-er. He was not supposed to die young. Or even middle-aged. He had at least a century left, like most other citizens of this moon.

When I met Cal that first day in lab, he was crouched on the floor, trying to fix our microscope.

"Hey, Ver! Can I borrow your stick for a second?" he said to me, blue eyes clear and shining, one side of his mouth lifted in a smirk. "I lost a screw under the scope."

Blushing at his directness, I handed over my cane. He retrieved the screw, and together we calibrated and rewired the machine. My heart pounded so loud and fast I worried he would hear it.

Since then, the questions we have asked of the universe have nudged my life toward the light, assuring me that it has a purpose. No matter how short it will be.

Now his soul is among the stars. Not here, where I need him.

Wiping my eyes, I walk toward the spires of the first-year dorms, my soft shoes making no noise, my cane tap-tapping on the quartz-paved path. Weeping cherry blossoms and their reflections in the ponds shine snowy white against the black background. The vibrant green dot of G-Moon Two, surrounded by smaller pinpricks of stars, glows in the sky above it all. When I first arrived at the Institute, with its multihued crystalline towers, I wondered how anyone got work done in such a stunning place.

Then I learned that the science bestowed meaning upon the beauty. Geologists know that for several million years after G-Moon One's formation, its distance from Pangu oscillated from near to far, leading to heating and cooling cycles that enabled the melting, growing, and remelting of gigantic multihued crystals. The architecture here is gemlike because of the sparkling abundance of raw material. Ecologists carefully selected organism combinations from the embryo vault to populate G-Moons One and Two, creating self-sustaining ecosystems: the mangrove lakes and dense maple forests on the other hemisphere of One; the rice paddies and cornfields of Two, serviced by communities of microorganisms living in the soil and pollinating bees buzzing through the air.

Science can explain why things are the way they are, how we arrived here, and what we will accomplish. Or what everyone else will accomplish, without me, if I do not manage to stop the disease that will soon take my life.

Now that Cal is dead, I am alone in that mission.

I am alone.

I crane my neck back to view the beanstalk-shaped Biological Laboratories skyscraper, which we call BioLabs. White quartz corkscrewing up into space. To the right, its neighbor, the spherical sapphire Mathematics Center, glints like a marble. I raise my eyes higher, to the starry night. To verdant G-Moon Two. To yellow, pockmarked G-Moon Three.

Home. How lucky I was to escape. I panicked as primary school graduation neared, fearing I would have to work in the factories like Ma and everyone else in my town. An apprenticeship at the Institute was my only hope of doing the science to save myself, but I had never been in a real laboratory before. I relied on the knowledge I had siphoned out of science articles and three years of pipetting solutions into chipped glassware— the best my school could offer.

I applied to the Institute and sent holographic messages to Cal's lab. Explaining my health issues, begging for a chance. Finally Jaha, the lab manager, called and said she would support my application. As soon as we heard each other's accents, we lapsed into our dialect. I could have flown. A fellow Three-er would watch out for me!

At the beginning of my apprenticeship, she brought me snacks, offered encouraging words at every opportunity. But after a few weeks, Jaha could not be in the same room with me. "You seem to have it together," she would say, excusing herself.

I could not help loving her husband. No one had ever made me feel like I belonged to them before—not even Ma. Especially not Ma. From the start, I was Cal's. But it did not take me long to learn that no matter what I did, no matter how much ground we broke, he would never belong to me in the same way.

That is the only thing I hated him for.

CHAPTER 5
Aryl

The first thing I do in the second-year dorm is run to the bathroom and hurl. Gargle water, spit it out. Scrub the hands that touched Cal's dead body, the hands that couldn't save him.

I leave the bathroom, stepping into the fluorescent lighting of the corridor. Despite my efforts, it stinks in here. I carry the stench of death inside me now.

Doors up and down the narrow hallway slide open. My fellow apprentices stand on their thresholds to stare. Small hexagonal mirrors on the curved, honeycombed ceiling reflect twisted images of my friends. The scintillating light makes me feel as if I'm tripping on party powder.

"Aryl? What's happened?"

"Say something, Fielding, is this a joke or what?"

"We heard an investigator *died*." As usual, Rhea wields a blunt knife in conversation. Her short silvery hair is damp; she must've showered after doing her before-bed mobility and flexibility exercises. Just as I should've done, if Cal hadn't . . .

I'm hit by the memory of when I moved my stretching mat into lab. Cal wasn't a fan at first—he said it smelled, it took up space. But after I taught Jaha exercises that kept her limber throughout her pregnancy, Cal thanked me profusely.

I press my legs together in first position, hoping the familiar stance will calm me, but it only makes my knees bounce with nervousness. I look into Rhea's expectant green eyes. They're so big and shiny that I see my face reflected back at me. There was a time I convinced myself I saw deeper feelings in those eyes. Sometimes I think I still do.

"You know you can talk to us," Rhea says. She comes toward me, arms stretched out. I let her hug me, but I pull away when I taste death in my mouth, smoky and putrid. I don't want to contaminate her.

There's a sob as another person stumbles into the hallway. All our heads turn toward the intruder, and my heart sinks.

Devon Kye is never a welcome sight. Tonight is already vacked enough without adding him to the mix. "Devon, go to bed," I say, voice flat.

But that only makes him cry harder. Annoyance rises in me, jabbing through the numbness. I'm gassed off at him, but if I were a decent person, I'd pity him instead. Devon's tiny, only slightly taller than Ver. He's got shiny, sallow skin and short, greasy black hair that clumps together. His investigator keeps apprentices in a basement lab fifteen hours a day, so sleep's hard to come by and hygiene's even more of a stretch. Devon's also scrap at experiments, though he manages to churn out enough decent theory to keep his investigator off his back.

It's a shame that Devon's from the same moon as my parents, because he makes me look bad by association. Out of all the second-years at the Institute, we're the only Two-ers. He's from Oryza, a small city near my parents' home village. So I've defended Devon in the past, even stood up for him when the discdisc boys hazed him. But tonight I don't have the time or energy to deal with him.

"What do you need?" Rhea asks Devon gently, even as she backs away.

Devon's black eyes don't leave me, and it's making me squirm.

"*What*," I shoot at him, not even bothering to make it a question. Can't he tell I want to be left alone? Can't they all?

"I'm sorry," Devon whispers in that rhythmic, quick-stepping accent, just like my parents'. "I'm sorry about Cal."

His words burn on impact. The tears are coming—but I won't cry in front of these people. I can't let them see that I'm not invincible.

My flexitab vibrates on my wrist with an incoming call. *Dad*, says the screen. I duck into my room. Whispers hound me as I close the door.

When I answer the call, two sets of holographic heads and shoulders pop up from the flexitab—a man and a woman with solid builds and round, worried faces. The projections are so opaque and vividly colored, it feels like my parents are sitting in front of me.

"Sweetgum, are you all right?" Mom says. "We heard about . . . a crime at the Institute."

As far back as I can remember, Mom's been loud-voiced and quick, rushing around as she cooks and cleans for my parents' boss. Now she's quiet and still.

"They . . . they think I killed him," I say. "Cal Eppi."

"The Institute called us," Dad says. Even over holo, my father looks solid and intimidating. He's been a doorman for years, and that means doubling as a bodyguard. "I'm sorry, sweetgum. We know you didn't do this."

I wonder if he means *We HOPE you didn't do this.* Dad's years of experience in security mean that he can't ignore the evidence against me. But he has to know there's no chance I killed Cal—that no child of his could do something like that. I need my family's faith like a seedling needs water. I can't count on anyone else's.

"We have to talk about next steps," says Dad, always the practical one. "Respect the police, do as they say. They'll find any excuse to put you away, or to send your mother and me back to Two. I'm afraid of what will happen at your trial if we let it get to that point."

The "objective" computer-run trials on One aren't kind to people like us. When machines are programmed by humans, they absorb human biases.

"Dad, you've told me this a thousand times," I say. "I've done my best to follow the officers' directions."

"Did anyone try to hurt you?" There's a threat in his voice.

I shake my head. Both my parents heave sighs of relief. I look past them, at the familiar mess of our family's apartment. I calculate the time in Celestine—it's nearly 5:30 in the morning. My brain jolts with confusion. "Mom, shouldn't you be at work?"

Senator Titania Mercure eats her breakfast at 6:00 when she's home, which means Mom has to be up and ready to make it for her. Titania has represented Celestine in the Senate for more than twenty years. She relies on my parents to maintain her mansion; when I was a kid, she told me that even the best-programmed AI can't match a real, breathing human who's paid to make your house a home.

My parents look at each other, as if silently debating who should tell me the bad news. Dad's the one to speak. "Titania has suspended our employment, sweetgum. Without pay."

"Because of me?" Horror is yanking on all the parts of my face. I've always been proud of my low resting heart rate, but now I can feel it pounding at a dangerous speed. I didn't expect this of Titania. She knows me! Or she used to.

"She's had her security unit . . ." Mom swallows. ". . . put us under home supervision. Ester"—my younger sister—"can attend school, but they'll escort her here straight after dismissal. Titania says these precautions are necessary, until things clear up."

"So you're basically under house arrest," I say. "That's illegal! Titania can't do that without a hearing—"

"Titania is not just anybody," Dad says. "The police will back her up if it comes to that."

Titania is one of the Senate's biggest supporters of the police force. Every chance she gets, she votes to give them better pay, better weapons, and more power in criminal cases.

"Clear your name, Aryl, and come home when you can," Mom begs. "If you can. Please."

The holo of my parents disappears. My fingers go limp, and the flexitab slips through them, landing on the floor.

How are two adults and a thirteen-year-old girl supposed to survive without money, without freedom?

I didn't commit the crime, but authorities *think* I did. And that might be my fault.

If I'd been pulling my weight in lab, I wouldn't have needed to catch up on work tonight. I wouldn't have planted myself right where Cal was killed.

Mom's hands are worn raw, with no sensation left in her fingers because of all the times she's burned herself in the kitchen. Dad's right eyebrow is split by a scar he got fending off extremists who tried to attack the Mercure mansion. My parents have worn themselves down to give me a future full of possibilities. And this is how I repay them. I've cursed them with the kind of life they swore I'd never have.

CHAPTER 6
Ver

"You're finally home, dear girl. At 3:05 in the morning! Are you still human, or has some nocturnal animal's DNA been annealed to your genome?"

Charles's deep voice greets me as I step into my first-floor dorm room. It is a bare white box, but it is mine. The only decorations are products of Charles's imagination—the best his AI brain can give. He projects rotating starry images on the wall next to my bed. They lull me to sleep most nights, but they are useless now.

"I heard about the alarm in BioLabs," Charles goes on. "Apparently there was a gas leak. Now that I know you're not burned or dismembered, I can delete that data from my memory."

That means he was worried. I spend more time in this room with Charles's incorporeal voice than outside with people. He knows all my needs and routines. One might call him my friend, but I am hesitant. Friends should have bodies.

"Cal died tonight, Charles," I say.

I crumple onto the bed and close my eyes, which are swollen and sore from crying. But the image of Cal's limp body is burned into my brain. Yellow hair tumbling over the floor tiles. I open my eyes again.

"Oh, no," Charles says, his tone nuanced and humanlike. At his command, the fleecy comforter creeps up my body and embraces me. I cry into it with abandon. Charles can run it through the communal wash-dry circuit later.

"It hurts so much. Why did it have to be Cal? It feels like someone is stabbing me in the heart."

"I wish I could empathize. I lack both a heart and the experience of being stabbed."

Aiyo. I look up at the ceiling, to where Charles keeps his hard drive, and I envy his simple existence.

"How can I improve your emotional state?" Charles says.

I have no reply. A memory of Cal fills my mind: the night he used the lab's audio system to play a selection of soft, jingling keyboard songs popular in his mountain hometown. During our stretch breaks, he would drag me up from my stool and we would dance. Me, doing what I could. Him, jumping and swinging his hips, waving his bionic hand in light-up mode high in the air. A human fluorophore. Extinguished now.

"Would you like me to search the Neb for entertainment?" Charles offers. The Nebula is the cloud system that contains all known information, each pocket behind varying amounts of firewalls and paywalls.

"Find me something peaceful," I say. "And from far away."

"I know just the thing."

Charles projects holographic images of heavenly spheres: Pangu, our dim, burnt-orange star. The gas giant planet Gui—eleven times the size of Jupiter, back near Sol—so massive that it causes Pangu to wobble in its rotation. Gui's three moons: sparkling One, covered in crystal formations, green plains and forest, and humanmade lakes as reflective as mirrors; green Two, with its tropical crops at the equator and its yellow corn and wheat fields in the temperate regions . . .

And Three. Yellow, dusty, un-terraformed. My home is pimpled with craters and habitat domes that contain entire cities. I pass my hand through the projection, picturing desert sand falling between my fingers.

On Three, we say we were born in Pangu's shadow. It is not scientific; stars do not cast shadows. But to some, the saying *feels* true. When it comes to our future, we know little and decide nothing. Thick clouds of space dust obscure every possibility.

The police may soon have a judicial computer cluster and human jury put me on trial for murder. Although the process is meant to be unbiased, taking into account all known details about the victim's life, the cluster rarely disagrees with the police. The human jury usually follows the cluster.

If this happens, the state could lock me up in the penal colony of G-Moon Three, the one people call the Sandbag. At the northern pole, where it is so cold that the carbon dioxide exhaust solidifies when the camps pump it into space. The guards put shocker implants in the back of prisoners' mouths. If you are disobedient or try to escape, you are electrocuted. There is only rudimentary medical care, and specialized medications are not permitted. If they put me in a tiny cell, I will be in more pain than should be legal. Pain so intense, I will wish it would hurry up and kill me.

I felt that pain, before I started my medication. An alien land of agony. I refuse to return.

"Three is too close," I tell Charles. "Show me someplace farther, please."

He zooms out from the Pangu System, across the black sky to Proxima Centauri B, a red dwarf. Its single rocky planet houses a million humans who stomp around at 1.3 times

24

Earth-gravity. They do not seem to be feeding themselves well—the Senate ships them tons of food in exchange for their valuable metal ores.

Humans settled Proxima three hundred years ago, about forty years before they reached the Gui moons. It was by chance that my ancestors woke up from their cryo-chambers here, not on that dense rock orbiting Proxima.

"Even farther," I tell Charles. "Take me away from every place I know."

Charles pans across the sky at light-years per second and shows me Sol, orbited by its four rocky inner planets, asteroid belt, and four outer gas giants. My muscles unclench; I rest my hands over my heart and feel my ribcage expand, then contract, over the underlying pulses.

Earth, the third planet from the sun, is barren. A steaming, swampy marble covered with gray clouds, long since abandoned by humanity. A million poor souls still live on its moon, though their infrastructure is shaky and their cities are subterranean. Our ancestors—those who could afford spacecraft passage— left Earth's orbit centuries ago, taking with them shiploads of seeds, bacterial and archaeal samples, fungal spores, and frozen animal embryos. They survived long journeys to faraway planets and stars. To Mars's green, lake-dotted surface and Jupiter's icy moons. To Proxima and Alpha Centauri, to the Gui Moons.

My ancestors made it here, while so many others perished.

These are the things I tell myself when I hate the universe for gambling with every cell in my body. Ripping membranes and molecules. Putting them together again in all the wrong ways. *I am lucky to be alive.*

Tonight, the thought fails to comfort me. Every *thump thump* of my heart kills me, because Cal's is no longer beating.

CHAPTER 7
Aryl

"Five and a six and seven and go!" calls the captain's groggy voice.

Rehearsal started at 6:00, as usual, which meant people had to get up at 5:30 to make it to the studio in time. No way would I let a dead investigator or the police's demands get between me and dancing. I'll be here until they drag me away.

I'm paying for my lack of sleep, though. As I stretch my arms out, fingers spread wide, each limb feels twice as heavy as usual. Even the shock-absorbent floor can't fully soften my landings. I shoot a hand above my head, shift my ribcage right, pop my hip out on the other side. Leap, step, turn turn turn.

My teammates know. Some are giving me *why-is-she-here?* stares. I feel their eyes waiting for me to miss a move—or to drop Rhea, whom I've just lifted in the air, one leg extended behind her. That would be catastrophic. She's the daughter of a gemstone mining tycoon who'd get me convicted of a second crime.

I won't mess up, not with all of them watching, and not with Rhea depending on me. Together, her lightness and my long lines make us shine. Whenever I watch playback of our performances, my eyes are drawn to myself and Rhea, no matter how neutral I try to be.

But something's off. It's not that I can't do the steps today—it's that I have no reason to. I can't *feel* anything worth putting into movement. I've always danced my joy, my longing, my heartache, and my anger. I've burned so bright, I've lit up stages large and small. I've reached to the back of an auditorium and snatched people's attention.

But what about numbness? How do you express *that*?

"Stop, stop." The team captain, a fifth-year apprentice named Kandel, is shaking his head. He carries so little body fat that even his neck is sinewy with muscle. "Fielding, you're not getting enough height on any of your jumps."

Rhea shoots me an annoyed look from where she's resting, hands on her thighs.

"And since when have you all gotten so lazy on your lifts?" Kandel says. "Quit slacking off. We're two weeks away from a performance in Lucent City's biggest arena. You can't be out of shape now."

So it goes. His comments discourage me, and that only makes me sink deeper into the pit I feel opening up inside. It makes me miss Rori, my old teacher. He always knew what to say to get me soaring, whether it was gently critiquing a technical detail or painting an image of what he wanted with his words. He charged his other students a fortune, but knowing my parents' situation, he trained me for cheap.

"Take care of your mind, Aryl," he used to say. "It's your paintbrush, and your body is the canvas."

How can I dance when my parents are locked down and out of work? And what about Ester? Her classmates will be as cruel to her as mine have been to me, but with extra thirteen-year-old zest.

Everything I wanted yesterday seems out of reach now. To

27

finish my apprenticeship, audition for one of the big Lucent City dance companies, and dance until my body gives out, returning to science as my backup career. I see parallels between the nano-scale movements of proteins and the human-scale movements of dance. The long experiments in science and the infinitesimal moments of moving onstage balance each other. I can't live without this dance team, this movement—but it could all be gone by next week.

All because of Ver's twisted, unrequited love, or whatever it was that made her kill Cal. Maybe Cal was cruel to her too, when none of us were around. Maybe she secretly hated him and wanted to get close enough to murder him.

After practice ends, Rhea and I stretch each other out. I try to ignore the others on the mats, who don't hide that they're watching us.

My hip flexors feel like wooden blocks. Rhea pushes my hips forward and wrenches my thigh backward to put tension on the muscles. She's strong, for someone so small.

"I was worried Kandel would say worse to us," she says. Her eyes are concerned. You can read her whole heart through those green-tinted windows. That's why she was the first one I trusted on the dance team, surrounded by the children of gazillionaires, senators, and Institute investigators who saw me as a farm bumpkin. At first, most of them ignored me. But everything changed when Rhea took a liking to me. Then they all started jockeying to grab a meal, to go out at night.

"Kandel's the least of my problems," I say. The police want to question Ver and me at 9:00. It's 8:44 now, so I need to leave soon."

"Listen, Aryl." Rhea's eyes cloud over. "How long will you be dancing like this?"

I stare at her, heart pounding. "Like what?"

"You know, all lifeless. You can usually bend people's hearts. When I asked you to be my doubles partner last year, that was why. I just . . . I hope you don't make me regret it."

Words won't come. Dread weighs me down. *Cal is dead.* The law will pin the blame on me, the daughter of aliens with the height in her step and the glint in her eye—unless I can convince them it was Ver.

A week from now, will I still even be free, let alone dancing?

CHAPTER 8
Ver

Many natural venoms work by breaking the complex electrical circuit that is their victim's nervous system. They seal off ion channels so that the cellular conduits can no longer conduct sparks of sensation or send signals to act.

The fifty-something detective from the Lucent City Police explains that this is what happened to Cal. The chipped digital badge adhered to his uniform reads *Detective Roderick Xenon*. He is burly and round, with an asymmetrical mustache and beady, shrewd eyes. He does not look like he has gotten any more sleep than I have. He reclines in Cal's office chair, which bothers me, even though Cal barely used it. Cal was always in lab with me. Still. That chair is *Cal's*.

"After a careful examination, we've concluded that Calyx Eppi died of tetrodotoxin injection," Detective Xenon says, rubbing his mustache.

"TTX?" I say, blinking. "A potent nerve block derived from pufferfish." I visualize toxin molecules sitting like plush pillows atop the sodium channels in Cal's neurons. "We do not keep that in our lab. We have no use for it in our studies of cellular aging."

Aryl lets out a slow, measured laugh. I start at the sound. Her ladderlike abdominal muscles contract under her tight, sweat-stained dance clothes. Before Xenon can ask her what is so amusing, Aryl says, "True to form, Ver. You didn't lose a second to show that you're the smartest one in the room."

My nose wrinkles in distaste. Aryl blows sandstorms of insults at people she dislikes. Despite that, she is one of the most popular second-years at the Institute—probably because people's spirits bow down to her before she even opens her mouth. She has luminous bronze skin and mahogany ringlets that fall to the middle of her back. Her face is oval, with a wide nose, full lips, and large catlike eyes. The tallest girl on the Institute's dance team, she can fold and extend her limbs in heart-stirring ways that make me ache to inhabit a functional body. When I am around her, I am not sure where to look because it is all so perfect.

Xenon speaks with an eerie calmness. "Miss Fielding, please focus. To answer your question, Miss Yun, some of the Institute's neurobiology labs would have TTX in stock. But that leaves me with a bigger question."

He takes a sip of his caffeinated lychee juice and gives us an impossible-to-read smile.

"I asked myself today: How would a healthy, competent thirty-two-year-old man have died by TTX injection? Surely not by chance. Murder is a possibility I cannot rule out. Murder committed by the only other people in Eppi's lab last night."

I glance from the detective to the two chunky security robots flanking him—yellow-eyed stacks of metal on wheels. They are less intelligent than your average lab mouse, but far more obedient. Sentient enough to follow simple orders but not smart enough to think for themselves. After an AI rebellion decades ago, the Senate banned the manufacture of corporeal robots capable of reprogramming their kin. So we have domestic AIs like Charles, who have brains but no bodies, and server robots with bodies but rudimentary intelligence. Xenon's could not pick up sarcasm if you hit them in the face with it. But they will cuff me the instant Xenon says the word.

I clear my throat. "Sir, do you have security footage of the lab during the incident?"

"Not of the lab itself," Xenon says. "As you know, investigators don't allow independent holo recordings of their work. We've reviewed the outside corridor footage, though. No one entered or left Cal Eppi's lab between when Miss Fielding arrived at 0:34 in the morning and when the alarm blackout began at 1:12. By the time the blackout ended at 1:15, Calyx Eppi was dead."

An asteroid drops in my stomach. All my muscles—the ones I can control and the ones I cannot—harden into stone. The police do not just *suspect* us of murdering Cal. They are *sure*.

My eyes dart to meet Aryl's. Hers are bulging with panic. She tugs on one of her ringlets and begins chewing at the end of it.

"If you're wondering who caused the death of your beloved mentor, girls," Detective Xenon says, "keep looking at each other. Because at least one murderer is sitting in this room."

CHAPTER 9
Aryl

I straighten my back and stare down my lab mate.

In lab last night, there were three people: Ver, Cal, and me. I didn't kill Cal, so it had to have been Ver. I need to convince Detective Xenon of that. If I don't, my family will stay locked up in a tiny apartment they soon won't be able to afford. And that's if we're lucky.

"Did you really inject Cal with adrenaline?" I hiss at Ver. "Or did you draw TTX into that syringe *by accident?*"

Ver is opening and shutting her mouth like a fish gasping for water. "Please-ah, sir," she says to Xenon. Her accent thickens in her panic. "I was trying to revive him. I injected adrenaline on the ventral side of the neck."

"Ah, yes." Xenon takes another sip of his lychee juice. "We found your injection site in Eppi's skin and checked the syringe. It's clean. And the TTX was injected on the *dorsal* side of the neck, to the left of the midline."

Ver exhales, but Xenon's not finished.

"Then the killer apparently threw the syringe across the lab—we found it near the clean room entrance, almost five meters from the body. With genetic fingerprinting of that syringe, we found both Eppi's and Miss Yun's DNA."

Ver shoots to her feet, though I can tell she instantly regrets it, leaning on the arm of the chair and rubbing her lumbar spine. I didn't know she was capable of moving that fast. Or of getting this angry. "I found Cal dead, huddled on the floor, after Aryl had already been back in the lab for thirty seconds. Forty. Long enough to put on gloves, smear a syringe in a culture of my bone marrow cells, and stick Cal."

So we're going at it now, huh? "First of all," I snap, "why are you growing your own bone marrow cells on petri dishes, anyway? Did the Institute approve the protocol for that?"

"That is none of your business!"

Detective Xenon observes us, eyes narrowed.

"Secondly," I say, "if I killed Cal, why would I have jabbed him in the *left* side of his neck? I'm right-handed. And you were the only one with him when the alarm first went off."

Ver pounces on this question, ignoring the earlier one. "Aiyo, do I look strong enough to wrestle down a healthy man? Or tall enough to hit him, *boom*, in the back of the neck?"

The angry little girl has a point. She barely comes up to my shoulder. I'm the same height as Cal but much stronger. The better nutrition on One likely helped me grow big enough to look like a plausible killer. *Thanks for all the fish, Mom.*

"You dropped a sample," I fire back at Ver. "I saw his face once the emergency lights came on. He looked like he was going to smack you."

"Cal would never," Ver says, lifting her chin. But she doesn't sound sure.

"Perhaps another piece of evidence will help you remember the truth." Xenon's voice has a gruffness that wasn't there before. "Miss Fielding's DNA was found on Investigator Eppi's lab coat—"

"Ever heard of CPR?" I interrupt. "I was trying to *help* Cal. Obviously I failed. If I'd known you'd use that as evidence to frame me, maybe I wouldn't have bothered."

"Oh?" Xenon's bushy eyebrows lift. He sets his drink aside, like he means business now. "Other biology faculty tell me that you and Investigator Eppi had a strained relationship, Miss Fielding. They say that even after all he's done for you, you couldn't sit down and respect him."

Did he just imply that Cal helped me, a dense offworld girl, out of the goodness of his heart?

Xenon taps his stylus against his flexitab. "Miss Fielding, do you deny that you had a difficult relationship with Investigator Eppi?"

"We all did," I say. "Cal expected giga progress from us, even in experiments where we had no clue what we were doing."

"He only pushed us because he wanted us to succeed!" Ver says.

"Yeah, sure," I say. *No one asked you.* "If he really cared about us, he would've—"

Xenon stands up in one swift motion. He moves like a much younger man. I shrink back, my heart pounding.

"For all I know," he says, "you girls killed Investigator Eppi together, and this whole argument is a farce to ensure that just one of you lands in prison. You were the only ones at the scene when Calyx Eppi died. DNA evidence implicates you both. So does history with the victim."

"Sir—" Ver says.

He silences her with a glare. "You are both under arrest. Helpers, cuff them and take them to the station."

The police bots' yellow eyes light up, and they roll in front of Ver and me. Ver gives no sign of resistance except for a stuck-out lower lip. I force myself to stay still, even though I want to kick the metal chunks away from me and jet out of here.

The cold titanium handcuffs clamp around my wrists. I close my eyes and picture my parents' faces. I won't watch myself become a prisoner.

CHAPTER 10
Ver

All else being equal, the same number of molecules of a lighter gas and a heavier gas will take up the same amount of space.

The Lucent City Police Department loves this law. They keep their prisoners in holding pods suspended by floats full of helium, the second-lightest gas. (Hydrogen, the very lightest, is too flammable for this purpose.) The floats are tethered to the ground level of the hexagonal police station by a narrow, bendable stalk, which contains a miniature elevator that can fit, at most, two people. Back and forth we drift, thirty meters above the city, our motion dictated by the air currents. The swaying stirs up nausea in my belly.

With just one tiny window, this two-person cell would be impossible to escape even if I were as strong as Aryl. She sits on her steel cot, stretching her triceps as if preparing to fight, refusing to look at me. In such a small space, she seems even bigger.

The only other thing to look at is a cracked, blank screen on the door. We have both tried to activate it by touch and by scanning our fingertips and retinas, but it remains dead.

Watching Aryl, I think of how in healthy people like her, micro-damage strengthens muscles. Rip through layers of actin and myosin by stressing the tissue, and the fibers will grow back thicker.

Aryl has put her muscles through countless small traumas. Her legs are solid and strong beneath her black leggings. Her metallic-gold tank top shows her muscular upper back, the skin rippling like a pond struck by a pebble. More than once, I have wanted to touch it, just to know what so much strength feels like. When I first saw her, all I wanted was to move as she did. So easy! Not only when she dances, but when she glides into lab and stands, stork-like, on one leg while pipetting solutions.

Only now do I see the danger in her. She could have killed Cal easily. Cal was tall, but soft and skinny. If she chose to, she could kill me too.

As it stands, though, she is the best hope I have of getting out of here. And I need to get out.

I am getting dizzy. I have not taken my medication since this morning—the police robots confiscated my pillbox. If I spend the night without medication, I will not be able to keep my balance tomorrow.

"We should agree to tell them nothing," I say. "If neither of us says anything to incriminate the other, we can both go free."

Aryl's eyes cut into me. "You expect me to fall for that? So I can cover for you with the police, and meanwhile you'll tell lies about me to save your own skin? Don't be ridiculous."

"Aiyo, have it your way." I should not have expected that we would be able to work together. We have hardly spoken more than a sentence to each other in lab. "But you will have to work very hard to cast suspicion on me. I have done nothing wrong."

Aryl sits up and gives me her signature eye-roll. "Why should I believe anything that comes out of your mouth? You were the last person to stand next to Cal. He trusted you, and now he's dead."

"So what is my motive?" I hurl at her. "What reason could I possibly have for killing the one person on this moon who trusted me?"

"I don't care what your reason was. *I* didn't do it, so it had to be you. I found Cal flat on his belly, already gone. And I don't have a motive either. I wasn't a fan of Cal, but he gave me the opportunity to lift myself *and* my family's hopes. I needed him too, Ver."

I think on this. "Yes. You did. I should have seen it earlier."

"Yeah. Both of us had too much to lose if he died."

And both of us *have* lost. Just look at us! "They are going to question us. One at a time. My proposal stands: We should not tell lies about the other to make her look guilty. It will only reinforce their idea that we murdered Cal together and are now quarreling." I cannot resist clarifying, "This does not mean I want to collaborate—I will only refrain from trying to implicate you."

"Fine. Let's do that." Aryl is nodding, a good sign, and I hope she follows through. "Besides, if we stick to the simple truth, it might help the police solve a damn murder for once . . ."

A buzzing sound cuts her off. A moment later, Detective Xenon's voice projects through our tiny pod.

"Ver Yun, come to the interrogation room."

I rise slowly as our locked cell door slides open, giving me access to the elevator.

"Hey," Aryl calls. "Good luck in there."

The words come out fast and hard, like she is cursing me. But I allow myself to think—for my own sake—that she means them.

CCC

"Let's start with the basics," Xenon says. He has made me sit on a high stool that seems specifically designed to hurt my back. He stands over me as he consults his flexitab. "Name: Ver Yun, or Yun Ver in the Three-er convention. You're sixteen years old, born in Honey Crater, G-Moon Three. Both your parents are alive and well?"

Breathe. Inhale, exhale. I focus on a small area of mildewed wall tile on the far side of the windowless room and wonder what fungal species are growing in the cracks.

"My mother works in a textile factory," I say.

"And your father?"

"I do not know where he is. Probably on the other side of G-Moon Three. May we move on?"

"Don't deflect, Miss Yun," Xenon says, mispronouncing my surname again. He makes it sound like *yum*. It should contain the ü sound, but I let non-Craterers get away with *yoon*. "I need to verify your profile. Your father left you and your mother when you were six years old, correct? Is he still involved with the drug-trafficking rings?"

I hate that when people think of Three, what comes to mind is poverty, cheap clothing, chemical fumes, mass-produced robotics, and drugs. That is typical when your home moon is the manufacturing center of the planetary system and workers smoke, drink, and pop Happy Patches to numb the pain from repetitive-motion injuries. My mother has carpal tunnel in both hands, the most common malady in the clothing factory where she works.

Three does not have a terraformed atmosphere like One and Two, so we live inside residential bubbles, one per municipality.

Every time Three-ers ask for terraforming, the Senate tells us we should be grateful for what we have. Factory production has not been automated, so we still have jobs. That shuts people up, because we know that One's robotics companies could install machines to replace many of the factory workers. I have heard One-ers make similar arguments about Two—machines could do the farming for them. The Senate protects the jobs of the outer moons' residents as a favor, or so they say.

I tell Xenon, "The police ran my father out of Honey Crater. He is probably still selling homemade liquor to people so desperate for cheap alcohol that they do not care if the methanol blinds them." My face is flushing—I talk about my parents as little as I can—but I know the humiliation is just beginning.

"Thank you for your honesty, Miss Yun." Xenon's voice has softened. Out of pity, perhaps. His eyes dart to my cane. I brace myself for the next question. "Would you mind describing what happened to your legs?"

Exhale. Inhale. *Say it.* "RCD," I whisper.

Usually those three letters drop on people like a bomb, halting their questions. But those are Three-ers or scientists, people familiar with the disease. From Xenon's blank look, it is clear he has no idea what I am talking about.

My voice goes cold. "Rapid Cellular Degeneration. I am breaking down, one molecule at a time." The ends of my DNA are shortening, so the rest of the strands are not protected. Deletions, insertions, mix-ups. Proteins folding wrong, until they can no longer do their jobs. "My case attacked my musculoskeletal system first, which is why I need a cane. But it affects my vision and hearing now too."

Ultrafast, unevenly distributed aging. The disease of

diseases, capable of flipping any body part's "off" switch at any time. No one knows why my body decided to rebel like this. RCD occurs frequently on G-Moon Three, striking about one percent of the population. It is rare on G-Moon Two and never intrudes on G-Moon One.

I will not live past thirty, may not even live to be eighteen. There is no known cure.

"That sounds terrible. I'm sorry." Xenon looks deep into my eyes. I feel like he almost trusts me now. "Do you have a medical diagnosis I could see to verify your illness?" He holds out my confiscated flexitab. "You can show me now, or we can find it later in our search."

My hand tightens around my cane. The knuckles bleed white. This has always been difficult. But if it makes my innocence more believable, then I will show my body's history to anyone who will look. I take the device, scan in, and pull up my copious medical records: full-body scans and prescriptions for drug cocktails that Ma worked overtime to pay for. And still we are in debt.

Xenon glances over the file, nodding. He avoids my eyes, his mouth frowning. "This is . . . this is not an easy life, Miss Yun. Aren't there more specialized drugs you can try? All I see here are anticoagulants, stabilizers, and painkillers."

I shrug. "It is what I can afford." Two years ago, an RCD drug called Telomar hit the market. G-Moon Three welcomed the drug with open arms, but clinical performance has been poor, especially for middle-to-advanced cases like mine. And the drug is too expensive to not work.

"This disease explains your interest in Investigator Eppi's lab," remarks Xenon.

"I have always loved science," I say, a defensive reflex. As a small child, I would peek under rocks and explore the arid gorge outside Honey Crater, looking for dead bugs in the thin blades of desert grass. I took them home and identified their species so I could learn about them. Species so different from us that we can only imagine their experiences.

"Yes, but it seems to me," Xenon says, "that your illness is a major reason why you work in this specific lab. A lab that's largely funded by ExSapiens Biotechnologies."

I suppress my impatience. Everyone has heard of ExSapiens, the company dedicated to eradicating disease and injury across the moons. My anti-inflammatory medicine is an ExSapiens drug—no side effects, no vomiting. As far as I know, Telomar has been their only failure. And they provide most of the money that Cal uses—used—to run his lab.

"I wanted to work at Cal's lab because of *him*," I tell Xenon. "Because he discovered antichronowaves . . ."

Xenon cuts me off. "I've heard of chronowaves, but *anti*chronowaves?"

"Yes. They move in reverse from the time continuum. Cal has demonstrated their potential to slow cellular damage and aging."

When I applied to the Institute, I listed Cal's lab as my first and only choice. I wanted to learn about my disease. I also wanted to know why so few One-ers get sick in the course of their century-long lives. Above all, I wanted to search for a cure—or at least an effective treatment that could prevent the agony of advanced RCD.

In my worst moments, Cal would take my face in his palms, stare into my eyes, and promise me we would find answers. My panic would trickle away. My heart would slow until I could count the beats again.

Sometimes I loathed that Cal had so much power over me. Sometimes I wished that he was cruel or old or . . . distant, so that everything could be simple between us. But I would not have accomplished so much in so short a time with an investigator who expected less of me. Or even with Jaha, who was overly solicitous, always too eager to help me, until she realized I rejected most of her offers. People clucking over me makes me feel even more self-conscious about being disabled.

"Aryl Fielding told me that you worked with Investigator Eppi late in the evenings," Xenon says, watching my face. "At any point, did he make inappropriate comments? Or touch you?"

I blink. It takes me several moments to process his words.

"All these cases come across my desk about older men preying on young girls. Did he ever make you feel uncomfortable?"

"No!" My voice shakes. "Cal advised me on my experiments, most often with other people in lab. Sometimes we worked later than the others but he never . . . He stopped me from falling over sometimes. He helped me carry things."

I do not say that Cal helped me extract my own cells, an intimate act I will never share with anyone else. *It's okay, my girl*, he'd say, taking the needle out of my arm. No one had ever called me that before. Not even my mother.

"Everyone I've asked says you were his favorite," Xenon says. "That must've meant you enjoyed being in lab."

"I did," I say. Tears are blurring my vision again.

"I wonder," Xenon says, "if perhaps you wanted something from Investigator Eppi that he couldn't give." He leans toward me, his hard features growing soft. "I see this case half a dozen times a year. The suspect killing someone because that was the only way to possess them."

"I got everything I needed from Cal, sir," I say.

It is a lie.

"I hear you're . . . a lone star, Ver, at the Institute. A girl on a new moon. It makes sense that you wouldn't have many friends. But you had Cal. Caring, handsome, brilliant. Someone who spent hours with you every night."

I hate where this is going. I am dizzy with pain, the kind biology can neither explain nor cure. It is difficult for my mind to pick out words that express what I mean to say.

"Cal was my mentor. Nothing more," I say, tears falling freely. "He was a good man."

Xenon sighs, and I hear his frustration seeping out. "That's what makes this so puzzling, Miss Yun. If he was such a good man, then why didn't you let him live?"

CHAPTER 11
Aryl

Ver comes back with her face blotchy and red. My heart wants to comfort the poor girl, though my brain wonders whether she's stuck to our agreement. I hope her tears are real—hope she didn't spend the last half hour shoveling suspicion off herself and onto me.

My own interrogation starts calmly enough. I lounge on the stool, thinking that the room is too small to hold me, the robot helpers, the desk, Xenon. From where I'm sitting, I could do a grand-battement and kick any one of them.

"Aryl Fielding," Detective Xenon says, reading off his flexitab screen. "You're seventeen years old, born in Celestine, G-Moon One. Correct?"

"Yeah." Thinking of my jewel of a neighborhood makes me wish I could zip away on a vactrain. When I was growing up, my family's apartment was the safest place on the three moons to me. The floor was always strewn with my stuff or my sister's; the air smelled like the coconut milk my parents used to cook our food. Outside, other kids from Two played discdisc with tattered balls and sticks while older migrants cracked sunflower seeds over their chessboards.

"Beautiful city, Celestine, with that blue, blue lake," Xenon says. "I'd love to retire there, away from this crystal desert. So, both your parents are alive and well?"

"Yeah," I say, heart palpitating at the mental image of their faces. Alive? Definitely. Well? Nah.

"And you have one sister," Xenon says. "Ester Fielding."

"She's thirteen and smarter than I'll ever be."

Xenon's face breaks into a smile. "My daughter's thirteen. Tough age. Lots of changes. Thank Pangu they make those new extendable clothes that grow with kids' bodies."

No way will Mom and Dad pay hundreds of Feyncoins for smart clothing when Ester can wear my hand-me-downs. But I don't need to mention that to the detective.

He squints at my profile on his screen. "Your family's not originally from this moon, correct?"

I've never liked that question—it makes me feel like I don't belong on the only moon I've ever known. "My parents are from Broadleaf Falls, G-Moon Two," I say quietly, like it's something to be ashamed of.

Mom played chess, Two's moonwide pastime, for money. The bets went higher and higher, giving Dad anxiety spells, until she finally won enough games in a row to afford spaceliner tickets to One. Even now, when I watch Mom play against her friends, she makes her pieces dance across the board—hunting, surrounding, and gobbling up her opponents' pieces.

"Have you ever gone back to Two?" Xenon asks.

I hate this question too—for the opposite reason. It makes me feel like I'm not a real Two-er either, even though I grew up eating the food and celebrating the holidays and being embarrassed by my parents' offworld habits, like haggling with robot cashiers.

"No," I say. "Spacefare isn't cheap."

"How did you come to work in Calyx Eppi's lab?" Xenon says.

"Coincidence, mostly."

The detective waits for me to say more, but I don't. It's satisfying to withhold the things people want. During the early stages of my friendship with Rhea, a bit of mystery made me feel powerful. It kept her coming back to me.

"Some information my partner and I have gathered might help you elaborate," Xenon says. "Senator Titania Mercure's son, Ford, is a fourth-year apprentice in the same lab. Your parents have been members of the Mercures' household staff since you were two years old."

"That's true," I say, my stomach turning. As a kid, I couldn't have pictured Titania hurting my family. Or my friendship with Ford unraveling the way it did.

"Oh, I'm sorry—how could I be so insensitive?" Xenon smacks his forehead. "We also learned that Senator Mercure has terminated your parents' employment and put them in home confinement."

He's trying to provoke me. I straighten my neck and spine. One wrong move, and Xenon will take it as aggression.

Picture the person who matters most to you in all the moons, Rori used to say during our dance lessons, straightening my shoulders, my spine. *They're balanced, right now, on the top of your head. Don't let them fall.*

"Please, sir," I say, playing the helpless victim. "If you could help my family—they won't survive long, shut up in the apartment like that . . ."

"Senator Mercure's household is her domain, not mine," Xenon says. "Can't you contact her yourself? You have easy access, it seems."

He has to know that I can't just *ask* Titania to release my parents. "Excuse me?" I say, frowning.

"She liked you enough to help you secure a place at the Institute, no?"

I've kept my cool so far, but now my jaw clenches and my teeth grind. Sure, I had a connection, but I still studied hard to earn my place at the Institute. Took exam after exam, squirming, electrodes wired to my brain to track my neural activity. Faced test administrators who pushed me to do impossible calculations and proofs, some of which had no answers, just to see when I'd break. I went through the same process all my lab mates endured: Ver, Kricket, and even Ford. Titania's own son had to do it; obviously her employees' kid wasn't exempt.

Xenon smiles, obviously pleased that he's angered me. But I won't let him win.

"Senator Mercure knows my family well," I say calmly. "She knows we're all hard workers. When I applied for my apprenticeship, Senator Mercure put in a word. I'm grateful for her high opinion of me."

Titania Mercure was in a good mood the day she called the Institute on my behalf. She might be the most unpredictable person I've ever met. As if to retaliate for my parents practically raising her son, she would alternately spoil and discipline Ester and me. I didn't know whether I'd get an expensive gift or harsh words—a synthetic silk scarf with a moving jellyfish print, or a tirade for playing with Ford in the wrong neighborhood and "endangering" him.

Xenon leans in closer. Can he see the tangled feelings under my skin? "You and Ford must be close, then. What was his involvement in Calyx Eppi's murder?"

I wait a beat to make sure he's serious. When I can tell he

is, I let out a laugh. "First of all—Ford and me, close? Not a chance. Secondly, what makes you think he was involved?"

"I can't discuss that." Xenon's face gives nothing away.

My guts twist. *Ford, what did you do?*

He was with Rhea last night, but I don't volunteer that information to Xenon. Instead I say, "Ford and I haven't been on good terms for years. Since before he entered the Institute."

Like stars jetting away from each other after the Big Bang, we've only grown more distant since childhood. His mom has corralled the G-Moon One senators into voting for tighter inter-moon migration laws, for protection of G-Moon One's natural landscapes, and for a tiered education system that lets neurologically better-developed kids go to better-funded schools. That last law made Mom wring her hands: I was never the smartest kid, but I knew how to grind. My family worried I'd have to go to some scrap school that never sent anyone to the Institute.

"How are you and Ford as lab mates?" Xenon asks.

"We . . . tolerate each other," I say. I won't play Xenon's game. I won't mention that I think Ford's become a total stalactite—a One-er whose ego is as fragile as calcified stone-drippings. Or that I think Cal Eppi was one too. He got himself a lab half full of offworld girls. He married a Three-er woman and made her his lab manager. I've overheard several men at the Institute say obedient Three-ers make the best wives. It made me cringe on Jaha's behalf.

"What about the fourth lab member?" Xenon says. "Krick Kepler. How were your interactions with him?"

I shrug. The boy we call Kricket is a sixth-year. He's the oldest in our lab, but we don't give him the respect that seniority usually inspires. "I don't know him well," I say.

"We have his pranks on record," Xenon says. "Adding stinking aldehydes to his roommate's face lotion, et cetera. We'll look into his involvement in this case. Moving on . . . You and Calyx Eppi had a tense relationship, as we've discussed."

"We had our moments," I say evenly. "But he always looked out for me. He even bought me dinner once or twice."

I neglect to mention that before Cal dragged me to his favorite Two-er restaurant he'd withheld a week's pay because I'd been performing with the dance team and skipping lab. That night, he set a trap. Knowing I was always hungry and out of money, he bought me all the food I wanted, and as I ate, he moaned about how he was losing patience with me. Then he walked me back to lab and hovered over my shoulder, nitpicking my pipetting technique. Maybe he'd bought me food so that I'd feel I owed him extra labor. I didn't.

"But science is not your only skill," says Xenon. "Your Institute profile says that you're an accomplished dancer on the Institute team. Impressive."

I know he's sweetening me up to get information out of me, but I feel a smile coming on anyway. I can't help it. When I jump and glide and turn, the moment is mine, whether there's music or not. I'm at my most powerful, making everyone in the room feel as I feel. I don't belong on One—people have made that clear. I wouldn't fit in on Two either. So I've made the stage my home, training to defy gravity. I've paid the price: callused and bloody feet, pulled hamstrings, a shoulder with a painful click. And time. Thousands of hours of time.

"You're capable of lifting up to sixty kilograms—the weight of a fellow dancer—above your head," Xenon says. "You would make a formidable opponent, Miss Fielding. Especially for a man who's spent the past fifteen years in a lab."

Before I can react, he reaches out and clenches a hand around my bicep, smiling. "Built strong, aren't you? Your parents must be proud."

The fact that he's touching me makes me want to vomit on his uniform. Once people learn that Mom and Dad came from Two, they spew all kinds of nonsense about the agricultural collectives; they want to know if my family worked the fields or packaged the crops for shipping offworld, as if those were the only two options. Or they bemoan the pickers' harsh conditions and low pay, and *oh*, how they wish they could do something to help!

I yank my arm out of Xenon's grip. "I couldn't have beaten up Cal. Didn't you check? There were no bruises on his body."

"Oh, but there were, on his chest," the detective says, the intensity in his voice growing. *That was from the CPR!* "Tell the truth, Miss Fielding. You subdued Investigator Eppi and held him down by the chest while your collaborator, Ver Yun, administered the lethal injection. She used her intimacy with the victim, and you used your strength. DNA evidence proves it."

I'm shaking my head, but Xenon isn't finished.

"Miss Yun was uncooperative, so she didn't get this opportunity, but I'll make a deal with you. Tell me everything about her role in Eppi's death, as well as your own, and when you're both convicted, your sentence will be half what Miss Yun gets. Confess now, and you'll still have a life ahead of you when you leave that jail cell."

It's tempting. Ver and I have no alibi, no money, no defense. The judicial computer cluster will definitely convict us of killing Cal. I could tell this officer what he already believes and leave with the hope of a future.

But admitting guilt—even if it could get me a shorter sentence—means giving up. I'm not someone who does that.

"Explain something to me, detective." I keep my voice low but taut as any braced muscle. "Why would Cal's own apprentices kill him? Even if we thought we could get away with it? Without him, we'd have no place in this world and no promise of anything better. I'd be a service worker like my parents, and Ver would rot on Three. Tell me why we'd vack our only hope of making something of ourselves."

I curl my cuffed hands into strong farmworker fists and enjoy watching Xenon flinch.

Instead of answering my question, he signals for the bots to take me back to my cell. "Miss Fielding, this interview is over. I can read your crimes in your eyes."

CHAPTER 12
Ver

I know there is no hope as soon as I see Aryl's face. Aiyo, her features are quivering with rage. Her usually radiant skin has gone bloodless and sallow.

"That prune's holding us here until the trial, whenever that is," she seethes, melting onto her lumpy cot. "And we can't do anything to change the outcome if we're shut up in here . . ."

The screen on the back of the door turns white and displays a message.

"Bail is online," I say. My body trembles when I see the figure by my name: three months of my paycheck.

There is a *swish* sound as Aryl kicks her leg out in front of her. She grabs it with her cuffed hands, pulls it toward her face, and stretches her hamstring. She tilts her head back to read the bail posting, upside down.

"Four thousand Feyncoins. I don't even have two thousand," she says.

"Your family?" I ask.

Aryl flinches and looks away. "Let's not go there."

Before I even have time to be curious, a cramp hits so hard I cannot speak. Pounding, expanding in my gut. These pains come out of nowhere after I miss my medication, especially when I am menstruating. I lie back on my cot in the fetal position and rock myself. I wish for Ma, how she would drape herself over me when every part of me hurt. Squeezing the pain out.

"Ver?" Somehow I register Aryl's voice, her warm hand on my shoulder. But I am still voiceless.

In pulses, the pain subsides long enough for me to open my eyes. Gradually it ebbs away to a point where my central nervous system is online and allowing me to think. Strange that I can be fine in any given moment, then in galaxies of agony the next. It depends on how I slept, what I have eaten, the movements I make, the drugs circulating in my bloodstream, and my emotional state. A panic attack, for instance, will bruise me from the inside out.

"I have to get out of here," I say, even though every word wounds my pride. "The security bots confiscated my medications."

Aryl's face changes. Her eyes widen with pity, which I hate, even when it gets me what I want. She masks it with sarcasm. "Well, unless your people on Three have an illicit fund that'll cover your bail . . . ?"

I do not smile. "Why does everyone think I am either poor as dust or drug-ring royalty? I give every spare Feyncoin from my paycheck to my mother. She spends it all. So I am trapped here."

Aryl arches one eyebrow into a parabola of judgment. I regret my words. This girl knows too much about me already. Now she will assume, correctly, that my mother spends much of my money on drugs. Happy Patches, squares that adhere to the roof of the mouth and dispense painkilling opioids and mood-boosting nicotine. They are expensive, and legally available only to patients with chronic pain diagnosed by a physician—which is also expensive—so most people get them on the street.

"My parents are always sending money to my aunts and uncles on Two," Aryl says. "I've seen how much pressure it puts on them."

I blink at her.

"My cousin hurt his back lifting lumber," Aryl continues. "Two lumbar hernias. He's on painkillers. The surgery's expensive and might not work."

"Keep him away from patches," I say.

When Ma is flying, she cares about nothing else. When she stops, the pain in her hands and back returns, and all she wants is to fly again.

She was not always this way. Once she was fiery and loving, determined that I would leave Three and earn a better life. When I was small, Ma used the extra money from her paycheck to buy me real eggs from G-Moon Two, so I would grow up strong, or at least smart. None of that mass-synthesized albumin goo from the food factories for me, though Ma herself ate it all the time.

"Sounds like you're speaking from experience," Aryl says.

Again, I say nothing—which any reasonable person would take as a *yes*—and watch her face change. She looks disgusted with herself for baiting me.

"I'm sorry," Aryl says softly. "I was hoping you wouldn't say something tragically alien like that, but then you did."

For the first time, I think her words match her thoughts. "We can be as tragically alien as we want with each other," I say.

To my surprise, we both start laughing. The sound is manic. Like we are announcing to all the Gui moons that we are the killers the police think we are. Feeling that you do not belong on the moon you stand upon is never funny. But it is a relief when someone else knows what that is like. Even if she is the only other suspect in the death of someone you loved.

Beep! Beep! The room's buzzer sounds. The laughter dies on our lips. Did someone hear us? Will we be punished for making noise?

"Hello?" I call out.

"Oh, Ver-hai, don't be scared," singsongs a sad, sweet voice. A voice with a regional Three-er accent, heavier and thicker from the weight of loss. The last voice I expected to hear.

Aryl rockets to her feet. "*Jaha?*" she cries. "Please believe me, I didn't do it—"

"I know you didn't, Aryl-hai," says Jaha, affectionately calling Aryl "child." "That's why I came to the station. I've paid bail for both of you. I'm taking you home."

☽ ☽ ☽

White is the best color at self-defense. White objects reflect all the visible wavelengths of light, absorbing nothing, and send the photons scattering.

On Three, it is also the color of mourning.

Jaha Linaya has arrived at the police station dressed in white from head to toe, a sash thrown over one shoulder, crossing a structured bell-sleeved dress. Star-shaped earrings sit inside her dozen ear piercings. A glowing LED hoop loops through her left nostril.

This is the drabbest I have ever seen her look. Her everyday outfits are colorful. Her long braid is space-dark; her skin, a deep shade of brown, usually glows. Today, shadows like slashes sit beneath her enormous black eyes. Makeup cannot cover her exhaustion. She looks like she can barely hold herself upright. Something more than the infant girl strapped to her chest is weighing her down.

Despite these warning signs, Aryl cannot stop smiling. She looks *too* glad to see Jaha. As if we will all troop back to lab and simply put this murder accusation behind us.

"Miranda, tell them the rules," Xenon says to the green-haired officer on his left. Although she looks young, her face is narrow, her eyes cruel. Her badge reads *Det. Miranda Card*; she must be a junior colleague of Xenon's. Why else would she take his orders?

She shoots him an annoyed look before turning her frightening eyes on Aryl and me. "Ms. Linaya's bail payment has been processed, and you're free to go until your trial, which will take place five days from now. I'm working with Detective Xenon on your case, and I swear on all our lives, justice will be done."

The words barely register in my head. I have less than a week to clear my name. An impossible task.

"Don't try to run off. We'll be monitoring your locations with every scan of your identifying features," Detective Card adds. This means our fingerprints and retina scans, which are needed to pass through transport checkpoints. "And we'll retain possession of your personal effects until after your trial." So we will not get our flexitabs back. Or my medications.

Card approaches me, and I try not to flinch. *Click, twist, snap!* Her hands are rough as she unclasps my cuffs. Aryl gives me an uneasy look. She is probably thinking that as terrible as Detective Xenon's interrogation tactics were, Detective Card's might have been even worse.

"If they're declared innocent at their trial, I want all that money returned to me," Jaha says to Detective Card. Card snorts mockingly and walks off with Xenon.

That was too easy. So easy, I am disturbed. Jaha showed up just as my body was beginning to fail. Just when Aryl and I had found the one common denominator between us.

Now that I walk free, I worry that the usual chill between Jaha and me will return. But she hugs me and Aryl one at a time, loosely, so we do not crush baby Dimmi. The hugs seem to be equal in magnitude; Jaha is careful not to show a preference for one of us in public.

When I see the baby, face scrunched up in sleep, I feel like crying. Dimmi is nine months old, and her little pink mouth looks just like Cal's. The miracle of inheritance. Will this child ever know how amazing her father was?

Aryl and I follow Jaha out of the station and onto the busy street. The balmy evening air soothes my lungs, a welcome contrast to the dry, filtered stuff blasting through the police station.

"I've gotten you two out, but Cal's stuck in the medical repository." Jaha's voice is flat, her eyes cold spheres of glass. "They're cutting him open. Taking samples of this, biopsies of that. They even asked me for the backup password to his hand, since it can no longer be activated by his voice." Her voice breaks. "I'm sorry. I don't mean to unload on you two."

Aryl puts a hand on her arm. "Don't worry about it."

Jaha takes a deep breath, as if pushing the reset button on her emotions. "Ver-hai, how are you feeling?"

Even though the solicitousness is embarrassing, I appreciate that she has asked. Has broken the silence between us. If I were not sick, what would we talk about? The fact that I was hopelessly in love with her husband?

"Fine," I lie. My spine has gone crackly-stiff. Sparks of pain are shooting down my legs. I want to ask Jaha to call a hovercab, but I am hesitant to ask for favors. It will be a short walk to campus anyway.

"I've ordered more of your meds," Jaha says, taking in my slumped posture. "The police are keeping the ones you had. They want to examine them chemically. The new ones should be delivered by drone to our home tonight."

"Thank you," I say flatly.

"We're going to your apartment?" There is dramatic surprise in Aryl's voice. I wonder if she is feigning it—if she knew the invitation was coming.

Jaha nods, as if this was obvious. "Don't you want some time away from campus? Your dorms are surrounded by reporters wanting to interview you. I've got food, privacy, and doors that lock."

As always, Jaha is prepared. But I cannot trust her.

When I first got to G-Moon One, she ordered ergonomic leg supports for my lab bench. She nagged the Institute housing officers to make sure I was given a ground-floor room in the part of the dorm complex closest to BioLabs, and she pressed for frequent maintenance checks of the BioLabs elevators to make sure they would never malfunction. She moved the lab supplies I used most onto shelves at my eye and chest level so I could easily reach them.

But that was before Cal started talking to me more than anyone else. Before he began ordering drone-delivered dinners for two during our late nights in lab. As the person who reviews lab finances, Jaha knows about that.

"There's something else," Jaha says now, lowering her eyes. "It's not easy to admit. But I need people with me at home. I don't want to be alone."

Aryl winces but nods. She tries to catch my eye. I give nothing away.

I cannot worm out of this one. Jaha has paid for our

freedom, at least temporarily, and in return, she is asking for our company. If I know anything about Jaha Linaya, it is that she is too smart to make underwhelming bargains like that. She wants something more from us.

Aryl might be ignorant of her plans . . . or they could be working together. Jaha has helped Aryl cover her truancy in lab, doing menial procedures for her while she was out dancing. It would not be beyond her to cover for Aryl now.

I will not sleep tonight.

CHAPTER 13
Aryl

"It's so good to have people here," Jaha says, taking Ver's lavender jacket. As she brings it closer to the wall, a hook forms out of the polymer. "We haven't had guests in months. Medea, remind me how long it's been?"

Jaha's voice carries a faint Three-er accent, but at first listen, she sounds as if she's from One. Sometimes I wish my parents had adjusted to this moon as well as she has—acting like One-ers, sounding like them.

"No one outside the family has set foot in this apartment for seven months and six days," chimes a monotone voice that seems to come from everywhere. "Hello, visitors. I am Medea, the Eppis' home AI."

"Hello," Ver says dryly. I blink, amused. Most One-ers ignore home AIs. There must not be many on Three.

Jaha and Cal's apartment isn't the kind of place where you could host parties—even five dancing people in here would be a stretch. But the walls are sunny yellow, and the living room window has no blinds or curtains. The floor is cluttered with everything from baby toys to appliance packaging to adults' shoes and jackets.

It feels safe.

Still, I keep an eye on Ver, worrying that she'll trip on some knickknack. If she gets hurt when I'm around, the police will assume I'm at fault and think I'm even more of a brute. That's the only reason I care.

Ahead of me, Ver's stopped in front of a pair of scuffed black boots, the laces threadbare. Cal's boots. He wore those on chilly days. His feet were small—I never noticed that when he was alive. Feels apt, though. Parts of that boy from the mountains never grew up.

Jaha wades through the clutter and deposits Dimmi in her cradle in a corner of the living room. Dimmi starts to wail, prompting a groan from Jaha.

"I've got her," I say, stepping over to the cradle and rocking it side to side. From when I was four until I was about ten, my parents spent all their time at work, leaving me to watch Ester. I could get peace from my sister's wails if I played with her or gave her a spaceship plushie or fed her.

I scan the floor for toys, grab a tattered pink elephant that's been loved to within a hair's width of its life, and hold it out to Dimmi. She keeps crying. Maybe she's cold? I lift her up, take the fleecy blanket from underneath her, and wrap her inside it. When I pass her the pink elephant again, she stops crying. Babies are all different, just like any other humans, but when it comes to needing warmth and comfort, each one is the same.

In the kitchenette, Jaha's heating up freeze-dried vegetables and precooked quinoa on the stove while she talks to Ver. She looks animated, grateful for non-baby company. She always was talkative in lab. Sometimes I'd move to the library to read and write so we wouldn't chat for hours about dance and clothes, or the puzzling ways One-ers behave toward us.

"Things hadn't been easy," she says, unprompted. "Funding

was running low, and we didn't know when we'd get more from the Institute or ExSapiens. Cal was making budget cuts at home to pay off interest on lab equipment—I had to stop buying produce farmed on One." She grimaces. "But it's not like Cal spent any time here. I took care of this whole place—and Dimmi—by myself."

"Trust me, we know," I say, remembering how I played physical therapist during Jaha's pregnancy.

Ver scowls at me, probably warning me not to insult the dead man.

I add, "I'm sure Cal only wanted the best for all of you."

But he wasn't working overtime to survive, like my parents. He was doing it because, for whatever reason, he wanted to.

"He was always irritable when he did come home." Jaha doesn't disguise the pain on her face. "Then, late at night, he'd tell me he was sorry. That he felt he wasn't enough as a man or a father." She's tearing up.

"Auntie, you don't have to tell us any more," Ver says, her voice sickly sweet.

"I think you're both innocent," Jaha blurts, looking us square in the eyes. "You didn't kill my husband."

It takes a second for the surprise—and the relief—to wear off.

"Thanks, I guess," I say.

"Then what did kill him?" asks Ver.

Jaha doesn't miss a beat. "Stress. Cal was frustrated and humiliated by his lack of progress. He felt he'd made no significant breakthroughs since he and I discovered antichronowaves all those years ago. I tried to remind him that discovery isn't linear, that something would come if we kept working . . ."

My face wrinkles. "You think Cal was depressed?"

Jaha nods.

"You . . . think . . . Cal *killed himself*?" Ver says.

"I don't know!" Jaha cries. "I don't know." In a hurry, she takes the food off the stovetop and transfers it onto three trays, burning herself in the process. She winces and sticks her index finger in her mouth.

The home AI folds down the table from the wall, I put Dimmi back in her cradle, and we sit, watching our food let off steam. Spongy quinoa and overcooked spinach that's brown and shriveled like mulch. Ver looks hungrily at the food but pokes it around her plate, squinting as if it's poisoned. Maybe that's her careful Three-er brain at work. People from Ver's moon are not known for trusting others.

As for me? I haven't danced all day, so I can't work up an appetite for this mush. My muscles feel limp and underutilized, my stomach still full from my last meal. I watch Jaha mix the quinoa and spinach on her own plate until it looks like green diarrhea, and I try not to gag.

But just as I pick up the spoon, there's an announcement from the AI. "Jaha, someone's at the door."

"Tell him we're not home," Jaha says, her LED nose ring winking aggressively.

"I would," the AI says, "but his insistent posture tells me he'll wait outside until you let him in."

"Give me a moment." Jaha rises and goes to the mirror. Taking scarlet lipstick from her pocket, she smears it onto her mouth, dabs light brown cream under her eyes to hide her dark circles, and tucks stray black hairs into her braid. Once her stage makeup is set, she lets out a deep breath. "Okay. I'm ready."

The door slides open, and the most muscular person I've

ever seen lumbers into the apartment. The cheap material of his suit stretches over his thick limbs. He seems to be bald, but he's so tall I can't see the top of his head. When I see his round face, I'm shocked by how young he looks. Maybe twenty-two or so. His glowing eyes—too blue to be true—rake over all of us, seeming to assess whether or not we're threats. They linger the longest on me, traveling up and down my body, before he blushes and turns away. I'm mildly annoyed, but I'm used to it.

Another man follows the large one inside. He's tall, thin, and golden-skinned, probably a few years older than Jaha, with straight black hair tucked under a close-fitting, neon-orange knit cap. His posture is terrible, his gait loping and unsure. But I know better than to underestimate the brain under that questionable orange hat, or to believe someone dressed so casually can't be important.

I recognize him. *Everybody* recognizes him. I stare, wondering if he's real.

"Scrap, Jaha, you look rough," says Pauling Yuan, founder of ExSapiens Biotechnologies, in a warm, scratchy voice. "Your face paint doesn't fool me. Come here."

Jaha lets out a croak of a sob, and Yuan's bodyguard looks on with mild interest as Yuan embraces her, resting his chin on her head.

I've seen Yuan on holo all my life. I've heard Cal talk about the time they spent working together when they were both apprentices, before Yuan got famous. Now the man himself has appeared at my dead boss's apartment and is hugging his wife.

I look out the window and fling a prayer to the stars that Pauling Yuan is here to help us too.

CHAPTER 14
Ver

After an atom absorbs energy, each of its electrons surges to a higher quantum excitation level, careening around faster and faster, in ever more complex orbitals. If one is excited enough, it can break free of the atomic nucleus and jet off.

This is how I feel with Pauling Yuan here. As if I will rocket off the ground. Aiyo, I have not been so starstruck since I first met Cal!

Pauling Yuan started ExSapiens as a young Institute alumnus, and it quickly became a success. With his earnings, Yuan funds labs like Cal's, builds hospitals in the poorest parts of Two and Three, and donates money to schools for their science programming. Sometimes he pays to treat poor babies' multiple sclerosis or muscular dystrophy with ExSapiens gene therapy. After Cal told me they were old friends, I hoped that Yuan would visit our lab one day. I always wanted to meet him.

But not like this.

"Thank you for coming, Paul," Jaha says, putting her voice in a straitjacket so her accent won't leak out. "Tea?"

"Yes, please," Yuan says. "And for you, Osmio?"

"Of course," the bodyguard rumbles. His fluorescently blue eyes scan the kitchen cabinets. "Sencha, please."

Osmio can see *inside* the cabinets! Did he get special eyes installed, to become better at his job? In addition to its medications, ExSapiens is famous for its enhanced synthetic body parts, though that is quite a crowded market.

"Sencha will do for everyone, then." Jaha dumps tea leaves into mugs and fetches hot water from a nozzle on the wall. Osmio holds his mug, comically small in his hand, blows on the liquid's rippling surface, and sips daintily.

When Jaha hands a cup to Yuan, he looks at the cannister of sugar on the counter and asks, "May I?"

Jaha nods, and Yuan stirs in four spoonfuls.

"I'm sorry for barging in," Yuan says, sipping his tea. They settle onto the sofa, while Aryl and I remain standing near the wall. "And I'm sorry I didn't come by more often before all this happened."

Jaha swallows, a lump in her throat. "Don't be. Cal loved doing science with you when you were apprentices. Always said you trained him better than his own investigator did. Between that and funding our lab, you've done more than enough for us."

"Looks like he paid it forward with his protégés. You bailed these two out?" Yuan says, gesturing at me and Aryl. "Good. Can't have the police arresting defenseless girls on a whim. Picking the most obvious culprits is sheer laziness."

My heart quickens. *Pauling Yuan thinks we're innocent.* With him backing us, perhaps we stand a chance.

Osmio's eyes follow Yuan's finger as if by reflex, and he gives Aryl a shy smile. She rolls her eyes.

"Their trial's in five days," Jaha says.

Yuan nods. "I've donated to the LCPD crimes unit so they can perform the highest-grade autopsy. I hope that'll lead to a more thorough investigation."

"You can't just throw money at the law," Jaha mutters.

"Listen, I want to make sure that Cal's legacy lives on in these kids," Yuan says. "And that they don't rot in prison just because of where they come from."

Next to me, Aryl looks so relieved she might cry. I would feel the same if Jaha were not acting so strangely. Pauling Yuan has spent millions supporting Cal's research. It makes sense that he would want to give Aryl and me a chance at exoneration.

"Ver, Aryl, can you give us a moment?" Jaha says. Hands twitching with nervousness, she shoos us into the darkened master bedroom. She casts a harried glance at Osmio, but he seems attached to Yuan through some covalent bond. Interesting that Yuan brought a bodyguard to see an "old friend"—is he suspicious of Jaha too?

I am alone with Aryl in the bedroom. It feels uncomfortable, even though she frightens me less than Jaha. Despite the darkness, I can tell that the room is octagonal. The circular bed takes up most of the floor space. It is perfectly made, with not even a dent in the sheets.

My chest heavy, I wonder what Jaha and Cal talked about here. Did he tell her last week that I said, "I am so glad to have you, Cal," as my heart seemed to burst through my mouth? Did he tell her how he responded?

"You're a gift to the lab, Ver, and to me," Cal said crisply. We both knew what I had tried to confess. "But I can't wait to see what you accomplish on your own."

The message was clear. It hit like a two-ton pendulum. I would leave Cal eventually. I was temporary; Jaha was permanent. I was his apprentice; she was his wife.

I was foolish to ever think otherwise.

CHAPTER 15

Aryl

Ver and I back away from the door, and the AI shuts it all the way.

"Look!" Ver whispers, pointing to three midsize screens on the wall. Security feeds. One shows the door of the apartment building, one displays the entrance to the unit, and one, a newer model, is of the living room. I bet Cal and Jaha installed that one to keep an eye on Dimmi.

Our eyes lock onto the screen with the living room feed. Even though Ver's close enough for me to feel her body heat, she's leaning away, as far as her spine will allow. She's scared, I think. Scared of me. Of my strength. A little intimidation is good in a situation like this, but I still feel ashamed.

In the living room, Osmio is standing stock still, watching Jaha with focus and cunning—so differently from how he looked at me.

Jaha turns her head slightly toward the camera, and I wonder if she actually hopes we're watching. Yuan is smiling at Dimmi's crib. He gets up, peeks inside at the baby, and dangles his finger in front of her face. Dimmi coos and grabs at his hand.

"I'd love to have a kid," Yuan says, sighing. "But I don't have the time, with work. My wife says she wants one, and that she can take care of a baby alone, but she shouldn't have to."

Jaha's nodding, looking wistful. "Cal always worried he wasn't doing enough for Dimmi. Or for me. But it was too hard for him to change."

"That's what I'm afraid of, if I become a dad," Yuan says. He sits back down next to her on the sofa and picks up his tea.

"And once you have a child, Paul, there's always one more thing to be afraid of," says Jaha.

I suspect that's exactly how my parents feel. Scared, all the time. But they couldn't have imagined that their own daughter would hurt them the way I have.

"Jaha, we're family. We always have been. If I can do anything to make things easier for you, please let me know."

"Thank you," Jaha says, her voice hollow.

Yuan unrolls his neon-green flexitab. "There's something I want to show you." He bends to whisper something to her, and a tear rolls down Jaha's cheek. She wipes it away on her white sleeve.

"Maybe . . . maybe Cal *did* kill himself," I mutter, moving closer to the holo screen. "Busted self-esteem . . ."

Jaha is scrolling on Yuan's flexitab, reading some kind of document.

"Cal would not kill himself *like that*," Ver says, shaking her head. "TTX is a bad way to go. If Cal wanted to die, he could have ordered sodium pentobarbital—legal euthanasia, much less painful. And he is licensed to purchase it. But why would he even consider suicide in the first place?" Ver's whisper sounds desperate. "He had a big future. Research was going well—I *know* he was excited! You have to believe me."

I nod, slowly. "He had a baby girl too."

"Some parents do not stay for their baby girls," Ver says. I can hear her throat closing up.

Where did that come from? Though I'm dying for her to elaborate, I bite my tongue.

"Investigators *do* stay for their experiments," Ver says. "He would not have left me to finish mine alone."

"Maybe he thought you could do it independently. Didn't he call it a side project?"

"He is humble," Ver says. So she admits it: Her project *was* a big deal. Or it would've been, if Cal's death hadn't put an end to their experiments.

In the living room, Jaha picks up a stylus with her left hand and signs the document on Yuan's flexitab. They get to their feet, and she bows her head in thanks. She's smiling through the tears. Why?

"I'll have my assistant process this right away," Yuan says to Jaha. "The funding is yours now, which means the Institute will approve your promotion in no time. Congratulations, Investigator Linaya. I expect great things."

Osmio takes this as his cue to move toward the door. Yuan bows to Jaha and follows his bodyguard out of the apartment, standing a little straighter than when he came in.

Watching him, I feel dizzy, as if I've done too many turns across the stage without spotting. The bedroom swirls like the Milky Way, and without thinking, I grasp Ver's narrow shoulder to stay upright. But only for a moment.

I whisper, "Investigator Linaya."

Jaha is next in line for Cal's position. An understudy poised to become principal dancer. *Why didn't I see it?*

Because I didn't want to.

"We are such dense matter," Ver breathes, one hand clamped over her mouth. Her other hand clenches around my wrist, and a warm sensation spreads through my belly. "You know why Jaha wants us to think that Cal was depressed? So that no one suspects *her*."

"She wasn't even in lab last night."

Of course, neither was Ford. And Xenon asked about *his* involvement.

"Jaha has always, *always* wanted to be Cal," Ver insists.

"You think Yuan isn't aware of that? He's known Jaha since she was our age."

"He was Cal's friend, not Jaha's. Besides, I think he brought a bodyguard because he is afraid of her. Did you hear how cold Jaha became when he mentioned that the police will do a rigorous autopsy?"

"But she bailed us out."

"To take suspicion off herself," Ver says. Her hand floats off my wrist and back to her side. "What is something no one would expect a killer to do? Free other suspects who had already been arrested."

This twisting logic is giving me a headache. But Ver may have a point. Jaha said she and Cal have been having money problems, so how'd she scrape together thousands of Feyncoins to free us? Maybe we can't trust anything she's said.

And I have to admit it: Jaha's the perfect murderer. She's the person closest to Cal. She knows all the ins and outs of the lab. She has more to gain from Cal dying than anyone else: his job, his money, full custody of their daughter. It's easy to believe that resentment was festering. Loneliness, from all those nights Cal spent away from her. And who knows what was going on inside the walls of this apartment when he did come home?

"I don't want it to be Jaha," I admit. "She's the best person in lab. Helped me when everyone else thought I was too dense to get anything done."

Ver bites her lip, not missing the accusation. Everyone loves Jaha, except maybe her. Sometimes I've even wished we worked for Jaha, not her husband. People always forget that she and Cal have the same qualifications. They don't know that Jaha's better at building scopes and rigs and relationships—at least with me. Cal refused to help when I got stuck on a problem. Jaha slyly sent books and articles to my flexitab that would steer me toward a solution. She not only accepted that I had a life outside of lab; she came to my dance shows and helped me book cheap tickets home to Celestine. She cared for the mouse colony while I was away. When Cal and I had our worst spats, Jaha would force a compromise.

Despite all this, Cal was the investigator, not Jaha.

What if this ideal wife and lab manager planned to kill Cal for a long time, while playing the roles that would deflect suspicion? Shivers tickle my spine.

The walls of the dark octagonal bedroom seem to inch closer. And I know that no matter how good Jaha has been to me in the past, I can't spend the night here.

CHAPTER 16

Ver

There exists a good hypothesis for why prey animals like rabbits have evolved to have eyes on the sides of their heads: so that they can scan a wider field of view for predators. The ones who lacked panoramic vision got eaten the quickest and could not pass on genes for their close-set eyes to the next generation.

Tonight, I am prey. I did not see what was right in front of me.

"We have to go," Aryl says. Her hands twist nervously behind her back. She wears her feelings in her movements, I have noticed, a habit that could get us both in trouble.

In a blink, she and I are back in the living room, gathering our things. I step, step, step as fast as I can. *Whoosh.* Nearly smash my hip into the table! I have to be more careful. An injury would mean untold amounts of pain. And I cannot work to exonerate myself if I am bedridden.

"We will look more suspicious if we are not back in our dorms tonight," I say to Jaha, breathing hard. "And all your help will go to waste."

She looks unconvinced. "You're already here," she says. "Wouldn't it be dangerous for the two of you to walk to campus alone at this hour?"

"No," I say. Aiyo, what moon does Jaha think she is living on?

"I'm sorry, Jaha, but Ver and I are tired," Aryl says, sounding reluctant. "We'll sleep better in our own beds."

"Thank you for everything, Investigator," I say.

Jaha lifts an eyebrow, and I realize I have made a mistake. "Jaha will do. After all, you only ever called my husband Cal."

Her smile makes my neck prickle. Thankfully, Aryl steps between us. I am glad that she is here. If she wants to protect me—which I hope is true—she will do a good job.

"We'll all be able to think better tomorrow, after we've slept," Aryl says. "See you soon."

"Whatever you say, girls," Jaha says. "Good night."

The AI slides the doors open. I rush out of the apartment as quickly as my feet and cane will take me, Aryl at my heels.

CHAPTER 17
Aryl

I walk a short distance behind Ver, under the pale blue street-lights. It's dark out, the clear skies studded with stars. One of them winks down at us as asteroids float by, blocking its light, then moving along. The hilltop neighborhood around campus is quiet, but strains of thumping music and beams of light trickle out from the dorms. People are having fun without me—something I'll have to get used to.

Rhea's out there, somewhere. She's got Ford and our friends, while I've got Ver, the nerd who was Jaha's husband's favorite.

I've never bothered to look at my lab mate before, not really. Now I see the curve of her skull and neck, accentuated by her short hair. Perfect seashell ears. Her walk, cane and all, is a rhythmic sway.

Ver glances over her shoulder, her thoughtful black eyes flashing, probably wondering why I'm staring at her. I smile, trying to seem unthreatening. With Jaha's costume-change into investigator, both of us are less sure that the other is a murderer than we were this morning.

I catch up to her, executing leaps from one foot to the other, fast as I can. I picture Rori watching me. *Walk like you're dancing. Run like you're dancing. Live like you're dancing,* he said at our last lesson.

Ver doesn't walk any faster or slower. She lets me fall into step beside her. That's a start.

"So, you and Cal," I venture. "What was it like between you? When you were alone?"

"Oh." Ver winces, but her face quickly settles into a neutral expression. "Teacher. Student. Typical."

"Don't give me that," I say. "You've been acting like you've lost your dad. Or your boyfriend. Someone you orbited, you know?"

Ver bites her lip, stops walking, and looks at her feet, like the reconstituted penguins you see in life museums. "I would not care if my father died," she says. I remember her saying, *Some men do not stay for their baby girls.* "But Cal was not like a father."

"Meaning . . . ?"

"No caring father would push me to risk my health every day by working so much. But Cal taught me who I want to be. It was as if I was a sprout and he was my sun. He helped me grow, and I grew toward him. Nothing . . . happened between us. It was not like that."

I take a deep breath before saying, "Did you want it to be?"

Ver looks at her feet again. "I am not sure." She shakes her head. "Truly. I have never been sure."

I have a hard time wrapping my head around the idea that Ver Yun, Three-er science robot, could have feelings for anybody, let alone someone as out-of-bounds as our boss.

It's . . . creepy. And sad, given how hopeless her crush was even when he was alive. Now that he's dead—tough luck, Ver.

"What *were* you two working on so late at night?" I sound

jealous, even though I shouldn't care whether she was in love with Cal or not. I'm thinking of when Ford started visiting Rhea's room. The pain of pining for an unavailable girl, getting slapped in the face by reality every couple of days.

Ver pauses. "I cannot tell you."

"I thought we were starting to trust each other," I say.

This prompts a smile from her. A sly but pretty one. "A bit soon for that, Aryl."

"Was it something to do with your, um, injury?" I say, gesturing toward her cane.

Ver starts walking again, faster now, practically throwing herself forward. All the grace is lost from her movements as she tries to leave me behind.

I keep up without any trouble. We reach a fork in the path; the left-hand side leads toward the second-year dorms, the right side to the first-years'.

I think of how Jaha has just become an investigator, of how she wanted to keep us in her apartment tonight. "Listen, I don't think you killed Cal. Really."

"And I know *you* didn't," Ver says. "You had nothing to gain."

I could hug her for believing I'm innocent. "Then why don't you tell me some of the truth? Your truth."

Ver looks up at me with big, teary eyes. "That has hurt enough people already," she says, turning away and hurrying toward her dorm.

CHAPTER 18
Ver

The lens of the human eye bends light rays together, forming an image on the retina that the brain can process. The lenses in my eyes have been slightly squashed out of shape because of my disease. Tonight, as I stare at the eyesore someone left on my door, I wish RCD had attacked *only* my visual system, so I would not see this.

THREE-ER WHORE. Jagged, uneven letters, scrawled in carbon paint.

Gou, which of my neighbors could have done this? I have barely spoken to any of them, because I am no good at the chit-chat that is popular on this moon. So no one knows me well enough to know that I am not a murderer who seduces her investigator victims. Is that what they think I learned on Three?

It is not just the police who think I killed Cal. It is everyone. Everyone except, perhaps, Aryl Fielding.

For a moment, I consider going to the second-year dorms. To Aryl. I remember how her strong wrist felt in my hand, the sensation of safety I experienced when she stepped between me and Jaha.

Aryl is gorgeous. A lot of girls on Three were too. I have always liked looking at them. But in Honey Crater, gay women are pariahs. They are equal under the law, just like everywhere else in the Pangu System. But people glare at them in the tram station and the market. Gang leaders and factory owners, nearly all of whom are men, give these women the worst jobs without saying why. And they tend to show up dead before their time. I have never let myself look too long at another girl.

Stop it, stop it. Aryl is the other suspect! I must control myself. Just like I did with Cal.

I enter my room. The cursed door clicks shut behind me. I slump against it.

"Charles?" I say.

No answer. Aiyo, no wonder. My voice came out at perhaps ten decibels—too low an amplitude to set off his verbal processing software.

"Charles," I try again, louder this time.

"Hello," he greets me.

My heart jumps into my throat. "Who did this to my door?"

"You *are* aware that I lack cameras facing the hallway, in order to protect your neighbors' privacy."

So unhelpful! I smack the padded wall with my cane and gently lower myself until I am seated cross-legged on the floor. I pick up the palm-sized notebook I sometimes use to do lab calculations by hand. The reusable green paper pages are coated with an acrylic that allows ink to be wiped off.

TTX injection, I write on one page. *Left side of the neck, dorsal.* I rip out the page and use a magnet to put it on the wall.

Aryl got to Cal before I did and gave CPR, I write on the next page. *Aryl is right-handed.*

Aryl did not like Cal, but she seems to understand why I loved him. The more I talk to her, the less she seems like a killer. She was framed, like me. But by whom?

Next suspect. *Jaha is replacing Cal as investigator.* I think back to the apartment, to the setup of the room where Jaha sat facing Pauling Yuan. *She signed the funding paperwork with her left hand.*

Jaha is left-handed! But Jaha was not in lab the night Cal died. Or was she? The police could have missed something, or lied to us about what they found on the security feed from BioLabs. But I cannot access those files with the resources I have. I will have to find another way to keep digging into this woman, sneaky as she is, like dark matter.

Who else has a motive? Other investigators, jealous of Cal's talents? But each lab focuses on a different research area. There is very little direct competition within the Institute, and splashy collaborations are frequent. I can rule out Cal's colleagues and his sponsor, Yuan. Cal might have been burning through funding more quickly than he should have, but someone who already has everything would gain nothing from killing his old friend. Not to mention that he is funding Cal's autopsy.

That leads me to Cal himself. *Cal is*—I cross out the error: *was right-handed. Had too many responsibilities and too much pressure.*

My hand trembles as I write. If Cal did this to himself, I will feel worse than if it was a murder. It would mean I failed to save him from himself.

Guilt kicks me in the chest, even though I know that is not how suicide works. No amount of love, money, or achievement can help someone when their thoughts are spiraling and their brain chemistry is altered. I have seen it on Three, where Ma's depressed factory coworkers fell like timber, unable to access medication or psychologists who could help. When I was younger, Ma would wring her hands, wonder how she might have helped them. But more recently, all she has said was, *And so it goes.*

No, no. Suicide does not fit this situation. When we were in lab together, Cal's eyes would light up blue like the hottest, brightest stars in the galaxy. When he talked about his life, it was with love.

I cannot stop looking for what really happened to him. Even if it takes me the rest of my short life.

CHAPTER 19
Aryl

I sleep like the dead and drag myself out of bed the next morning on stiff legs. The feeling that I've forgotten something tugs at me, but my foggy brain can't figure out what it is—until Rhea comes stomping along the path toward me with Ford Mercure in tow.

My heart surges with affection for her and resentment toward him before hardening into the usual envy I feel at seeing them together. It's no surprise that Rhea chose Ford, with his light brown skin that tans coppery under Pangu's light, his long narrow nose with a slight bump, his tight black curls that dust his shoulders. *He's what Rhea wanted, what you couldn't give her.* Wealth, class, handsomeness, maleness.

I try to catch Ford's eye, remembering how the police questioned me about his involvement in Cal's death. He looks away. *What are you hiding?*

Rhea, on the other hand, is staring me down. She plants herself in front of me, one fist on her hip. "Where were you this morning? I was partner-less at practice." Wisps of light blond hair have escaped her hair gel, and sweat's soaking through her pale blue dance top. Several passersby stop to stare. *That's her,* they whisper as they look at me.

Even though Rhea has to tilt her neck back to see me, I feel small. "Rhee—"

"You're innocent until sentenced by the cluster, Aryl. Free to do whatever you want. What's your excuse for skipping practice?"

It's as if someone has pulled a stopper out of me. "I saw my investigator die, got arrested, spent a day in jail, and learned that my parents got fired and put under house arrest. Sorry if I wasn't available to be your personal forklift."

Rhea gives me a doubtful look. Dance is our world. Nothing matters more to either of us, or so we like to pretend.

I blink back tears, turning to Ford. "Did you know, Ford, that your mom's holding my family hostage?"

Ford flinches. "It's a temporary suspension of their employment," he says. "A safety precaution."

"You've had your whole life to figure out that my parents would never hurt anyone," I say. "Not to mention Ester. She's suffering too. And you're letting it happen."

"My mom also has to think about her coalition in the Senate, her constituents . . ."

"Oh *no*," I say, throwing sarcasm over my grief for pride's sake. "What if voters find out her housekeeper's daughter got framed for murdering the person who held the key to her whole future? How embarrassing *for her*. This has scrap to do with your mother's reputation, Ford. Unless *you* did something to Cal—"

"Shut up. You're the one who got arrested," Rhea says.

I glare at her. "Don't tell me to shut up."

"Excuse me?" Rhea gasps. "I was giving you the benefit of the doubt. I was still willing to dance with you even after what's happened. But you can't *expect* people to assume you're innocent.

I don't blame Senator Mercure for taking precautions."

"Thanks for weighing in." So the last year and a half have come down to this. As soon as my friendship stops being convenient for her, she's back to seeing me the way she sees all other Two-ers. As a criminal.

"Look, I'm sorry, Aryl." Ford angles his body away from us and speaks to the ground. "But my mom knows what's best."

After listening to Rhea rip me apart, this is all he can offer? What a coward. My voice breaks as I ask, "Best for who?"

Before Ford can respond, Rhea steps between him and me. "Aryl, you're being incredibly ungrateful. I've done so much for you. So has Ford. Without me, no one would know who you are. Without him, you wouldn't even *be* at the Institute. This is how you thank us?"

Ford looks sheepish now, as if he wants to interrupt her. But I know he won't have the backbone.

"Scrap, Aryl," Rhea goes on. "Turns out my first impression of you was right."

"And that is?" I ask. Even though I want to sink into the ground, I stand taller, daring her to say it. I know what's coming: the final confirmation that I've never been good enough, and will never be good enough, to gain her respect.

As for her love? Forget it.

My heart is pounding in my temples, and Rhea's face swims before my eyes. Ford looks at the ground, his cheeks going crimson.

But Rhea won't say out loud that I'm a brutish alien. Instead, she smiles coldly. "You know what you are."

A dancer stands tall not only because of muscles and bones, but because of a force deep within her, propping everything up from the inside. Call it dignity, or pride, but it's more important than any one body part.

Mine has been destroyed.

I trudge to BioLabs, feeling as if I'm collapsing in on myself. Rhea made it clearer than ever. Everything I had here was given to me, an act of charity. And now I'm losing it all.

The moment when Rhea first asked me to stretch with her at dance practice plays through my mind. Her hands were cool and soft; mine were callused and sweaty. After, we went to dinner at a nanotech gastro-joint, the kind of restaurant I'd never known existed. Real human servers, not bots, waited on us. Synthesized edible crystals combined with garden-grown plants electrified my tastebuds. As the courses rolled in, Rhea asked me nonstop questions about my childhood. She was fascinated by everything, from the food Mom cooked to my audition at Rori's dance studio. By the time she paid for dinner, I was in love with her.

Every time we could talk privately, I gave her more of me. As a hint that I liked girls, I told her about Eva, the dancer I'd dated before she left Rori's studio to become a professional. About how my parents weren't surprised when I brought her home—just glad I'd found someone I liked. I knew they'd be happy for me. On Two, they'd seen all kinds of relationships. Since sharing and acceptance are part of the culture, Two-ers display their true selves in full view of their communities. Rhea smiled at this story, but there was no flash of recognition in her eyes. No jealousy either. Still, I hoped that time would make her realize she wanted me too.

Rhea and I spent the next month dancing, in rehearsal and on stage, swinging our hips together at parties, posing for holos with our cheeks mashed against each other's. But then she started dating Ford. Every time she talked about him, her hands fluttered with a delicate nervous energy that broke my heart. I had to accept that she didn't like girls, or just didn't like me. That I'd mistaken her warmth and generosity for a crush.

But was it even generosity? *Look at all I've done for you . . .*

Did she hang out with me just to prove she was a charitable person? To advance on the dance team by choosing the strongest partner?

The questions hound me as I approach BioLabs. A crowd of reporters surrounds the main entrance, flexitabs flashing, holo cameras buzzing around like bees.

"Aryl Fielding, should the public believe the charges of murder against you?"

"When will Jaha Linaya return to work? We have questions for her."

With my eyeprint, I unlock the building's door and slip inside. No one follows me.

In a corner of the hallway, I sink into a squat and let my head hang between my knees. When I feel calmer, I take the elevator and enter Cal's lab. The lights are dimmed, and a section toward the back, where Cal breathed his last, is still cordoned off by yellow police lights. The police would've wanted to shut down the whole lab, I think, but I can imagine the Institute fighting them to let us keep working. Science halts for nothing and no one.

The space is empty except for Krick Kepler, parked at his usual workstation, surrounded by monitors, typing furiously.

Kricket doesn't look well rested, but then again, he never does. A mixture of freckles and pimples covers his pallid skin. His carroty mane is pulled into a thick, wavy ponytail. He's of average height, but his stalk-like legs are too long for his body, and his pants never fully cover his ankles. I'm not sure when or where he picked up the nickname Kricket, but it suits him.

He looks away from the desk-to-ceiling monitor displaying a short script with scarlet error messages as output. "Hey, Fielding. Weren't you in jail? How'd you get out?"

"Bail." I glance over the lines of code and say, "You forgot to indent this loop," pointing to the error. Kricket's never been great at the parts of research requiring finesse. Might be why he's been an apprentice for six years instead of the usual five.

"Hey, thanks," he says, fixing the mistake. "Wait a second . . ." He dives down, retrieves his backpack, and rummages around in it until he produces a shrink-wrapped muffin studded with fuchsia goji berries. "I got you this. Can't imagine you've been taking care of yourself."

"Thank you," I say, accepting the muffin gingerly. I like Kricket, but I'm wary. He's not known for his generosity, and he *is* known for mischief. After he and Ford argued in lab last year, Ford had an explosive diarrhea episode brought on by phenolphthalein, a pH indicator and strong laxative. A few months ago, one of the Institute's meanest discdisc players pushed Kricket into the big pond on campus on the coldest day of the season—then, to his teammates' great amusement, peed ultraviolet for a week after swallowing concentrated anthocyanin.

Despite Kricket's practical jokes—if they can really be called that—he's always been decent to me. Since he's been working here the longest, he answers the questions we're too embarrassed to ask Jaha or Cal.

"Where's Jaha?" I ask now. Ver, I assume, is sleeping off the past two days. Or avoiding me, because my nosiness last night upset her.

Kricket glances at his shoes. "They took Jaha to the police station this morning," he says. "Two officers. They just wanted to question her, though. They're not about to arrest the Institute's newest investigator."

Does Jaha's questioning mean I'm a step closer to redemption—and my family to freedom? A swoop of hope courses through me, followed by a smack of guilt. Imprisonment would tear Jaha away from her daughter. My freedom would be at Dimmi's expense.

I unwrap the muffin and examine it closely—not that I'd be able to tell if Kricket laced it with anything. But my belly is rumbling up a storm, and I can *smell* the honey in the dough . . .

"It's clean," Kricket says with a laugh. "No spare organic compounds in there."

Reassured, I take a bite. My sister eats muffins from the bottom up, saving the smooth top part for last, but I'm not so meticulous. It'll all look the same in my stomach.

"So it's just us this morning?" I say to Kricket, stating the obvious as I glance around.

"Yeah. Ford's going back to Celestine."

"He is?"

"I heard Senator Mercure sent a spaceliner to pick him up."

"That's so . . . Titania," I say, shaking my head. Even in Ford's last year of primary school, Senator Mercure would holo-call to check that Mom had packed him a lunch, and if he'd forgotten it at home, it would then be drone-lifted to the cafeteria, as if Ford was incapable of buying school food. "But won't running back to Celestine make Ford look suspicious? The timing's weird."

Does she think the police will arrest Ford? Given Xenon's interest in him, I can't count him out as a suspect. But Ford and

Cal seemed neutral toward each other, so I can't imagine what Ford's motive for killing Cal would be. And he has the perfect life—why ruin it with murder?

"Senator Mercure is probably afraid the killer will strike again." Kricket shivers dramatically. "She must be scared for her baby, all alone in Lucent City!"

I don't indulge his mockery of our colleague. "More likely she doesn't want him to get caught up in the media circus."

Kricket nods. "Like you said, though—leaving the Institute makes him look like he has something to hide."

"He has an alibi," I say. "Wasn't he at some gala that night?" With Rhea.

Kricket shrugs. "Yeah. But that doesn't mean he's clean. And just because you were in lab doesn't mean you're not."

A rush of emotion makes the muffin turn to mush in my mouth. I lunge forward and hug Kricket while he splutters in surprise.

"Thank you. Thank you," I say. Now I know what I need to do. "Can I borrow your flexitab?"

CHAPTER 20
Ver

Humans are the only mammals who can willingly delay the onset of sleep. Every other warm-blooded, hairy creature shuts down whenever the need strikes.

I have kept myself awake for too long, and now my body must compensate.

For seventeen hours, I sleep through Aryl's voice messages on Charles's communications platform.

Ver, come to lab. This is important.

Ver, are you really still sleeping?

Are you okay?

ANSWER ME. PLEASE.

Eventually there's a *bang-bang-bang*ing on my vandalized door. Aiyo, what does she want?

"Someone has arrived," Charles says. "Should I let them in?"

I sigh. I revealed too much to her last night. But there is no way to avoid meeting again. I peek in the mirror and run my hands through my disheveled hair. I tell Charles yes.

"Hey." Aryl hovers in the entryway, the sole of one foot wrapped around the other ankle. There is relief in her voice.

I lower myself onto the floor, so that I am surrounded by my scattered notes. Aryl approaches and sits next to me. She touches the back of my right hand, as if to check that my body temperature is still hovering around 310 Kelvin.

"When you didn't answer my messages, my mind jumped to horrible places."

"Because of my health?" I say, my voice going sharp.

Aryl shrugs. "All the stress can't be good for you."

"I am fine," I lie.

A shadow falls over her face. "What happened to your door?"

Humiliation burns through me. If I could melt down the door with a blowtorch, I would.

"Do you have any idea who did it?" Aryl asks.

I shake my head. "No. It could have been anyone. Anyone who thinks I hurt Cal and wants to intimidate me into confessing. Anyone who thinks Three-er girls claw at powerful men for a living."

Aryl moves closer to me, and when I don't move away, she touches the back of my hand again. I shiver. "I grew up on this moon. I know how cruel people can be."

People were cruel to Aryl? The girl cannot walk a hundred meters without some popular apprentice greeting her. Without someone looking her up and down and gaping.

"Have you looked at yourself?" I say. "What is there to be cruel about?"

Pain suffuses Aryl's face, raw and terrible to see. A glimpse into the girl I am urgently curious about. "People like us, who are different—we represent everyone who shares our blood." Her voice is hoarse with emotion. "We can't afford to make mistakes."

I look down at our hands, her long and graceful fingers. Like stem tendrils in various states of unfurling.

Aryl clears her throat. "My parents work for Senator Mercure. She's put them under house arrest without pay."

Anger shoots up my sore spine. "How is she allowed to do that?"

"The rules don't apply to some people," Aryl says. "Speaking of which . . ."

Aryl updates me on Ford's flight and Jaha's questioning by the police. I slide my hand away from hers and try not to think about why she grabbed it in the first place.

"I knew I was right about her!" I mutter under my breath. "But we still need to find evidence that *we* are innocent. The police are wondering if it was us *and* her, not us *or* her."

"We have to look into Ford," Aryl says, nodding. "After Kricket told me Ford ran off, we used Kricket's flexitab to call Ford at least ten times. No answer."

I massage my temple, where a headache is gathering force. "He cannot dodge us forever. We have to clear our names. Not just for us. For our families."

And for what remains of our dreams.

CHAPTER 21
Aryl

GO BACK TO THE FARM.

The handwriting's the same as the message on Ver's door. We've come here for respite from that graffiti, to sit down and strategize, but we've only found more of the same.

Heads peek out of doors. Snickers echo. Several apprentices lean against the walls, watching Ver and me. Rhea, who's leaving the showers wrapped in a towel, runs a hand through her damp silvery hair, smirks at me, and vanishes into her room.

"It wasn't any of us, if that's what you're thinking," says one of our dance teammates, before following Rhea.

The scene around me blurs. Memories take over: That time when I was eight and wore a Two-style hemp dress to school and got pushed down in the mud. That time I was thirteen and Ford's first girlfriend told me to wash my hands before I touched Ford's food so I wouldn't stink it up or give him an infection. Mom never let me serve the Mercures, so I don't know where she got the idea that I was Ford's waitress.

GO BACK TO THE FARM. The child inside me is screaming.

I want to ask my *friends*, some of whom have been in the dorm all morning, why they didn't stop this from happening.

I want to decompose into a dirt mound on the floor. I want to run away.

But I don't do any of that. Instead I turn to Ver and say, "Hey, we match now."

Ver's shaking so hard, the tip of her cane is bouncing all over the floor. She takes me by the arm with her free hand and heads back toward the elevators. I let Ver lead me out of the building and across the Institute grounds, past people curiously watching the two murderers, until we make it to the campus store. Inside, Ver clatters through the aisles, and I follow. She points to items on the shelves; I snatch them up and carry them.

We buy a liter of steel-colored paint, a roller, and a brush for twenty-seven Feyncoins, pooling the money from our dwindling accounts. The mindless robot cashier logs our purchases and says nothing.

Returning to the dorms, we cover up the hateful graffiti on my door. It's late, and the hallway has cleared.

We go to Ver's dorm and do hers. By the time we're done, our eyes are wet. My heart feels full of too many things, like it's gotten too big for my chest and might break a rib.

"What was the point of cleaning up their mess, anyway?" I say.

Ver lifts her eyes to mine and shrugs. "To show them they will not win so easily."

Cutting words are no match for Ver's spirit. I can't believe I've been viewing her as a rival, a possible enemy, instead of realizing what an incredible ally she'd make. I hope she'll stay at my side until all this is over.

CHAPTER 22
Ver

Early the next morning, Xenon and Card invade the dormitories like a virus taking over a host cell. They leave my door open when they enter my room, and several of my hallmates peer inside, smirking. They have probably come to find proof that I planned to kill the person I loved most.

"Glad you've been enjoying your freedom, Miss Yun," Card says. "Home AI?"

". . . Yes?" Charles says.

"Lift up her desk, throw her clothes out of the closet, flip up her bed."

"You do not have the permissions to execute those commands."

Card sneers at me. "Miss Yun, lift your desk."

A cold sinking feeling in my stomach collides with white-hot anger in my chest. I glare at Card and try not to cry.

"You can't?" Card says. "Xenon, do we need to get her vitals to confirm this?"

Bang! Charles has raised my desk to the ceiling and turned it sideways so that my notebook, styluses, and personal care items rain down on the officers. "I have lifted the desk as you ask. Do you require me to move any other furniture?"

"Argh!" Xenon rubs his temple, where a stylus has clocked him, and resorts to tearing the rest of my room apart on his own. *Crash, clang!* Charles drops the desk back to its usual position.

Card is looking at the notes magnetized to the wall. "You're investigating on your own, I see."

She talks to me as if to a pet. *Good girl!* But they have found nothing incriminating—even after flipping my whole life upside down.

Xenon barks, "Miranda, stop speaking to the suspect. Keep looking."

Frowning, Card lowers her bright green head and captures images of my notes with her flexitab.

"Listen," I say. "Did you notice I covered up my door with paint? There was graffiti on it. On Aryl Fielding's door too. Abusive messages."

"Do you have holographic evidence to prove this?" Card says flatly.

"You took our flexitabs," I remind her.

Xenon shoots Card a disapproving look for talking to me, and she turns back to her work.

I refuse to let them ignore this. "You can 3D-scan our doors and read the words under the paint. As keepers of the peace, you must punish whoever did this."

Xenon scratches his mustache, stepping back to examine my door. "Miss Yun, killing an investigator has consequences, and this is the least of them."

"The police owe me protection—as a witness—before my trial," I insist.

Xenon leans down until his face is level with mine. "Listen, Miss Yun. Think about what you've gained by living on this

98

moon. Have you been physically hurt since you arrived here? Since your arrest?"

I glare at him, putting on a poisonous expression that people have said makes me look like a snarling cat.

Card snaps, "Answer him, girl."

This woman's behavior puzzles me. She obviously does not enjoy taking Xenon's orders, yet she falls in line as soon as she finds someone smaller to bully.

"Yes," I say flatly. "You took my medications."

"You lying little errorcode," Card says.

"The correct answer was *no*, you have not been harmed by anyone," adds Xenon.

They did not want the truth. They wanted to feel righteous.

Xenon straightens to his full height. "You should be grateful. You leave your moon and come here, to the best research institute in the galaxy. To Lucent City. You enjoy its safety and its luxuries—and then you kill the man who brought you here. We take this job seriously. If you are found guilty, Miss Yun, we will make sure that you never see Pangu's light again. That you stay in its shadow forever. And that people like you can no longer destroy the cities you did not build."

He will relish sending me to the penal colony, the one place he believes I belong. Ninety-seven percent of the Sandbag's inmates are from Two or Three, even though those moons hold less than half the population of the Pangu System.

What the detectives do not know is that the sands of G-Moon Three are composed of silicon dioxide, often in the form of yellow quartz. Quartz, just like the most magnificent buildings in Lucent City. Only the size of the pieces is different.

My heart is still pounding as I walk to Aryl's dorm room. *Galunk, galunk.* So loud and obvious, I want to tear it out of my chest.

As I knock on her door, I see that our handiwork has resulted in a messy layering of the steel-colored paint. It is ugly. But it marks this space as *hers* again.

"Come in," Aryl's home AI says in a monotone.

I do and nearly run into a desk, which is half-blocking the door. A shoe rack is flipped over, and a landslide of soft dance shoes flows toward the bed, where it meets an ocean of instant spicy rice packets. Someone has dumped cheap jewelry on the mattress. Aryl's rings and necklaces are the kind that project holograms of flowers and complex geometric shapes. I can barely tell that the bedsheets, stained and discolored from years of use, were once stark white. Her home AI makes faint clicking noises as it moves objects one by one back into their rightful spots.

"The police searched my room," Aryl huffs. "Xenon had a field day with my foam roller collection." She looks terrible. Her blood must be a cortisol cocktail.

"They were in my room too."

Aryl pushes aside a lunch box and sits beside me on the bed, so close I can smell the coconut oil in her hair. One curl dangles between her exhausted eyes. She locks her golden-brown gaze on mine, and a faint smile lifts her lips.

"Ver, come with me to Celestine."

My body freezes, but my heart has climbed into my throat and is contracting rapidly. "Running away will only make us look worse . . . Oh." I clap my hands together as it dawns on me. "You do not want to run. You want to talk to Ford."

As I say his name, Aryl flinches, but her face quickly returns to a neutral expression. "Yeah. He won't answer messages. Xenon asked me twice if Ford worked with us to kill Cal, back when we were in custody. The police might have evidence against him. *Legitimate* evidence. He probably would've been arrested already if not for his mom."

Ford, a killer? He never showed hostility toward Cal. But rich One-ers are skilled at masking their feelings. Ford was so polite to me when I first arrived that I thought he wanted to be my friend. Then I realized he acts that way with everyone. Even people he dislikes.

I am trembling now, just as I was when I realized Jaha could have killed Cal. Between her and Ford, we must be right about one of them!

"Let's go. Now," Aryl says. "There's a vactrain to Celestine every hour."

Travel to a faraway city, alone with Aryl? She and Ford have known each other for years, and Celestine is her native environment. What if I am wrong about her innocence, and this is some kind of trap?

"What about Jaha?" I ask.

"She and Ford could've been working together. We're more likely to get information from Ford than from Jaha. And even if Ford's not guilty, he might know something useful. His mom has access to classified information." Aryl looks at my worried face and sighs. "Ver, I can go alone, if you're not comfortable coming with me. But I hope you will."

She is not forcing me to go, not trying to do me in. And everything she says makes sense. My brain returns to homeostasis, and my heart lowers itself back into my chest cavity.

"Ford knows everybody at the Institute," I say. "Not to mention his mother . . ."

"The most powerful senator on the moons," Aryl says. "Prison warden to my parents and sister." Pain flashes like lightning across her face. She must be worried sick about her family. Maybe that is why she is so desperate to go to Celestine.

"Will Ford agree to see us?" I say. "What if he calls the police?" Two murder suspects showing up at the Mercure estate is not a smart move. The place is surely protected with layers of security. The Mercure family has total power in their own domain. They may not even need the police.

"Ford will talk to us," Aryl says, lifting her chin. "I'll make sure of it."

CHAPTER 23
Aryl

The vactrain ticket costs me the last forty-nine Feyncoins from this month's pay. And that's a bargain, considering how much extra "service" we're getting here at the station.

As soon as we scan in our eyeprints, a red beeper goes off, indicating that "RESTRICTED TRAVELERS" have been detected. Three police officers go through each layer of our bags with infrared, metal, and biohazard detectors, and one officer pats down our bodies. I'm used to this—a security unit always searched me before I saw Titania Mercure—but Ver screws her eyes shut and cringes away from the officers' hands.

I'm itching to peel the officers off of her. Seeing her so uncomfortable hurts.

She's the only one who understands what I'm going through. Rhea and Ford have each other, whatever that's worth. I have a small, sick Three-er girl from the middle of nowhere. The old me would've thought I'd fallen so far. Now, I'm grateful for anyone who will stand by me.

After the police clear us, we check the departures display and walk to our platform. Pangu's orange light slants in through the glass ceiling and catches floating dust motes brought in from all over One. The station is constructed of curved sheets of transparent carbonglass, warrens and burrows layered onto one another. Two stories underground, we reach the sealed airlock that leads to the vacuum tunnel where our train will run.

There's not much to look at except a holographic ad playing on the tunnel wall: an image of a titanium smart leg with blocky quads and striated hamstrings, plus a slimmer "female" version. Below the image are the words *EXSAPIENS: Optimizing the human body, faster than evolution.* The company's logo—double-stranded DNA helices wrapping into the outline of a tall, slender human form—hovers in the background of the holo.

I'm always astounded by how much those bionic features cost. Lots of companies make them, so I guess there's a high demand. I think it's crass to *buy* superhuman strength and install it onto your body instead of working to build it naturally like I have. For all the good that's done me.

Our train arrives, hurtling down the tunnel and squealing to a stop in the airlock. It's oblong, perfectly clear on all sides, with reinforced glass that's strong enough to hold up to the air pressure from inside.

The cars are nearly full. The shiny doors swish open with a bright tinkle of music, and we enter the one parked directly in front of us. On a weekday like today, most people inside are middle-aged business travelers wearing sweat-wicking smart suits made of beautifully draped fabric. Ver and I look tattered in comparison: two girls on the run.

We find a rare empty row, one that two other boarding passengers are eyeing. But when they see Ver's cane, they choose other seats. Ver flushes with embarrassment. "Here, you go in first, Aryl. Take the window seat," she says.

"No, thanks," I say. She shouldn't give up something she

wants just because strangers were decent to her. "This is your first time on the train; you *have* to look at the view, at all the rock formations on the mountains. My sister and I used to spot ones that looked like animals."

Ver shrugs, scoots into the seat, and peels a red banana she bought at the station, nibbling on it like a squirrel to make it last. As I sit down next to her, elastic seat belts automatically fasten over our chests, and excitement and nostalgia fill me up.

I close my eyes and imagine my family by my side. A few years ago, Mom and Dad finally saved up enough money for us to visit the tundra. To get there, we rode a vactrain like this one. With glee, Dad explained how the lack of air resistance allowed the train to zip along at supersonic speeds. Mom laughed, said maybe I got my start in science from Dad; he was always the one to learn how things worked and fix them when they didn't. Then Dad reminded Mom that thanks to *her* brilliant mind, she'd made hundreds of Feyncoins playing chess. They'd started snuggling while Ester and I looked away in disgust.

I'm taking Ver to my old city. Only Ford has seen me in Celestine. I never would've let Rhea or my other Institute friends witness how I used to live, when I was only the daughter of alien housekeepers.

My hand rises from my lap to grab Ver's. I catch myself, and it floats back down. *Where'd that come from?* A week ago, all I felt for Ver was resentment—for being the perfect apprentice, for being what I should've been. Now, with her about to enter my world, it's hard to remember what gassed me off about her in the first place. She's a clear thinker and a bad liar. I know she's keeping information from me, but I also trust her enough now to not force it out of her.

"Ensure all seatbelts are securely fastened," the train's AI reminds us. Ver tugs at her own belt, reaches over, and pulls on mine. She smiles at me but says nothing.

The train rises slightly above the track, as if the whole apparatus has filled its lungs. Held in place by the 360-degree magnets covering the tunnel, it lurches out of the airlock, hits the vacuum, and zooms off. It's soothing to watch the speedometer on the ceiling climb from 100 kilometers per hour to over 1,200.

A minute later, the train has left the underground tracks beneath Lucent City. Still enclosed in a transparent tunnel to maintain the vacuum around the vehicle, we surface onto sprawling green plains dotted with small towns. Each one is constructed with crystals mined from G-Moon One's crust, and the different colors and shapes make the communities look like jewels spilled out onto the landscape.

Ver's nose is pressed to the glass, and she's smiling. Who wouldn't, surrounded by so much beauty?

As I watch her peaceful face, the exhaustion of the past few days catches up with me. I let the gentle gliding of the train lull me to sleep, knowing that I'll be in familiar territory when I wake.

"Aryl?"

The soft surface beneath me is rocking, trying to shake me off.

I straighten my neck, look down, and gasp. I've been napping on a folded unitard propped up by Ver's shoulder, putting pressure on her joints and muscles.

"Oh! Sorry!" I say as she rubs her deltoid and trapezius.

"You were only there for a few minutes," Ver says, like that means I didn't hurt her. "Nothing to worry about."

I look at her shoulder, imagining a bruise forming. My eyes wander up to the curve of her neck before I realize that she's watching me too. She smiles but says nothing. I snap my gaze to the window, heart pounding, and try to mind my own business for the rest of the trip.

At Celestine, we disembark from the vactrain, walk across the open-air station, and board a turquoise tramcar for the Lakeside district. The tracks are held up by towering tropical trees and run along branches that extend seamlessly from one trunk to the next.

I know this route by heart: snaking among the dense buildings of downtown, passing over parks full of magnificent flowers as big as your face, where children play at all hours. The midday light streaming through the large paneled windows is golden and the windows are open, letting in the humid, warm air. Colorful birds ride the whirls and eddies of wind that the tram creates in its wake. I ache to take the tram all the way to the end of the line, Meteor Valley, where my family lives. But we need to deal with Ford first.

The Mercure mansion is at the north end of the city, on the edge of Lake Celestine. It's a spiraling four-story wonder shaped like a conical snail shell, with massive white double doors where the snail would poke its head out.

I try to keep calm as we approach. *It's just Ford's house.* I've come here a million times in my childhood to play hide-and-seek in its innumerable rooms, but I've never shown up uninvited, with a fellow murder suspect, to find out if *Ford* committed the murder. Ver, skulking behind me, reminds me of that.

"Stop here," I say abruptly. "Don't get zapped."

The air seems to pulse with energy. Ten meters from the house, there's an electric fence. Anyone who's not a Mercure has to check in with the staff to avoid a shock.

This is where I'd usually call Dad. My hand automatically reaches to unroll the flexitab the police confiscated.

But Dad's not here anymore.

"Stop right there!" someone shouts in a distinct Two-er accent.

A wide-eyed young man rushes onto the path, pointing a laser gun at us. At me, specifically. He's tall and solid, like a security guard should be, but he still looks less intimidating than my father. It's his boyish, scared face. Titania probably hired him just this week to beef up the security detail in Dad's absence.

"We're Ford's friends," I lie, holding up my hands so the Two-er guard doesn't shoot. *Why do we fear our own?* "Is he home? Tell him Aryl Fielding and—"

"No guests allowed while the senator is away," he says. "I don't care who you are."

A second figure is rushing toward us on the paved path.

"Hey, drop that!" Ford barks, and the guard lowers his weapon.

I can breathe again. Ver's shoulders come down from her ears. Ford approaches us, his body tense, like he's ready for a fight. I glare at him. His long, curly black hair is still wet from the shower. He's wearing a crisp white shirt made of what looks like the softest waterproofed, wrinkle-proof cotton money can buy. The water's beading on its surface, and despite his disheveled appearance, he still looks holo-ready.

The guard holsters his weapon but keeps one hand on it, just in case one of us decides to assault Ford, I guess.

"What are you doing here?" Ford asks quietly.

"What do you think?" I say. "We came to talk to you. In private."

I jut my chin in the guard's direction. Ford makes eye contact with the young man, who retreats only slightly—not out of earshot.

"We have questions for you," Ver says. "At least ten, the last time I checked."

"Not here," Ford whispers. "That guard isn't leaving my side as long as I'm on the grounds. Mom's orders." He comes close, puts his lips to my ear: "Meet me at 14:00 at Meré's."

"*You* want to go to Meré's?" I whisper. The one time Ford ate at my family's favorite street stall with us, he coughed his way through the entire meal. Mom had never put chilies in the food she fed him and the senator.

"I want answers too," he says, straightening. His voice is lower, even slightly threatening. "You two aren't the only ones in trouble."

CHAPTER 24
Ver

At high heat, the Maillard reaction transforms food molecule by molecule. Amino acids and sugars fuse and form aromatic rings, resulting in browning and crisping.

The oily, savory, sweet, and spicy smells wafting through the bustling street stall make it clear that Meré, the eighty-year-old Two-er migrant behind the counter, understands this reaction—and more. Her hands scuttle about as she adds ingredients to a deep black pot, stirs with a wooden spoon, and serves browned vegetables over mashed cassava. To protect her face from the splashing oil, she wears a flat, transparent visor.

Crack, sizzle, clang! Followed by contented slurping from the fifteen or so customers in the tent around us, most of them eating in small groups.

Beyond the stall, I hear chatter in at least two dialects. People on balconies yell across the street at one another as they hang clothes out to dry. Every sound echoes off the closely spaced apartment buildings, all made of low-grade crystals: streaky ultraviolet fluorite, dull green olivine. This neighborhood, Meteor Valley, is just a kilometer from the Mercure estate. But it is like no place I have seen. To think, Aryl grew up here!

"Two orders of fish balls with okra and onion, one mild, one hot!" Meré's voice cuts through the neighborhood noise. "And breadfruit fries!"

Aryl rushes forward and takes the boat-shaped metal platters from Meré's hands. She brings them to our corner table and digs in as soon as she sits down. Crunches through chili peppers without flinching.

I cautiously bite an onion slice. The flavor explodes in my mouth. It is as if the cook did not want to leave a single taste receptor inactivated. To be kind to my RCD-compromised digestive system, I have ordered my dish mildly spiced. *This is mild?*

Pangu's rays beat directly overhead. It is nearly time for Ford to arrive. My leg bounces from anxiety, my nervous system implementing what non-scientists call the flight-or-fight response. I can neither flee nor fight. But if I have learned anything from studying biology, it is that evolution is a messy architect. It leaves traces.

Aryl's free hand lands on my knee to make it go still, and the hair on the back of my neck stands up.

"It'll be fine," she says and removes her hand. "Remember— first, we ask him what he knows about Cal's death, see if we can find out why the police suspect him too. *Then* I bring up my family. That's when things'll get messy."

The stall goes quiet. People are staring at the entryway to the tent.

He has arrived.

Ford is wearing a white cap that hides half his face, but in this neighborhood of migrants he still looks foreign. "Hey," he says, taking a seat across from us. The string lights crisscrossing the ceiling of the tent create green and yellow and red speckles on his face. "Before you say anything," he adds, cutting Aryl off as she draws a breath, "I'd like to say for the record that I'm meeting you here, willingly, to show that I had nothing—*nothing*—to do with Cal's death."

"Kiss my blistered feet," Aryl hisses, and Ford scoots his chair so far back, he nearly falls over. "I don't owe you any gratitude. Especially after yesterday, when you stood there while Rhea insulted me—"

I slam my water glass down to make her stop talking. She stares at me. But we need answers, not an airing of grievances. "Ford, why are you hiding here in Celestine while the police investigation into Cal's death is ongoing?"

"I didn't want to interfere," Ford says. I have heard that practiced voice in lab. It means he prepared for this question. "Look, Ver, I couldn't have done it. I was at the grav-sickness benefit gala that night. See?"

Ford holds out his device. Holos of him at the gala pop up into the air. We shield them with our bodies so other people cannot see. Ford is dressed in an asymmetrically cut black suit that emphasizes the width of his chest, his arm around a pretty blond girl I recognize as one of Aryl's dance friends. This must be Rhea. The holos are time-stamped to just after midnight. Even as Ford turns up the contrast, they show no sign of being doctored.

If Ford's alibi holds, there is no way he could have killed Cal—at least not directly. My jaw clenches, but I will not let my frustration show.

"You had your share of spats with Cal," I say. "He told me your social climbing got in the way of your progress."

"Might be the only thing I have in common with Aryl," Ford says. "Look, I'm not concerned about my scientific career.

I'm headed for the Senate. Science is a stepping stone; people will respect me more if I finish an apprenticeship at the Institute."

"Good for you," Aryl says dryly. "Congratulations on having so many options."

"My point is, Cal's smart enough to understand that research isn't my highest priority. He wasn't standing in the way of my future, and we both knew it. There's no reason for anyone to drag my name into this case. Unless they're trying to bring down my family."

"You Mercures have a long way to fall compared to some," Aryl says.

"Scrap, Aryl, will you just hear me out?"

Aryl clenches her jaw and waits. I nod, gesturing for him to continue.

"Someone's framing me," Ford says. "There was an explosion in the BioLabs basement the night Cal died—that's what set off the building alarm."

"I thought the alarm was set off by a gas leak," I say.

Ford shakes his head. My spine tingles, as if someone has dropped spiders down my shirt collar.

The alarm was part of the plan—it caused the lights to go out, which could have allowed the killer to slip into the lab unseen by the hall cameras. It distracted anyone else who was in the building that night, sending people toward the exits while the killer was injecting Cal with TTX.

"The security cameras in the basement were switched off, so the police don't have any footage to go by. But they found a torn nitrile glove with my DNA on it near the explosion site."

Aryl has stiffened, her eyes pinned on Ford. "You set off an explosion? Why?"

"*I didn't do it*. It's a setup." Ford unrolls his flexitab—sky blue, with clouds rolling across it—from his wrist and shows us a file. "The police report states that, in the sample they found, my cells were not intact, and the ratios of genes present in the DNA were all wrong. Some regions were duplicated many more times than others. Since no one else's genetic material was found at the site, they're sticking with me. But I was never there!"

Aryl slams her hand on the table, making the fries jump. "How do we know you're not lying?"

"Wait," I tell her, studying the report. "Sequencing analyses are difficult to forge. And this document looks legitimate." The page resembles the documents we had to sign at the station—the right fonts and headings and designs. "This is a lot of information for Ford to volunteer, if he *is* guilty."

I squint at the text, at the haphazard sequences of Ford's DNA the police have acquired. "Ford, someone tried to replicate your genome many times over," I say. "But they did an atrocious job. Many portions read as nans." This means the individual nucleotides making up the sequence could not be identified. "Others have been transposed in the wrong places."

"Yeah. Someone wanted to make it look like I was involved," Ford says, jiggling his leg. "Probably Kricket. Copying a genome is so easy, but he still messed up . . ."

Aryl's hand, still resting on the table after she slammed it down, clenches into a fist. "Kricket? How about Jaha?"

"Jaha would not fail at something as easy as viral whole-genome replication," I say. To copy a genome, we only need to feed host cells to a modified virus, which churns out hundreds of duplicates of the DNA.

Aryl's eyes widen as what I am saying sinks in: Ford is

probably telling the truth. "Ford, you scrap pile. Something this important, and you didn't tell me right away?"

"I wasn't sure you'd trust me!" Ford says. "I know how bad it makes me look."

"We only have three days until our trial! Ver and I could've used this!"

I look between the two of them, confused. Why would Aryl expect Ford to share information? But there is the easy way she insults him too. The way they make eye contact despite their verbal animosity. I wish I could sort out what is going on between them.

"Ford, why were you not arrested along with us?" I ask.

Ford's shoulders slump. "Because of Mom."

Aryl rolls her eyes. "Titania's precious little boy."

I feel numb. Ford did not have to endure questioning or a jail cell. He will never face the possibility of life in the Sandbag, knowing that his body and his dreams will be destroyed. Not like us.

"Listen, Aryl, I'm on your side here," he goes on. "If I could be accused, and I know I'm innocent . . . then you and Ver could be too."

"Meanwhile, my parents are suffering with me." Aryl can't keep the bitterness out of her voice. "Don't you care? Mom and Dad made us share our falling-apart toys with you whenever you got tired of your shiny new ones."

Ford's face drains of color. He rubs his forehead with his thumbs. "I'm trying to help you, Aryl. I know more about this case than the police will tell anyone else. I know everything they know about that basement explosion. Along with the glove that had my DNA on it, they found concentrated benzoyl peroxide residue. That's what caused the explosion."

At high concentrations, benzoyl peroxide is a bomb. The unstable molecule splits violently down the middle at the slightest provocation, separating into two benzene rings hooked up to an oxygen with a single radical electron. But it is also a common substance that many labs use. In lighter doses, it helps to clear up pimples.

"Benzoyl peroxide is never sold or stored at concentrations above ten percent," I say, thinking out loud. "But its concentration increases when people are careless and store it for two, three years . . ."

Ford gives a short, sharp laugh. "I don't know anyone who'd *forget about a hazardous chemical*. This was deliberate, not an amateur mistake."

"So you think someone made a bomb on purpose," Aryl says. "But there are more efficient ways to do that than by leaving BP lying around. Ways that won't get you suspended after a lab inspection."

"Sure, but whoever did this probably figured that the accessibility outweighed the risks," Ford insists. "Most investigators barely go to the bench themselves. They don't know what's in their chemical closets and wouldn't notice if something wasn't where it was supposed to be. Not everyone's a control freak like our Cal."

The three of us go quiet.

I try to recall every face I have seen in the hallways since I started working in BioLabs. The ubiquity of BP means we cannot rule out anyone with access to the building.

After a minute, Aryl slaps her knee. "It's got to be him."

Ford and I make eye contact. When he is bewildered, he looks like a lost little boy. "Who?" he asks.

"Devon Kye," Aryl says, grabbing Ford's flexitab and

running a search. "A second-year, from Oryza on Two. He works in the lab that makes artificial skin out of semimetals. In the BioLabs basement."

She turns the screen to projection mode so we can see a holo of Devon's listing in the Institute directory.

"The night Cal died," she goes on, "I saw Devon in our dorm, crying his eyeballs out."

I snap to attention. Why did Aryl not mention this before? Because trauma interrupts memory consolidation in the brain? Or because she distrusted me? Oh, probably that.

Aryl peers at Ford's flexitab. "His profile says he's on leave. I'm surprised someone hasn't connected him with Cal's death by now."

She has a point. Devon's departure from the Institute is unusual, especially for a Two-er with little money to spend on spacefare.

Ford says, "I've never heard of this guy."

"You didn't hear about the time he accidentally dropped a vial of acetone and set someone else's experiment on fire?" Aryl retorts. "For whatever reason, he was pipetting outside the hood."

"Oof," I say. Devon is lucky no one got hurt.

"Oh, that guy," says Ford. "I've heard stories about what scrap his work is. Never actually met him."

"Ford, sometimes I know people you don't."

"Then why didn't you think of him earlier?" Ford shoots back. "Especially if he was bawling in the dorms right after Cal died?"

"Because I've had enough else to think about, thanks to your mom, okay?" Aryl's voice, thick with pain, cuts me to my core.

Ford seems lost for words.

"Aryl," I say, breaking the silence, "Devon seems too scatterbrained to even exist at the Institute. If he did cause the explosion, it could have simply been an accident."

"Or," says Aryl, "someone got him to set up the explosion because, if it got traced back to him, it would *look* like an accident."

I see what she means: even if the police connected Cal's murder to the explosion, they would not be able to connect the explosion directly to the killer. "You think Devon was an accomplice," I say. "Whether he knew it or not."

CHAPTER 25
Aryl

Meré shoos us out after half an hour, telling us other customers need a seat. Pangu is slowly cooking the midafternoon air, but Meteor Valley shows no signs of slowing down.

We leave the tent by the food stall and duck into an alley-way, where young kids are playing discdisc with a rubber ball and sticks. Ford looks uncomfortable, even a little scared. Ver stares at the kids, wide-eyed, as if she's worried they'll smack a ball into her or rob her. They're both being dense, but I don't say anything.

We holo-call Devon Kye from Ford's flexitab, but he doesn't pick up. Taking a call from Ford might put him on the suspect list.

"Maybe it's for the best," says Ford, looking uncertain. "Maybe instead of trying to contact Devon directly, we should report our suspicions to the police. They can take it from there."

"Have you *met* Detective Xenon?" Ver asks, tilting her chin up. "He wants Aryl and me in jail. He is not going to listen to us if we offer him another lead."

I beam at Ver for standing up to Ford.

"Don't rag on the police, Ver," says Ford. "They're good people, at least here on One—*I've* never had a problem with them, even when I got into giga trouble. Remember, Aryl?"

Yeah, I do. Ford went through a rebellious phase six years ago—around the time he stopped hanging out with me. He wore purposefully ripped clothes, snuck out at night to meet his friends, and smoked all manner of substances. The police brought him home several times, to his mom's horror, but Ford never got arrested.

"Pangu's light sure does shine on you," I say, deadpan, remembering the way Detective Xenon grabbed my arm to feel its farmworker strength. But as much as I'd like to shred Ford, he's still my best chance to get my family released. "Nice to get second chances, yeah? Speaking of which, can't you call your mom for just five minutes and let me talk to her about my par—"

Ford's already shaking his head. "Aryl, Mom would put me on lockdown if she saw me outside the house, or you anywhere near me. Even on a holo-call."

"You have to stand up to her one of these days. Does she know that half your lab is offworlders?"

I don't follow politics, because there's no point in knowing what powerful people think and why. I can't even vote yet. But I still know that Titania Mercure has always wanted people to stay on their home moons. She's got her reasons. First, G-Moon One is the typical destination for migrants, and the cities here are already crowded. Second, migrants like my parents and Ver, and even migrants' children like me, have a hard time fitting in. Worst of all, poorer migrants sometimes commit petty theft and graft. Those stories tear me up. Sure, people get desperate, especially in a world where they're at the bottom. But don't they understand how bad it makes all of us look?

"My mom doesn't *not* like offworlders," Ford says, but

he sounds unsure. "She always says Solstice and Coco"—my parents—"are the best help she's ever had."

"Yet she fired them and put them under house arrest," I say.

Ford bows his head, clasps his hands, and stares at them, as if the knot of fingers will solve his problems. "I'm sorry. I know my mom isn't perfect. And . . ." He trails off. I wonder if he's thinking about Rhea—what she said to me yesterday, how he didn't stand up for me. "It's so hard looking at you, Aryl. I know you think I've become just like her. But I haven't."

Ver's looking between us, clearly bewildered.

I cross my arms. "Then you have to do what's right and set fire to what anyone else will think of you."

Ford looks around to see if anyone else is watching us. When he seems satisfied, he says, "I know you're gassed off, but I do believe you're innocent and I want to help. Here, you can each have one of these." He takes two plain flexitabs out of a pocket. They're maybe ten years old—thicker than the newer models, and the holo projections aren't so high-res. "They're burners, routed through virtual private networks. Untraceable. They can talk to each other—only to each other—and access the Neb. My family uses them to message about sensitive topics. I've got one too, and I always carry spares. They're yours now."

"So *you* could trace us with these," I say. "Spy on us."

"The police are already watching you," Ford says, laughing a little. "And trust me, Aryl, your life isn't that interesting."

Ver looks from the burner flexitabs to me. She'll do what I do. It feels like trust.

"Look," Ford says, unrolling one of the devices. "These don't require you to scan in fingerprint or retina identifiers. And see, I've connected it to the Neb, but on my official flexitab"—he opens his newer, shinier device—"there's no sign of any other devices here. If you had your usual flexitabs too, they wouldn't know these things are here."

I find myself nodding. Ford knows what he's doing with computers.

"I think they are safe," Ver says. But I'm still wavering.

"Aryl, if I was going to betray you to the police, I would've done it already," Ford says. "And how will I ever get elected to the Senate if my childhood best friend goes to prison for murder? The optics would be terrible."

He's only half-joking, and it should gas me off, but I fixate on the words *best friend*. He's never called me that, even back when it would've felt true.

I let the pause stretch between us. Ford's face is calm and earnest. He's not fidgeting or filling the silence with nervous chatter.

"Okay," I say. I take one burner flexitab and hand Ver the other. "Thanks. I guess there are still *some* perks to knowing you." Even if he won't lift a finger to help my family.

"Should we try calling Devon again with one of these?" Ver asks.

I slap my burner flexitab so that it curls around my wrist. "Scrap calling Devon," I say. "Let's go see him."

Ver and Ford blink at me like I've suggested walking on Pangu's fiery surface. And to be fair, Oryza probably isn't much more hospitable. But I'm ready to escape this moon for a while. Celestine reminds me of the person I was and the person I should've become: a scientist-dancer who'd pull her family up with her. And Lucent City holds all the stages I could've danced on with the girl who didn't deserve me. At this time of year, the moons' orbits have aligned so that they're closer than usual.

"Aryl," Ford says, using the exasperated-big-brother voice I haven't heard in years, "I know you'll take any excuse to explore, but going to Two while you're under police surveillance isn't a great idea."

"Guess my pep talk didn't sink in," I say. "You won't intervene with your mom on my family's behalf, you won't put me in touch with her so I can talk to her directly, and you won't come with us to talk to one of the only suspects in this murder case who isn't one of us." I clap slowly, three times. "All hail Ford Mercure the Second."

A choked noise escapes Ford's throat. "Okay, fine. If you're determined to do this, we can take the *Mercenary* to G-Moon Two."

"What is the *Mercenary*?" asks Ver.

"The old family spaceliner," Ford says. "All the patrols will recognize it. No one will search you prior to boarding or stop the vehicle for inspection. They'll assume it's just me."

I consider Ford's offer. With four days until our trial, we need to act fast. If we leave in the next few hours, we should be able to make a quick trip to Two and be back in Lucent City by tomorrow morning.

"Deal," I say. "We're too broke to throw away three hundred Feyncoins on commercial spaceliner tickets. As long as you can get me back to the Institute in time for the next dance practice."

"No guarantees." Ford flashes a grin, and for an instant, the boy I once thought of as my brother comes back. "Ver? You in?"

Ver twists her hands. She opens and closes her mouth a few times before whispering, "I should not go."

Ford doesn't get the hint. "It's a really nice spaceliner.

Fully stocked pantry and drink collection, 360-degree interactive projectors for holofilm viewing, a workshop area—plus a detachable hoverpod for ground exploration."

Ver shakes her head. "I . . . I prefer to stay on One. My condition, you see. It can worsen during spaceflight."

The alley goes quiet. Maybe Ver's injury has complications if she goes into zero gravity, as counterintuitive as that is. Zero gravity is a therapeutic treatment for lots of injuries, especially spinal ones, but I know better than to tell Ver what's good for her.

Ver shifts her body to face me. Her expression is flat and unreadable. I stare deep into her eyes, trying to parse what she's feeling.

"While you are away, I can look for evidence on campus— talk to Jaha again," Ver says. "And I will think. Somehow, I feel . . ." She pauses, wrinkles her brow. "The answer to all this is so simple. It will make us kick ourselves when we finally see it."

But I don't *want* her to stay behind. I've gotten used to her quiet company and the comfort of not being alone in this mess.

"Think as much as you need to," I say. "But don't do anything risky until I'm back. Okay?"

Ver bites her lip and slowly smiles. "No promises."

After another few minutes in the alley discussing logistics, Ford lopes away, back to Lakeside. He'll program our destination into the *Mercenary* and pick me up after sunset. The ship's surface camouflage feature will work best when it's dark, and we don't want anyone taking footage of the departure.

Meanwhile, Ver and I walk together to the carnelian rowhouse where my family lives. Pangu is setting behind the roofline ahead of us, and in the distance, Lake Celestine glows orange like freshly welded steel. My neighbors, an elderly couple, are sitting on the shared porch space, looking out at the vegetable garden tended by the building's residents.

Sometimes as a kid, I'd pick ripe mini-cucumbers or purple tomatoes from that garden and bring them to Mom at the Mercure mansion. With a squeeze of lemon and a pinch of salt, she'd make the flavors come alive, and Ford and I would eat until our bellies swelled.

I brace myself as I look for my family's patch, the quadrant of the garden closest to the street. But it's just as vibrant as I remember, and I smile when I see it.

"We've been taking turns watching your family's vegetables," calls the old woman.

I bow my head and thank her before I scan my fingerprint to get into the building. We skip the stairs and take the narrow elevator, which barely fits two people and creaks past the first couple of floors.

My family's in a two-bedroom unit on the fourth floor. It's the same as when I left: cheerful green foyer and living room, the kitchenette a sleek forest of steel appliances. But when I see my parents, the guilt spikes up in me again.

They look sickly pale. Take a Two-er out of Pangu's light, Mom used to say, and she'll become a ghost.

Mom crushes me in a hug, sobbing into my shoulder. Floury dust flies from her hands. She's been making taro buns and the starchy scent is everywhere. It smells like love. Like the labor of a mother who cooks and cleans all day in someone else's house and goes home to nourish her own family. I'm filled with happiness, but my chest is heavy with the knowledge that it's temporary.

When Mom lets me go, I run into Dad's arms. Even though I'm taller than him, he's able to pick me up and swing me in a half-circle. He sets me down and flicks me in the cheek with his index finger.

"Ow!" I'm seventeen, and I still get cheek-flicks? But I've missed them so much.

"What are you doing here, sweetgum?"

"You told me to come home if I could. But we can't stay long."

Dad turns to take in Ver, who, in her nervousness, looks smaller and grayer than ever. "This must be Yun Ver."

"Hello," Ver says.

"She can't be here, Aryl," Mom says, shooting Ver an uncomfortable glance. "Family visitors only."

"Oh, Coco," Dad says, looking Ver's frail body up and down, "we can't turn this one away. What harm can she do?"

"Ver's helping me clear my name," I say. "We're working together. She'll head back to the Institute tonight."

Mom crosses her arms. "Go to Aryl's room. Both of you. We'll talk more once Ester's home."

Using hushed voices, my parents argue their way to the kitchenette. As I lead Ver to my old bedroom, she whispers, "Should I leave? They do not seem to want me here."

"They're just scared right now, but they're kind people."

She still looks uneasy as we duck into the room that I used to share with Ester. "My sister's redecorated," I note. The walls are a moody purple, and Ester's collection of cheap shoes, full of spikes and studs and glowing buckles, has taken over my half of the closet. But other things are the same. The two beds are parallel, still, with the familiar seafoam-blue sheets. The ceiling's covered with the stars and birds we drew there in glow-in-the-dark marker as kids.

"So much space," Ver murmurs. "What did you two do here?"

A sense of her loneliness hits me, and I feel sad for Ver and everyone else who's grown up without a sibling. I tell her about the talks Ester and I had before bed, staring up at our artwork, and the holofilms we watched on my flexitab before Ester got her own, projecting the scenes into the space between our beds.

One of the Mercures' security guards brings Ester home from school. Ver ducks into my closet so there's no chance of the guard spotting her, but I go into the living room to meet my sister.

Ester runs to me, her discdisc jersey fluttering. She's wearing the uniform, even though she can't practice after school.

The hug's different, since she's grown so much—nearly my height now. She's going to be even more of a tower than I am. "What happened to your eyebrows?" I ask, rubbing my finger into the deep purple arches above her eyes.

Ester wriggles out of my grasp and grins. "Got them antho-modded."

I should've known. To change the color of your hair as it grows, you get DNA injected into your hair follicle cells so they produce pigment. Anthocyanins, like the ones in blueberries, turn hair purple.

"It's pop-pop," Ester says. "You'd know that if you weren't so old, or so busy running from the police."

"I'm not running from the police, you little errorcode." She dodges my attempted cheek-flick just as my parents enter the room, hand in hand. Gross.

"Dinner's ready, girls," Mom says. She looks around for Ver. "I hope I made enough food."

With the guard gone, it's safe for me to let Ver out of the closet and bring her to the living room. Ester mutters something about how I love pulling girls out of closets. I muss her hair to shut her up. Thankfully, Ver just looks confused.

Once we're sitting on the floor around the low wooden table, Mom wastes no time collecting information about Ver. "Have you visited home since you came to the Institute?"

"Er, no," Ver says, her face closing off. "Too much lab work."

"So you live with your parents? What about grandparents, uncles, aunts?"

She's testing Ver, seeing how many of the Three-er stereotypes apply. I try to say "sorry" with my eyes, but Ver's looking down at her food.

"Just my mother," she says. "All my grandparents are dead."

Mom and Dad look at each other, silently passing judgment. But they can't blame Ver for coming to One. The long lifespans here are part of why *they* moved. On Two, people live to their eighties at most, dying from the hard work, from a diet of lower-quality crops than the ones they export. Something way worse is happening on Three.

As the meal drags on, it's excruciating to watch Mom keep questioning Ver, who stutters and eventually stops being able to speak altogether. Dad apologetically piles steamed cassava and roasted taro leaves on her plate, and Ver nibbles at the food like a rabbit.

The cassava is dry and tasteless in my mouth. I shouldn't have brought Ver here, shouldn't have let my mother treat her the same way One-ers have treated us.

After dinner, Ver thanks my parents with several little bows of her head and makes for the door. She'll set off for Lucent City. I offer to walk with her to the tram stop that'll take her to the vactrain station, hoping for a few minutes alone with her. I half expect her to brush me off, but she agrees.

It's dark out, though lots of older Meteor Valley residents are still sitting outside on their balconies, talking and eating sunflower seeds.

"Do you think your friends are worried about you?" Speaking slowly, as if warming up her voice, Ver looks up at me with curiosity.

"My friends?"

"All of your dancers. That girl, Rhea." Her voice twists around the name. She almost sounds jealous.

Can Ver tell that I've been stewing at Rhea this whole time? That I wish I'd never met her? *You know what you are.* "I'm sure Rhea's fine," I say coldly.

Ver's studying me as we walk. "She is your Cal."

I nod. It still hurts to think about how Rhea hoodwinked me. But being around Ver dulls the edges of the pain. She doesn't judge me for things I can't control.

"Message me when you get to campus," I plead as she boards the tram car. I need to know she's gotten back safely. "I'll meet you there as soon as I can."

At home, Ester holes up in her purple-walled territory to do homework, and Mom breaks out the papaya. I loved fruit nights as a kid but stopped "attending" when I got older. I preferred to go out to dance shows with my friends and girlfriend.

Kneeling with my parents by the table, I stab a toothpick into a scarlet cube of papaya and pop it into my mouth.

"Sorry if we gave your friend a hard time," Dad says.

"That girl? The one who's making Aryl share the blame for what she did?" Mom says.

I swallow, hardly tasting the fruit's sweetness. "Mom, you don't know her—"

"You don't either," Mom snaps. "I saw the way you looked at her. But you have to be cautious."

Dread is crawling up my spine. This is the first time Mom's told me to stay away from a girl.

"She's so desperate to seem innocent, she'll say or do anything. Including betray you. You haven't come across her kind before. Your father and I did our best to shield you from them. Three-ers will cheat instead of work, steal instead of buy, and kill rather than stand up for what they want. They don't know how to share, as we do. They're prejudiced; they don't accept anyone who's different . . ."

I want to clamp my hands over my ears. Every word is so unlike her. "Mom, stop."

"What? You know it's true. Dark—that's what those people are like, after being shut in factories their whole lives. The shadows poison them. Your father and I know. When we first arrived on One, we worked for a Three-er contractor. Always, he stole from us—a Feyncoin here, ten percent off a gig there. Stole, stole, stole."

"Ver's not . . ." I'm about to defend her innocence, or say that Three-er migrants might think Two-ers are just as rotten, but something stops me.

Maybe Mom has a point. Maybe I'm not the best judge of Ver's character. I was wrong about Rhea's. I'm not clearheaded when it comes to pretty girls with short hair and soft voices.

"Sweetgum," Dad says, spooning more papaya into my bowl, "we trust you to look after yourself. But this moon will always be less forgiving toward you than its native children."

"I *am* a native child," I say, but the words ring hollow. I've never even seen *myself* as fully belonging here.

"You know what I mean." Dad takes a deep breath and pinches his wide nose, which is what he does to keep from crying. "I believe you when you say you're working to clear your name. Just, please, don't sacrifice yourself for your friend. This family has come too far to watch you lose everything."

Mom reaches across the table and holds my hand. Hers are scarred and callused from years of domestic labor. The juxtaposition with my smooth skin almost makes me cry.

"Aryl, do whatever you need to do to prove your innocence," Mom says. "Whatever happens, we will always believe in the goodness of your heart."

Guilt turns the papaya to acid in my belly. The meaning's clear. My parents didn't raise me on One to see me sent to the Sandbag for a crime I didn't commit. They want me to sell Ver out—implicate her in Cal's murder so that I can walk free, just as Mom thinks Ver plans to do to me.

My alternatives so far aren't much better. Our other suspects are a brilliant and generous scientist who's been a mentor to me, the boy I grew up with, and a hapless apprentice whose life's been even rougher than mine. I need to be willing to send any one of them to the Sandbag.

Having a pure heart is, like so much else, a luxury I can't afford.

CHAPTER 26
Ver

Light detector cells in human eyes mostly correspond to three primary colors: blue, green, and red. Every other hue is an amalgamation of these—a fact that astonished me when I first learned it. Now, when I return to campus, it seems as if my eyes' blue and green photoreceptors are broken. I see only red, everywhere around me, as Pangu sets over the Institute.

The slanting crimson light makes the pond, the crystal sculptures, and the trees look as if they are burning. Fire, fire, devouring this whole place. So strange that of all the colors on the light spectrum, red carries the least energy.

A throng of people stands outside the BioLabs tower. At its center is Jaha, wearing a red blouse and skirt, her face the scarlet of burning lithium. She is surrounded by senior investigators.

I need to see what is happening, but I dare not risk getting injured by the crush of people. I approach the edge of the crowd, searching for a face I recognize. The one I find belongs to an old bear of a man whose lab invented an electron microscope with inconceivably precise sub-angstrom resolution. I would often see him chatting with Cal, offering advice.

"Investigator Faraday," I say, "what is happening?"

"The faculty combed through Ms. Linaya's communications," he says, his breath smelling of the onions he must have had with his dinner. "Accessed her private accounts through the Neb. Listen."

At the front of the crowd, Investigator Lark, who recently celebrated her one-hundred-and-twenty-fourth birthday, is holding court. She has a sonorous voice for someone with snowy hair, a hunched back, and skin like crinkled paper. "You wrote to your child's caretaker, 'My garbage husband won't clean the ****ing lab fridge, so you need to watch Dimmi an extra hour while I do it. Someday, I swear, I'll throw the whole man away.'"

Cal does not deserve such slander! He was never lazy and surely would have done what Jaha asked if it was needed.

Jaha smirks at Investigator Lark. "If you've never insulted a man, Stephania, then you haven't spent enough time around them."

The jab slides off. "To your sister," Investigator Lark continues, "you wrote, 'He barely knows how to run a lab! He flails, with slow progress and unhappy apprentices. If I'd been born a man on this moon, he would be answering to *me*.'"

Jaha blanches and goes silent. Her reaction can only mean she really wrote these things. The onlookers—investigators, and apprentices alike—begin to whisper.

Lark goes on. "You thought you deserved Cal's job, Jaha. So you got rid of him. And from the looks of things, you involved his apprentices."

Hearing this accusation should make me happier than it does. At least public opinion has found someone with whom Aryl and I can share the blame.

But something feels wrong about this. If Jaha had wanted

to kill Cal, she probably could have done so in a way that looked more convincingly like an accident or a natural cause. Why this way, at this time?

Her words are harsh, even shocking—but if Cal were still alive, they would sound like expressions of frustration or signs of strain in her relationship, not serious threats. Besides, if Jaha did plot Cal's death, she would have been careful *not* to say or write anything that could later draw suspicion. Without other evidence, I cannot connect those words with Cal's murder.

"Now that the employees of BioLabs have heard our findings, all investigators will hold a vote about Ms. Linaya's future at the Institute." Lark's words come out colder than dead space. "It is not our place to decide if Ms. Linaya is a criminal—only if she is to remain an employee."

Fifty or so investigators troop into the BioLabs building to cast votes in the conference room. Investigator Faraday gives me a nod before following his colleagues. The apprentices linger outside, waiting for the outcome, as Pangu casts lengthening shadows over us all.

Jaha walks toward me. My throat goes dry. I was not expecting to interact with her.

"Are you all right, Ver?" she asks quietly. "You left so suddenly last night."

I manage to nod. Casting about for something to say, I ask, "How is Dimmi?"

"Staying with my mother in Phoenix Port for the moment. At least until I find out if I get to keep my Institute housing. But listen, Ver. There's something I've been wanting to tell you. This isn't the ideal setting, but I might not get another chance."

I stare at her, unsure what to expect.

"I'm sorry I've been . . . distant from you the last few months. I envied your talent, your drive, the fact that I didn't have such an opportunity at your age."

I struggle to formulate a response. Thankfully, Jaha keeps talking so none is needed.

"I panicked shortly after you arrived, Ver. I thought there was room for just one hardheaded, cold-blooded science prodigy from Three. The longer you worked with Cal, the more you would accomplish. Soon you'd be the first Three-er woman to do this or that. I wanted it to be me."

Confusion scrambles my brain. "I thought you were jealous of me for . . . a different reason."

Jaha sighs and shakes her head. "Oh, Ver-hai, you are so many things, but you were never a threat to my marriage. My husband wanted all the data he could get out of you—nothing else."

She speaks so calmly, without hesitation. I cannot doubt her honesty.

I do not know how to feel. Juvenile and silly. Angry at Cal for using me like so much lab equipment. Shocked that Jaha put my real relationship with him into so few words.

But I also feel . . . respected? Jaha saw me as more than a silly girl chasing her man. She feared I would catch her dreams in a net before she did. Because she recognized me as her equal.

"It took Cal's death for me to see that holding you back is bad for science, bad for the future of our moons," Jaha says. "I need to make space for you and other offworld girls instead of walling you out. We have enough enemies on G-Moon One as it is. So let's keep you and me and Aryl out of prison, if that's all right with you."

Jaha's words slot into my mind. Her treatment of me in lab makes more sense now. So does her bail money—part of this new solidarity. But I hold on to a wisp of doubt. She *did* resent Cal, and me, yet now she wants to be my ally?

"Do you have any ideas for how to prove our innocence?" I ask her.

Jaha grunts. "About as many as you do." Not encouraging.

At last the investigators reconvene outdoors. Jaha pats my shoulder somewhat parentally and moves back to the center of the crowd.

Lark announces, "Nearly unanimously, with only two dissenting votes, we have voted to terminate Jaha Linaya's employment."

Jaha is trembling, her face spasming with emotion. I can see it from here.

"Ms. Linaya, you are not welcome here," says Lark. "Take your blood funding from ExSapiens. Take your apprentices, if they'll still have you. Take what's left of your humanity and go somewhere else—at least until the police put you back where you belong."

She means Three. The Sandbag. I flinch.

Jaha draws herself up to her full height, her eyes flashing like emergency lights. "How dare you judge me? You people, who have no idea what it's like, or how hard I worked to be here. This dream was so far away, it might as well have been across the galaxy. I started in a medical factory on Three, on an assembly line—can you imagine what that's like? Then I made so much of myself, with all the qualifications to be an investigator. But despite everything, all you see is where I come from."

Unexpected tears spring to my eyes. I know the home she left behind. I understand the astronomical escape velocity needed to break free.

"What if *I* had been murdered? You would've spared Cal this treatment."

Silence from the investigators. No one denies it.

"You think I trapped Cal into marriage so I could climb the ladder," Jaha says. "But you will never know the love I felt. I still feel it." She pounds her fist over her heart. "Everything I've accomplished, I could've done with or without my husband. He just made the journey more worthwhile."

My tears run down my cheeks and neck and soak into my collar. I cannot look away from her, cannot stop listening. Her words reverberate in my chest as only the truth can.

Jaha's voice is low. "There will come a day when I am recognized as innocent. A day when you will want me back. But I will never forgive you for grinding my name into the sand."

Her angry eyes scan the crowd, moving from face to face until they happen to land on mine. They are pleading, yearning for me to believe her.

I incline my chin ever so slightly.

Jaha nods back. Without sparing a look for anyone else, she marches off into the shadows.

CHAPTER 27
Aryl

Ford's always been a good multitasker. As his family's spaceliner zips between G-Moons One and Two, he's drinking fizzy kiwi juice while monitoring our flight path and deflecting messages from Rhea demanding he return to campus. I'm strapped into one of the seats across from him, a chair covered in lab-grown snakeskin, waiting to hear from Ver.

My parents begged me to stay at home longer, but I hugged them goodbye and swore them to secrecy about where I was going. I think they were pleased that I'm finally visiting their homeland—even though we all wish the circumstances were different.

Inside the *Mercenary*, it feels like nothing can go wrong. The tastefully subdued beige walls and quartz cabinets contrast with the corner Ford's turned into a machine shop. There's a workbench, mounted high because he's tall, a computer with a wraparound monitor, a sleek soldering gun, and labeled drawers filled with wires, nuts, bolts, and hand tools. Ford somehow squeezed an all-resolution microscope into one corner—a towering machine capable of imaging sheets of cells down to single protein molecules.

"Nice setup," I say.

"Thanks," Ford says. "Did you see the portable wave detector? I'm almost finished with it. Only have a few tweaks left." He points at an unfamiliar piece of equipment. Wires hang off the contraption, and complicated-looking lenses surround a silicon core where I'm sure giga precious elements are housed.

"I bet Kricket's way behind in building *his* detector," Ford says. "Not that it matters now."

"What?" I say, confused.

Ford explains, "A few months ago, Cal assigned Kricket and me the same project—building a portable antichronowave detector. It was a race. First person to finish would complete the research apprenticeship."

I grimace at Cal's casual cruelty. "But wouldn't the loser have to start a new project from scratch? Like a first-year." Wasting half a decade of apprenticeship.

Ford nods.

"That's pretty vacked of Cal."

"It is, but he's the boss."

"Ford, why didn't you mention this competition earlier?" I say. Kricket never said anything about it either—probably out of embarrassment. He's already been an apprentice for so long. Most people who aren't on track to publish original research by their fifth year leave the Institute, whether by choice, by loss of their lab position, or by suicide.

"It's not relevant to Cal's death." Ford's nonchalance is so complete, I can't help but groan.

"A portable antichronowave detector would be a huge breakthrough," I note, as if he somehow might be unaware of that. It'd mean that we could measure these mysterious, time-defying waves as we travel across planets, not just in our specialized lab. Worth killing over? Possibly. "Does it work?"

"Only when I least expect it to," Ford says. "Sometimes I get seemingly valid measurements in the weirdest places, like right over mountains, but—"

"Hold on," I say as my burner flexitab lights up with a message.

They sacked Jaha, Ver's written.

What?! I write back.

The investigators voted her out, comes the reply. *They found horrible things she wrote about Cal. But I do not think she killed him. If she had, she would have covered her tracks better—left no evidence of any problems between her and Cal.*

That's the Jaha I know. Used to living her life under a microscope. Too smart to commit a crime that could backfire on her. She had too much to lose.

So who did it? All I can picture is a faceless shadow, slipping out from behind a lab cabinet and sticking Cal with a TTX-filled syringe.

I clap a hand over my mouth and rock back and forth in the snakeskin seat. Only the strap across my lap keeps me tethered in the zero-gravity environment.

My hands remember the feel of Cal's still-warm chest. Of his heart, refusing to beat.

I'm hyperventilating. The panic is coming on strong, and I can't stop it—

"Aryl, calm down," Ford says. He's unbuckled himself and is floating next to me, shaking my arm. "You'll use up all my oxygen!"

The touch of his solid, warm hand brings me back to the moment. *Breathe. Look around you.*

I stare into Ford's brown eyes, past the layer of cool indifference, and see concern. It makes me remember the way he massaged my back and my sore feet before my earliest dance auditions and shows, even though he was eleven and didn't know what he was doing.

"Ford, when did we become strangers?"

He looks away—at Gui, a swirling blue mass coasting by outside the window, and says, "We were always meant to be strangers, Aryl. When we were young, we just didn't know it yet."

The words sting, but they're the truest ones he's spoken in a long time. The children of senators and farmworkers aren't supposed to cross paths, let alone walk the same one.

"When we were little, you barely knew the difference between me and your other friends," I say. "You let me play with your spaceship sims and ride the water slide . . ."

"Until I got different friends. Friends who made fun of me for being around you. I tried not to let you hear."

"I heard," I say, thinking of the time his discdisc teammate yanked me back by my hair and said, *Stay away from Ford, Hoehands.*

Ford winces. "I wanted to make it up to you when you followed me to the Institute. After I started hanging out with Rhea, I thought I'd see more of you." His voice sounds tentative. "I can't count how many parties I spent standing next to her, waiting for you to challenge me to climb the poles. But you never did."

"Why should I have?" I say. Seeing him at those parties, with *her*, only reminded me I wasn't in their league. "Friendships don't get repaired by osmosis. The guilty party has to at least apologize first. In our case, that was you."

Ford stares out the window, hiding his face. "Yeah. It's just . . . other people. I wanted them to like me, and being close to you would've made them ask questions. Even thinking about that made me so ashamed, I couldn't look you in the eye. Sometimes I still can't."

There's regret in his voice, and my first instinct is to tell him that we can pick up our friendship where we left off. But I'm also holding in resentment. It's bubbled in me for so long that I'm like a pipe about to burst.

"Is that why you're helping Ver and me?" I ask. "For absolution?"

"It's because I know you're innocent." There's an edge to Ford's voice. "You're not the person the police think you are. You're better than whatever demon lives in their heads."

I take his warm words and let them curl up next to my heart like a small furry animal. I've missed Ford so much. But I'm gassed off that it took a murder trial for him to come back to me.

As we approach Oryza, the *Mercenary* slows and dips, bringing me eye-to-eye with my parents' homeland. The place that runs through my veins.

Like every settlement on G-Moon Two, the city is surrounded by farmland—sprawling green fields of tropical crops, the jungle-like squares forming a chessboard, bordered by irrigation canals. Cassava, taro, plantain, coconut. Rice paddies, stepping up the low hills to the west of the city, as far as I can see. The fields are dotted with workers wearing wide-brimmed hats made of a thin bluish film to protect them from Pangu's UV rays.

Unlike the pastel crystalline surface of One, Two has a flat, smooth landscape, aside from the humanmade rice paddies and the black mountains of igneous rock rising to the east. The terraforming is simple, with sanitized square plots for farms, lakes, and residential communities. This moon knows it needs to feed the others and doesn't hide its purpose.

The *Mercenary* lands on the airfield about three kilometers from the city center. Two is windy, Dad has told me, because of the moon's high axial rotation velocity—one day is only twelve standard hours, so people are used to two sunrises in a twenty-four-hour period. That fast rotation makes it possible for crops in many locations to pollinate each other with or without bees and bats, which are in short supply. Mom's chess pieces were all weighted so that they wouldn't blow away.

I came from here, I tell myself.

Even after a lifetime of hearing my parents' stories, I'm still stunned. Everything on Two is foreign, from the rows of pine-apple and coconut palms to the small cubic dwellings of the workers. The purple-blue slice of Gui on the horizon looks too small, since Two's orbit is farther out than One's.

My parents are probably worrying about me. I brush my fingers against my burner flexitab, wishing I could message them, tell them I'm all right. But I can't contact them with this device.

I'm so sorry. I look back at One, hoping that somehow they'll hear me.

Ford and I exit the ship into the warm, humid air. Sweat beads on my forehead and the back of my neck, but a moment later the wind blows it away, keeping me cool.

Leaving the *Mercenary*'s AI to park the ship in a garage, Ford unrolls his flexitab and calls a cab to take us to a neighbor-hood on the other side of Oryza. My eyes bug out at the thirty-Feyncoin fare that appears on Ford's screen.

Ford shrugs. "We don't have time for two train transfers and a hoverbus."

The orange and black hovercab floats downward. It has wings and a tripod to land on, like some tropical beetle. After Ford and I board, it pushes off into the air, following lanes marked by yellow lights, joining hoverbikes and buses.

My nose is glued to the window, my eyes taking in the chaos of Oryza's morning bustle. The only consistent feature is color—saturated reds, greens, and sapphire blues. On One, people wouldn't just call you an errorcode if you painted an apartment building sunflower yellow; they'd knock it down to replace the exterior with crystal.

Here, the buildings are of all different shapes and sizes, and because it's so crowded, the structures are layered over and under one another like a 3D puzzle. People walk along the paths or bundle into auto-rickshaws pedaled by bots. Unlike hovercabs, these can't fly and are exposed to the elements.

Opening the window to get a whiff of the street food stalls below, I'm hit by a smell that's pleasant and awful and everything in between. Urine, smoke, fragrant herbs, hot oil, chilies, roasted meat. Compared to the richer neighborhoods of G-Moon One cities, where everyone stays indoors, Oryza's streets are arteries pulsing with people. It's like Meteor Valley—home—but amplified. And I love it. I wish I could hop down and explore.

But I need to stay focused. Devon Kye. The benzoyl peroxide. With three days until the trial, I need to prove without a doubt that I didn't kill Cal. Jaha hasn't been arrested, even though she's been sacked. Which means the police still need someone to blame for the crime. And I need to make sure it's not me. Or Ver.

The cab swishes onward. West of downtown is an assortment of prefabricated houses: flimsy cubes of plastic and carbonglass that can be towed from place to place. Each set of six units is clustered around a common area with a garden, rain tarp, and table—Mom told me that neighbors on Two share most meals and all gossip. Every house is painted in a feast of colors—orange, turquoise, lime. The work is done haphazardly, one glowing hue layered over another.

After flying past whole conglomerations of box houses, we touch down, raising dust from the ground, which the wind whips into the air. Two old ladies strolling the neighborhood look up at the cab with interest but keep walking. There's no one else around; at this time of the day, all the kids are at school and all the adults at work.

Ford and I walk to Plot 7, the address we found on the Neb. Devon Kye's cube is a deep, regal blue—probably the quietest color on his block—with one window on either side of the front door.

I'm squeezing my fists so hard that my fingernails carve out crescents in my palms. I rap on the door once. Twice. I kick it and hear a tumbling noise from inside, a small body tripping and falling. I go up on tiptoe, peek into the right-hand window, and see a human form curled up on the floor, hands clasped over its head. Devon.

A pair of dark eyes meets mine.

"Open up," I mouth through the window.

Fearfully, the boy inside nods.

CHAPTER 28
Ver

It is only a matter of time before I lose access to BioLabs. Even if I were not a murder suspect, my lab is in the process of collapsing. Without an investigator or a lab manager to supervise us, apprentices will be unable to keep working. But for now, my retinal scan still gets me into the building.

The police have changed the elevators' settings to prevent them from going to the basement, but the back staircase is clear. Step by painful step, I lower myself down the stairs. *Tap*, grab, *tap*. Have to distribute my weight among the handrail, my cane, and my feet.

On a normal day, I would rather eat food cooked by Kricket than do such acrobatics. But I need to see with my own eyes what Ford described. I exit the stairwell into a dimly lit hall and make a left.

The hallway outside Devon Kye's lab is blocked by glowing yellow lights, marking the area as a crime scene. Beyond the lights is a cavern, singed black. I can see bedrock where the walls have been blasted away. A metal door, blown off its hinges, lies twisted like shrapnel. The scene glitters with shards of broken glass. Farther down the hall is the chemical cart. I gag on the smells of alcohol, bleach, and other compounds I cannot name.

This is bad for my health. I must leave soon.

I walk up to the glowing yellow lights and lean against the wall for support. With trembling hands, I raise my burner flex-itab and capture one, two, three images. Feeling dizzy, I retreat and pull myself up the stairs, sweating, breathing hard, a single question ringing in my mind.

Who did this?

CHAPTER 29
Aryl

Devon unlocks the door, and Ford struts into the small plastic house like he owns the place. He walks past the pile of shoes on the threshold, without removing his own, and sprawls on the single green armchair. His loafers leave dust prints in his wake.

I hang back and remove my boots. It's rude not to. As I do, my burner flexitab lights up with a message from Ver. *Boom*, she's written. I open the attached image and suppress a gasp. What was formerly a BioLabs hallway is now a blackened mess.

What was Ver thinking, going into the basement to get this image? She could've fallen, or worse!

"Your parents at work, Devon?" Ford says.

Devon doesn't answer, keeps his head low. His stained blue shirt is zippered off-kilter—how did he manage that? His straight black hair sticks up in ten directions and his enormous dark eyes aren't focused. But then, they never are.

I perch on the right arm of the chair Ford's occupied. "Devon, we're not going to hurt you," I say. "But we need you to answer some questions about the night of Cal's death."

He settles into a farmer's squat on the dirt-streaked carpet. There's a pang in my chest—Dad does that too, when he's tired from standing and there are no chairs around. It makes me feel guilty, like I'm interrogating a cousin or a family friend. But not guilty enough to stop.

"You work in the basement of BioLabs," I say. "What do you know about the explosion that set off the emergency alarm two nights ago?"

"N-nothing," Devon says. "That night I was watching a holofilm at the arena with friends. The new historical about the Lunar rebellion."

The level of detail makes me suspect this is a fabricated alibi. Ford seems to agree. He's been lied to so much by people trying to impress him that he's developed good instincts. He catches my eye, and I nod.

Ford leans over Devon, flexing his shoulder muscles under his shirt. "Do you have receipts for the tickets?"

"I was with a friend of yours," Devon says, cracking a smile. "Krick Kepler bought the tickets *and* paid for the cab ride."

I lift an eyebrow and turn to Ford. "That doesn't sound Kricket-like."

Whenever I've gone out for food with Kricket, he's divided the bill down to the last tenth of a Feyncoin. While he's weaseled some of my purple yam fries on multiple occasions, whenever I ask for a bite of *his* dish, he'll say yes—if I pay him half a Feyncoin.

Devon's smile doesn't waver. "I guess some money is worth spending, to him. If it's on someone he thinks is cute."

I blink. I never would've pictured Kricket chasing boys. And I've never thought of Devon, who can barely remember where he's saved his lab notes, as anyone's crush.

Steering my brain back on track, I ask, "Did anything odd happen that day? The explosion that set off the alarm happened in the hallway outside your lab. You work with giga amounts of chemicals. Maybe one of your lab mates was involved?"

"Everything was normal, as far as I remember."

"Then why'd you come back to Two right after it happened?" Ford demands. "Why are you hiding in your house with the lights off?"

"I needed a break from the stress, okay?"

Ford rises from the chair and unfurls his body to its full height, towering over Devon. "Tell us what really happened before Cal's death."

The smaller boy gets to his feet, brushes his long bangs out of his eyes, and locks his gaze on Ford's upturned chin. "I have no idea what you're talking about."

"You have no idea about *this*?" I project the hologram Ver sent me. The hallway outside Devon's lab, black and littered with broken glass and twisted metal.

Devon stares into the burned abyss and shakes his head. "You know me. If I had any information, my brain would've scrambled it by now. Go bother someone else."

Ford walks forward, forcing Devon back until he's pressed against the wall. I frown. It's a cheap scare tactic. But I don't stop him.

"We found you already, Devon," Ford says. "The Lucent City Police will be next. And they'll do anything I tell them."

Devon's chest deflates. "Okay, so, that day, I was told the admins would be doing a safety inspection. Since our lab manager was out, I—I gathered some expired chemicals and left them on a cart outside the lab for collection."

He might as well have *LIAR* tattooed on his forehead. "You *know* the inspections are only on the first of every month," I say.

Devon shifts his weight to one foot. I notice that the other leg is trembling. "That slipped my mind. Honestly. I just did what I was told."

"Were you also told to leave the chemicals out in the hallway instead of *inside* the lab where the custodial bots could pick them up?"

Devon gulps. "I didn't think it would be a big deal. It was just some sodium azide that we use to keep our tissues from getting infected. And a strong base—one molar potassium hydroxide, I think. Nothing out of the ordinary."

I push closer to Devon, certain he's leaving something out. "What else?"

He looks at me as if we're wasting his time. "The only other thing was ten percent benzoyl peroxide in ethanol, okay? Like I said, not a big deal."

"BP gets more concentrated with time," I say. "When was the bottle opened?"

"I don't know, probably a few years ago?"

"Just bumping that thing could've caused an explosion," I say.

The color's draining from Devon's face. He steps away from the window so that he's no longer illuminated by Pangu. Ford and I don't budge.

"I . . . I didn't . . ." Devon stutters.

Ford's not sympathetic. "Who told you there was going to be an inspection?"

Devon's veiny throat bobs up and down as he swallows. "Krick," he says. "Krick told me. He must've made a mistake."

I let out a disbelieving laugh. "Kricket's been at the Institute for more than half a decade, Devon. First-of-the-month inspections are part of his circadian rhythms. He lied to you.

Whether you two were at the movies later that night is irrelevant. Something bumped that super-concentrated benzoyl peroxide, and it blew up part of the basement. That activated the emergency alarm—"

"Giving Cal's killer an opportunity to strike," Ford finishes.

"It wasn't me!" Devon says desperately.

"We know," Ford and I say together. If Devon had killed Cal, he would've left so much evidence that even Detective Xenon would've caught him.

Devon's thin lips are trembling, as if he's about to cry. "Are they going to kick me out of the Institute for this?"

I'm hit by simultaneous impulses to hug the poor kid and to smack him. "That's the least of your concerns." I nod at Ford. "Let's get out of here."

Kricket was involved in Cal's death. The fact that I have a clue buoys me as I turn toward the door. *Take that, Xenon,* I think, tying my boots back on. This gives me the slimmest of chances to set things right for the Fieldings.

Yet there's a wedge of discomfort beneath the relief. I had to hurt another Two-er. One of the only people like me to make it to the Institute. *We have to look after our own, sweetgum,* Dad told me, over and over, while I was growing up. And while I didn't always like his and Mom's friends' kids, they were the only ones who didn't mock me for being different.

Ford follows me out. Behind us, Devon sinks back into a squat on the floor, his head in his hands. As we leave, I hear a sob escape him, just before a gust of wind slams the door shut.

CHAPTER 30
Ver

I end my holo-call with Aryl and make my way to the older apprentices' dorms. Even though she told me not to. Begged me, her pleading voice carried by photons through thousands of kilometers of space.

"Please, Ver," she said. "I don't want anything to happen to you. Wait for me. We'll face him together. Please."

But every minute I spend waiting for her is a minute wasted. Sixty seconds that justice for Cal's death is still not done. Sixty seconds that I could be using to gather information so I will not die in the Sandbag. We have just three days to find the killer!

So I go, tap-tapping across the darkening courtyard. Each step feels shakier than the last. But waiting around means failing Cal, and failing myself. My sickness will *not* prevent me from saving my own future. I will face Kricket alone.

If I was healthy, Aryl would not try to stop me. Aiyo, if I was healthy, we might have found Cal's killer by now! What was her *Please, Ver* all about? Is she worried that if I get hurt, she will be blamed?

Or maybe she cares about me.

Aryl. Light-footed, magnetic girl, whose movements make shimmering auroras look clumsy. I never thought she would like me. Not even as a friend. My heart leaps up in my chest, then flutters back down. Vibrating, almost. I want to laugh like I have lost my mind. Maybe I have. I have never felt this way about anyone except Cal, a married man twice my age, and my supervisor at that.

I looked at girls many times before, on Three. But this time, there is the possibility of Aryl feeling the same about me. We could make something real happen, and on One we would be no different from any other couple. It would be new, and frightening, and perhaps . . . happy.

If we manage to stay out of the Sandbag.

My heart touches down from its flight and thumps, pumps away. Squaring my shoulders, I walk into the cylindrical tower of the smallest dorm—the one reserved for apprentices who take longer than five years to complete their research. The exterior is a soft, relaxing lavender, a half-hearted attempt to assuage the residents' fears that they will never leave. But it does nothing to soothe my nerves.

At the row of elevators, I scan my eyeprint. The smells of industrial quantities of bread and farmed fish waft from the first-floor dining hall, and I inhale deeply. A few older apprentices stare at me, but no one tries to stop me. I have not been terminated from the Institute. Yet.

Kricket's room is on the fourth floor. The corridors are older and uglier than those in my dorm, with lower ceilings and dull, scratched metal doors. Steadying my hand, I push the electronic bell on Kricket's door.

"Evening, Yun." Kricket greets me with a smile and ushers me into the semicircular room. He is prepared for this.

Every part of me trembles with fear. I hope Kricket will assume the shaking is a symptom of my health condition.

We sit across from each other on his yellow rug. I had not expected his room to be so neat—no clothes on the floor, no food or products or even stray hairs on the counter. He looks cleaner than usual too. His fiery ponytail is tangled and frizzy, but he has a shaved face and unstained, unwrinkled clothing.

"You look . . . good," I begin. My attempt at One-er small talk. "Holo-called your boyfriend lately?"

Kricket's milky-white face flushes, and he fiddles with the split ends of his ponytail. "Just now. And we're not dating yet." He tosses his hair over one shoulder. "I'm procrastinating, like I do with everything else. You know how it is."

I do not, but that is irrelevant. My words come out painfully slowly, but I manage to speak: "If you just spoke with Devon, then you know why I came here."

Kricket sighs. "Listen, Ver, I know you're desperate to stay out of the Sandbag. I wish I could help you. But I didn't kill Cal. I took Devon out to see a film at the Lucent Gaze Theater—we went late, 'cause it was cheaper."

He raises his flexitab, showing me the two tickets he purchased, plus the receipt. He is being so well-mannered and helpful, even though he is usually a safety hazard. I would be a fool not to question the change.

Just because he bought the tickets does not mean he went. "Tell me about the film."

Kricket's voice becomes icy. "The film was great. Nice 3D cinematography. But why are you asking me all this? Jaha's been chased off campus, and you're not going after *her*. Is it because you were in it together?"

My back clenches painfully. "How dare you . . ."

Kricket grins. He loves to irritate people. Whether they

are mildly annoyed or ready to dump him in the biohazard bin, it is all satisfying to him.

I press on. "You told Devon there was going to be an inspection and had him leave expired, concentrated benzoyl peroxide out in the basement hallway."

Kricket laughs. "Maybe. It was a joke. See, he keeps his bench messy. Everyone in his lab rags on him for it."

"So you knew there would be a bomb in the basement that night. All you had to do was preprogram a bot to bump into it and—*bang*! The alarms would shriek. The lights would shut off. The murderer could slip into Cal's lab in the dark. Could corner him and kill him while the rest of the building was emptying out. No one would hear Cal's scream over the alarm."

Kricket is shaking his head. "There's security footage from the theater. There are witnesses, besides Devon. I was there, not in BioLabs."

"You may not have struck the final blow, but you made it easier for the person who did."

Kricket smirks. "So what's my motive, Ver? Got that figured out?"

I say nothing.

"See, that's your problem. You were the investigator's pet. You wouldn't understand how *anyone* could want him dead. You can't know what it's like to work for six years with Cal over your shoulder, telling you that you aren't good enough, then giving up on you. He never cared about any of us. Not even you. To him, you were an experiment *and* an experimenter—two for the price of one!"

The truth in Kricket's words makes them sting even more. But I tilt my chin up, defiant. "Thank you for explaining your motive to me so clearly. Next question: Who were you working with?"

The smile slides off Kricket's face. He rises to his feet.

Aiyo, have I gone too far? If he decides to strike me, I cannot run.

Balancing my weight between my cane and the wall, I stand. Even so, I only come up to the bottom of Kricket's nose. "Careful, Yun." Kricket presses forward, forcing me back. Up close, he smells of musky cologne. "You should be grateful that I haven't called the police on you by now."

I am dizzy with fear, sick with it. Vomit comes up the back of my throat. He could kill me.

"Is this how you thank me?" Kricket whispers.

Everything that comes next happens in slow motion. My foot catches on the leg of his desk. My cane clatters to the ground.

Crash!

I fall, landing hard on my left hip. The pain steals the breath from my lungs. First the impact, then the needles down the sides of my legs. Someone plucking the nerves in my thighs and calves, many times per second.

When I open my eyes, Kricket is hovering over me, fussing, his long red ponytail dangling past his shoulder and almost brushing my face. "Scrap! Are you all right? Can you sit up?"

Using only my arms, I drag myself over to my cane. With its support I manage to stand, bracing myself against the wall with my free hand. The needles in my legs dig in deeper. Sciatica. Something is impinging my nerves, sending pain signals from hips to feet. Tears of pain and frustration run down my cheeks.

"Ver, I'm sorry," Kricket says, all his bravado gone now. "I didn't mean for you to get hurt. I swear. Do you need to go to the campus hospital? I can take you."

Ha, the hospital! They will lock me in a room to heal. Almost as effective as prison, in terms of getting rid of me. That is what he wants!

"I'm serious," he says. "If you're hurt, I'll pay for the treatment. For any new technology you need. If your legs don't work anymore, you can get new ones. Look, please, don't cry. Don't cry."

He moves closer, and I flinch away, repulsed. Aiyo, I do not want some flashy contraption like Cal's hand. I just want a body that will support a happy, whole life. My body is not replaceable. *I* am not replaceable.

Besides, my legs are not the problem. My whole body is decaying. He will never understand how much that knowledge hurts.

He helped murder the only person who did understand.

"Tell me who you were working with," I whisper.

He shakes his head. "I'm sorry," he says again.

Like the wounded animal I am, I turn tail and slink away. The tears on my face are obvious, and it humiliates me that he sees them.

CHAPTER 31

Aryl

"How many times have you called her?" Ford says, stretching out in his seat aboard the *Mercenary*. On a whim, he's had the AI change our seat coverings to silver synthesized fur. I think it's the softest thing I've ever touched. "Maybe she's napping. Pangu knows she needs it."

"Something's not right," I say, refreshing my burner flexitab. Still nothing from Ver. "I told her to stay in a safe place until I get back."

"She'll listen," Ford says to the ceiling. "Watch it, Aryl, you're slouching."

Grudgingly grateful for the reminder, I squeeze my shoulder blades together until my back's no longer rounded. When we were younger, Ford often picked me up from dance lessons, and Rori told him what to nag me about at home. I'm surprised, and touched, that he remembers.

"Ver likes giving orders, not taking them," I say.

Ford arches his eyebrows. "You can't keep trying to protect her from everything just because she's got problems."

His words lodge in my brain. Despite his flaws, Ford sometimes spouts truth. No one likes being treated like a helpless toddler.

Ford's still watching me, gauging my reaction. "Aryl. You like Ver, don't you?"

The *Mercenary* seems to heat up like something's burning inside. A week ago, I would've laughed off the suggestion. If I were to date Ver—if she liked me back, that is—I might as well resign from dance team. None of my friends would accept a broke girl who can't dance or drink or pole-climb like we do . . . and who also doesn't care about any of those things. But now?

"Do you have more taro chips?" I mutter.

Ford laughs. "Yeah, you like her. I don't blame you. I like how she hasn't groveled at me. And she's cute, for a suspected murderer." He reaches underneath his seat and tosses me a bag of chips in a clear biodegradable wrapper. It floats across the aisle to me. "Though I guess the suspected murderer part could be enticing, seeing as you're one too."

"Stop talking before I arm-wrestle you." I rip open the packet. "Or worse."

I wouldn't ordinarily snack like this. Salt and starches make me retain water, which interferes with leaping and turning. But considering everything else I'm going through, what do a few pounds of water weight matter? When I show up to dance practice tomorrow—er, this morning—I'll still perform adequately and escape scrutiny.

When I'm halfway through the bag, my burner flexitab vibrates. I stop crunching to check the new message.

Kricket confirmed that he convinced Devon to plant the bomb, Ver's written.

It's enough for me to know she's gone and done something dangerous, and my heart takes off at a gallop.

Are you ok—

"Don't reply right away," Ford drawls. "Give it two minutes. If she's fine enough to message you now, there's no rush."

Scowling, I put the flexitab around my wrist and cover it with my sleeve. Eat more chips. Fifty-two seconds pass. I write to Ver: *You questioned him, didn't you?*

She replies right away. *Yes.*

"Ver, *why*?" I cry out loud.

He created the diversion but did not strike the blow that killed Cal. He would not say who he worked with. It looks like a dead end.

"Ford, can you make this thing go any faster?" I say.

He looks at me like I've suggested roasting and eating someone's lab mice. "We're riding the gravitational slingshot from Two," he says. "Can't accelerate without missing One. Or crashing into Gui."

Space transport between the Gui moons takes advantage of the moons' high orbital speeds: once a ship locks into orbit around one moon, a kick from the engine at the correct angle will launch it toward another. It's fuel-efficient and safe. But it requires precise calculations involving the positions of not only the origin and destination moons, but also the forces of gravity from Pangu, Gui, and each of the moons.

"Give me one of those," Ford says, reaching across the aisle to take my second-to-last taro chip. He crunches into it and makes a face. "Your mom's were better."

The chip in my mouth turns to tasteless mush. My throat convulses; my eyes fill. I owe Mom an apology for imprisoning her, Dad, and Ester in their home and, so far, offering no way out.

"I'm sorry." Ford looks like he'll cry too. "I do want to help them. Once we're back on campus, I'll call my mom. I'll try to talk to her."

"I hope you really mean that."

"It's the least I can do. I have to start standing up to her sooner or later."

We fall silent, listening to the whir of the ship and the occasional clink of a small asteroid bouncing off the hull. Part of me doesn't want to go any faster. Despite the hurry to get back to One, I want to stay here, like this. When we land, he'll go back to being the perfect son of Senator Mercure. He'll hide behind his popularity, his mom's name, his money. I'll go back to being an alien girl accused of murdering a promising investigator.

And if we can't prove otherwise, I'll lose him again—along with everyone else I care about.

CHAPTER 32
Ver

The musculoskeletal system requires constant tending, especially if a person is sedentary like me. Muscle fibers are meant to slide and stretch—not freeze, swell, and form lesions.

Two years ago, when I started having pains, my school nurse sent me an exercise and acupressure guide meant to relieve the symptoms of muscle spasm and nerve impingement. "Ten minutes twice a day will double the time you'll remain mobile," he said. "That could mean years of walking instead of sitting in a hoverchair."

I memorized the guide. By following the directions, I could make myself feel slightly better.

Tonight, though, I do not want to stretch or massage. All I want is to crawl into bed, which I know will make the spasms worse. I do it anyway. Why should I not give up? I cannot prove Kricket guilty; I cannot figure out whom he is working with; I still do not know how someone managed to inject Cal with TTX. Nothing makes sense and everything hurts.

Out of all the things Kricket said, one juts out in my mind, cutting me again and again. *If your legs don't work anymore, you can get new ones.*

I wish I had told him how simplistic that thinking was,

made him feel enough to bring him to his knees. RCD will not stop with my legs. Organ by organ, it will shut down my body. I have seen people as young as twenty on Three, paralyzed from the pain. Living in sheet-metal shanties, unable to work. Unable to think, as the disease invades their brains. I always turned away from those haunting images of my future—a future that is already encroaching on the present.

Kricket does not know how it feels to have your body betray you. But Cal did.

Cal first told me about his injury one night when we were taking microscope images, high on the novelty of our progress and delirious from sleep deprivation. He told me how he had fallen during a difficult ropeless climb up a crystal rock face. Aiyo, the things fifteen-year-olds dare each other to do!

"The moment I got my replacement hand, I knew I would become a scientist," Cal said, adjusting the controls. "I was no longer restricted by what I was born with. I could become faster, work harder, and improve other people's lives in the same way."

Maybe that was why he never cared about anyone's natural limitations when it came to lab work. Including mine. After capturing my heart, he knew my brain and hands would do whatever it took to accomplish our goals. If he had kept me at arm's length instead of pulling me in, I would not have given everything I had to the work. To him.

Now, I do not regret working so hard, but I do regret the reason why.

That night, though, all I could do was continue to listen to him, mesmerized. Cal told me that, despite some initial ghost pains, he got used to his new hand. It could take his vital measurements from inside his body, as I learned when he ran to lab late and sweated so much his electrolytes were depleted. The high-speed computing functions let him sort through three-thousand-row spreadsheets of data without touching another device. I never saw him wear a flexitab. Why would he, when he had a processor in his hand powered by his heartbeat?

I remember Jaha asking Cal to delete financial documents and experiment records from his hand's hard drive, to save them on the secure lab computer instead. "Someone will fish information out of that hand," she cautioned him once. "Just walk by you with their little hooking device and scoop it up."

It was a paranoid Three-er thing to say, and Cal just laughed. "Someone could break into the lab or hack the server. The only place secrets are safe is inside our heads," he said. He tapped Jaha's temple, and she groaned.

If I had been murdered instead of Cal, the people investigating would be dense not to take my disease into account. It is my most obvious vulnerability. So why have Aryl and I not talked about Cal's hand?

Because she will learn more about me than I am ready for. Things that Cal found out slowly over the six months of our secret experiments. Things I have always wanted to hide.

Charles's voice pulls me away from my calculations. "Thinking hard, are you?"

"I cannot move much else besides my brain," I say, gesturing to my prickling, burning legs.

"My computing abilities may be of assistance. Or my six free petabytes of memory."

"Not necessary, Charles, but thank you. Just . . . please make sure I stay warm."

"That's easy," Charles says and increases the temperature in the room by two degrees Celsius. "You do know, Ver, that AI processors may be better suited to solving murders than your own brain."

I offer no reply. Not that Charles would know what my silence means. AIs manage information better than any human, but how well do they know *people*? How well can they understand the tensions, the jealousy, the love among six individuals who worked in the same lab day and night?

I wish computers could tell me who took Cal from us. From me. But they cannot.

Besides—Cal would say that if anyone could solve his murder, it would be me.

CHAPTER 33
Aryl

Ford drops me off at the airfield just north of the Institute.

"Keep my services in mind the next time you get in trouble," Ford says, patting me on the shoulder. The one that clicks sometimes. He gives me a light push out of the spacecraft.

The *Mercenary* takes off in a noisy haze, arcing into the night sky. City lights bounce off its golden exterior as the ship ascends, and its exhaust trail of hot hydrogen gas fizzes, like a shooting star in reverse.

I sprint toward campus, hoping to catch the last few minutes of dance practice. When the team sees me, frazzled and greasy from travel, they'll understand how hard I tried to make it.

I want Rhea to see me too. All her poison hasn't made me keel over—yet.

Two figures appear on the path before me, and I force myself to slow down when I see Rhea's stony face and Kandel's gassed-off one. All my happiness drains away; my body goes heavy with dread, and my leg muscles tighten.

"Practice is over?" I ask, deflated. "I'm sorry—I was hoping to join for the last few minutes. I rushed back!"

"You're out of chances, Fielding," Kandel says. "This is the second practice in a row you've missed."

"Not to mention," says Rhea, "your *values* no longer align with ours."

The words won't sink in. "But you know about my situation," I tell my team captain, trying to ignore Rhea. "Can't you sub someone in for me until everything's been sorted out?"

Rhea scoffs. "By the time everything's sorted out, you'll no longer be an apprentice here. Your Institute profile already lists your status as suspended. Weren't you notified?"

Maybe I was. Without my flexitab, I've got no access to my messages, no way to check whether I'm still getting paid.

"You're off the team," declares Kandel. "You're done."

The blows keep coming, beating me when I'm already down. I grieve the money I could've sent home to make my family's life more bearable. And along with the loss of my job, I'm facing a future without dancing. Without everything I've worked toward.

Live like you're dancing, Rori always told me. How am I supposed to do that now?

"Good luck, Fielding." Kandel shares a knowing look with Rhea. "I wish you all the best."

They step gracefully down the path, moving away from me.

"Who's going to be your charity case now that I'm gone?" I yell after them. "Who else are you going to lure with a dung heap disguised as friendship until they turn out to be too alien for you?"

Rhea doesn't turn around.

I stomp away in the opposite direction, raging at these scrap humans and the universe that produced them. Soon, though, that rage burns itself out. My feet drag on the tarmac. My spine curls. Joint by joint, I feel my body turning to stone.

Why should I even care how I move? My dance dreams are over. No more stages, no more music, no more applause. No more sharing my innermost feelings using only my body.

I don't want to live like I'm dancing anymore. I want to forget I ever could.

CHAPTER 34
Ver

Aryl shuffles into the lab. Slouching, distraught. I am lying on the office couch, insulation bags filled with hot water draped over me. I am trying to relax my coiled muscles. The trail of pain down both sides of my legs makes them hypersensitive to the touch. I feel like a fish, using my lateral line to detect mechanical stimuli. Except all the stimuli hurt.

The lab is empty except for us. I decided it would be safer to meet and talk here, away from the home AIs in our dorm rooms. Fond as I am of Charles, he is always listening. So I dragged myself to BioLabs, perhaps for the last time.

"I don't know what to say to you, Ver," Aryl says, executing a descending spin that ends with her seated on the floor, head on her knees. Oh, dancers. "You're hurt."

I roll onto my other side and raise my head to look at her. "I tripped in Kricket's room. My fault."

Aryl slides closer to me. Questions spark in her enormous eyes, which are puffy from crying. Something else is wrong.

"What happened?" I asked her.

She says quietly, "Oh, it's nothing. They kicked me off dance team. Just now."

"Aiyo. How unfair." She must be devastated. Dance defines

her body like my RCD has come to define mine. Who am I now without stillness? Who is she without movement? I reach out a hand and she takes it. Closest I can give to a hug.

"What does it matter?" Aryl says, slouching as she sits. The posture looks unnatural on her, and it saddens me. "I won't be able to dance in the Sandbag, and we'll be there in two days if we don't find the killer." She wipes her eyes with the back of her hand. "Anyway, Kricket. You were saying?"

"Something he said made me think . . . Cal saved all sorts of files on his hand, the artificial one. He took holos with it too. The police wanted to see something on there. Jaha said they tried to access it, remember? Back at the police station."

"Do you know the contents of those files?" Aryl asks.

Instead of answering directly, I say, "I think they could have put Cal in danger."

"Why?"

I can feel my face going red, but she rushes on before I can reply.

"Is it something to do with the portable antichronowave detector Ford and Kricket were racing to build? Cal pitted them against each other, put Kricket's whole future on the line. Did you know about that?"

"No, but Kricket's motives matter less to me now than his methods." Later I will need to ask her what else she knows about this detector. For the moment I try to stay on track. "If Kricket managed to access the files in Cal's hand, and if we could prove that, we would have something concrete tying him to the murder."

"Kricket's too bad with computers to have hacked an artificial limb."

"Maybe he was working with someone who could," I say. "Aryl, we need to get access to Cal's hand."

I still want to hide everything Cal might have on there about me—from Aryl, from all the Gui moons. But it is looking more likely that, if we are going to walk free, it cannot stay hidden. I *can* sacrifice my dignity for freedom. But it will require the kind of vulnerability that terrifies me.

"Cal's hand is in the medical repository," Aryl reminds me. "Along with the rest of him."

I refuse to visualize that. "Yes, so we would need to get to it and find a way to extract the files . . ."

"Ver, that's illegal!" Aryl shakes her head. "And an invasion of privacy, never mind that Cal's dead. Xenon would have a field day if he caught us."

I shrug. "Xenon already has a whole spreadsheet of charges against us. One more would not matter. We have forty-nine hours until the trial, Aryl. We need to act."

Aryl scrutinizes me, eyes narrowed. "This is a scrap idea."

"We have no better ones. Please, Aryl. We must try."

Aryl chews on her lip, thinking. "It's so dangerous, Ver, what you're proposing."

"So is this whole situation. If I get tossed in the Sandbag, I will die. If you are there with me, who knows what will happen to your family?" I must turn myself inside out to say those words. But it works. Aryl is nodding, though she still looks troubled.

"If we do this," she says, "if we can access Cal's files, we might find out how Kricket and his accomplice coordinated the murder. And maybe Cal took images that night. Of the last thing he saw."

Yes. But there is more. The documents that concern me. That concern all of us. "So, how are we accessing that hand?" I ask.

Aryl gathers herself, taps her fingertips together and grins mischievously, looking very much like Ford. There is purpose in her again. "I have an idea."

CHAPTER 35
Aryl

The Lucent City Medical Repository houses the bodies of people who've donated themselves to science. It's mostly staffed by simple wheeled robots and organizationally savvy, incorporeal AIs. But there are humans too: scientists doing research, medical apprentices pursuing their studies. To accommodate grieving members of the public who aren't comfortable chatting with AIs, those humans take turns staffing the front desk. Right now, a white-coated woman is stationed there.

"How may I help you, young lady?" she says in a surprisingly high, youthful voice. She's around ninety, and her hair's dyed brassy yellow. Ester wouldn't approve. *No one that age has natural blond hair,* she'd say. *Pick a wild color or leave it be.*

My own hair is straightened and colored platinum with temporary dye, thanks to Ver. People who look at me now won't see brunette killer Aryl Fielding. Just a blond Two-er girl in baggy farm clothes, fresh off the spaceliner.

It was comforting to feel Ver's hands combing through my curls. When I closed my eyes, I almost forgot why we were changing my appearance.

Glancing down now, pretending to be shy, I see a full glass of steaming cacao extract on the scientist's desk. No lid. Perfect.

I whip out my best Two-er drawl and say, "I'm looking for my great-great-great-uncle. Never got to say goodbye, you know—the rest of the family's on Two. I came to pay my respects."

"Oh, I am so sorry," the woman says. "What's his name?"

"Theodosius Tello." Aged 138 years, Mr. Tello was a real Lucent City resident, moderately wealthy. He died of a cold last week; Ver's dorm room AI, Charles, found the obituary in a Neb search. Scientists at the repository want to study how and why the cold virus so easily overwhelmed Mr. Tello's aged immune system.

"This is him," I say and pull up Mr. Tello's image—snipped from his obituary—on my burner flexitab. The scientist bends over it to look at his face. As she does, I scan her right eye.

Mr. Tello looks, conveniently, like my alter ego. Whether the thin platinum wisps of hair on his head were real or dyed doesn't concern me.

"Ah, yes, an interesting case." The woman looks from the holo projection to her own screen. "Let's see where he is . . ."

If she resents taking time away from her scientific work to handle reception duty, she's not showing it. Probably just glad to have a job. She must be one of those older One-ers who hasn't saved enough money to retire. Not everyone is rich, and plenty of people on One have to keep working into their eleventh decade. It's unfair, but at least they're not doing hard labor.

"We've moved the body out of the main holding room and into cryo-protection. He's in Room 18, Bin 23."

"Can you tell me the stats of the room?"

As she squints at the screen and reads off temperature, humidity, and construction materials, I pretend to squint with her—and pass my hand over her drink, sprinkling powder inside.

"Thank you so much," I say and move away from the desk with a quick, stomping walk.

My burner flexitab dings with a message from Ver, who's keeping track of my location on her own device: *The iris reconstruction is complete. You should be good to get in.*

I grin. We copied this software from one of the labs at the Institute hospital—one that studies iris pigmentation and open-sources their imaging platform on the Neb. With a few tweaks to the code, Ver and I got their reconstruction program to do what we needed.

The old woman's iris scan in hand, I follow the wall signs toward the holding room, where I know I'll find Cal and hundreds of other recently deceased people, all of whom are being picked apart by curious scientists.

"You're going the wrong . . ." the woman says, her voice slurring. I hear a small *thump*, the sound of a head connecting with a desk. When I glance back, it looks like she's taking a nap, as old people often do. The zolpidem is working.

She seemed sweet; I fight the urge to check that she didn't hit her head too hard. Zolpidem tartrate is a gentle drug. She'll wake up in a few hours, feeling groggy but refreshed.

I step up to the large black doors of the holding room and use my flexitab's holo-imager to project her reconstructed iris for the scanner. The doors swing open, and I close them behind me. Wind rushes past. This airlock has a high flow rate to help disinfect me. I put on a white coat, hair net, goggles, and gloves. The personal protective equipment conveniently obscures my identity. Hopefully any passerby will think I'm a scientist or a doctor in training.

Passing through another set of doors, I enter the holding room. The stench of formaldehyde and flesh sets fire to my windpipe. And it's *cold*. My breath is a vapor cloud. Every exposed hair on my body stands at attention. This place is a cramped, windowless refrigerator for hunks of meat.

Metal shelving for the corpses towers high on either side of me. I stay away, wary of accidentally touching something that was once some*one*. Blue-white overhead lighting casts an icy tinge over everything. In the middle of the room there's a medical examination table. And a body on top, covered in a white sheet.

Although every instinct tells me to leave, I stand my ground and breathe in lungfuls of air. Gradually my nose becomes desensitized to the smells, though I can't shake the sick feeling. Shuddering, I wheel a heavy biohazard waste bin over to block the doors.

I shouldn't be quaking over dead bodies. I've witnessed plenty of gruesome injuries in the course of my dance career. Lots of blood, and lots of feet: callused, blistered, broken, misshapen. Nothing fazes a dancer after she's seen her own feet. Or so I tell myself.

Each body-sized shelf is labeled with its dead occupant's name. I try to work out a pattern so that I can find Cal faster. They're not alphabetical by first name or last. Or by neighborhood or cause of death. Finally, I notice that all the people closest to the door died earlier today. Farther into the room are bodies from yesterday.

A soft knock sounds on the door to the holding room. Probably a staff scientist. But whoever it is doesn't knock too loudly, in case someone's doing an actual examination.

I've got a minute before I get caught, maybe two. I find

the bodies from the date that Cal died. And I see it: *Calyx Eppi, 04-09-2798*. His bin is at my hip level.

Bracing myself, I heave the plexiglass container—scrap, I'll call it a coffin—out of its slot and lower it to the floor.

I hear a voice outside the room, maybe asking the AI who's in here. I catch my breath and flip open the coffin's dark-tinted cover.

There's Cal.

Death has drained his skin of color. But his handsome features are still there, the lips parted to reveal his overlapping front teeth. He looks like a sculpture of himself.

Thankfully there's nothing in my stomach to retch.

The knocking grows louder. "Who's in there?" a voice shouts.

I grab Cal's left wrist and seize the bionic hand's translucent, whitish fingers. They lie limp, like dead jellyfish tentacles, but only for a moment. When I touch them, the cold bioplastic fingers shudder to life and squeeze, crushing mine. The hand is chilled. The knuckles bulge, the wrist flexes, and the fingers clamp down harder, harder.

My heart leaps into my throat. I'm in so much shock, I barely feel the pain.

The pressure on my fingers eases momentarily. The bionic hand's fingertips tap my skin at inhumanly fast speed, as if playing a keyboard. Next it grabs my wrist, grinding the tibia and fibula against each other, and vaults into the air to wring out my entire arm. I hold back a scream, try to yank my hand away. With my other fist, I pound the bionic hand from every angle I can manage. Ver will kill me if I break the screen or damage any internal components. But this hand will kill me if I don't fight back.

Finally it beeps softly and lets me go. My fingers prickle as blood rushes back to them.

The banging at the door crescendos. I press the bionic hand to Cal's chest, trying to boot it up—*Come on, Investigator, what were you hiding?* Even as its fingers continue to grab at air, I wrestle it down, grunting with effort. Whipping out the burner flexitab, I take a 3D scanning shot, moving the camera around until it's viewed the hand from all angles. Next, I'll need to fish for files.

As soon as I loosen my grip, the hand clenches into a fist. I duck down and to the left; it mirrors my movements. I go up and to the right; it follows me. Even as I jump back, it pops me in the chin. Galaxies appear in front of my eyes.

Forget the files. I need to get out of here!

Biting down hard on my lip to hold in a yelp of pain, I flip the lid back over Cal's body—and his terrifying hand—and deadlift him back into his bin.

I careen out of the holding room. Breathless in the airlock, I'm facing a middle-aged scientist with white hair and a black goatee.

"Stop! What are you here for?" he demands. "You know, we remove all valuables from the dead before we examine them. There's nothing here for you to steal."

My whole body is shaking.

"Let's see who you really are," the scientist says.

He reaches for my goggles. I block his hand, but he uses his shoulder to push me back against the door. My upper back takes most of the impact; I'm able to stay upright—barely.

Faking a concussion, I clutch the back of my skull and let my body loll. When the scientist reaches for my goggles again, I kick his shin as hard as I can.

"Auuugh!" he shouts in pain, jumping back.

I sprint out of the airlock, out of the repository, back into the daylight—just as an alarm shrieks inside. On the busy street, I slow to a walk and duck into a shaded alley full of trash receptacles. It's not pleasant, but it's private.

When I'm sure no one can see me, I clamp my teeth around my forearm and scream into it silently.

CHAPTER 36
Ver

Cuttlefish change the pigment and iridescence of their skin to seamlessly blend into their external environment. I remember learning this in my primary school biology class and feeling jealous of such a versatile creature. It is a pity that Aryl did not have this ability to disappear when we sorely needed it.

While I wait in the abandoned lab, I have been using my burner flexitab to watch news stories about the Lucent City Medical Repository break-in. Holo footage from the building's security cameras is all over the Neb already, showing a girl with straight blond hair getting pushed into a wall—*bang!* Clutching her head, she stomps on a scientist's foot and runs out of the facility.

How long before the authorities trace the intrusion back to Aryl and me?

Aryl stumbles in. She has washed the platinum blond out of her hair. The strands are forming curlicues once again. Her face is bruised, and her eyes are full of stories. Frightening ones.

I get to my feet, even though it hurts, and edge toward her. "What happened?"

"It . . . it . . ." Her eyes fill with tears.

I dig in my bag until I find half a loaf of sweet green tea bread, squashed but still soft inside its wrapper. "Here," I say, holding it out.

"You're amazing," she says and tears in. There is a blip in my heartbeat, a catch in my breath.

After several deep breaths, she is ready to talk. "Cal. His hand. He was dead—his face was like stone—but his hand, it punched me." She points to the bruise on her chin, a mottled purple and green. As I reach out to touch her skin, she shrinks away, curls up into a ball. "It was still alive, somehow."

"*What?*" I stare at her. Did seeing Cal's dead body disturb her so much that she hallucinated?

"It grabbed my fingers and twisted my arm around and punched me in the face."

Barely able to process this, I reach out a trembling hand and touch her elbow. "So . . . you were not able to search for any files stored in the hand."

"No, but I did capture a 3D image of the hand itself. I'm not *that* bad a scientist." She shoves the rest of the bread into her mouth, unrolls her burner flexitab, and projects a holographic image of Cal's bionic hand.

It is the same, down to the metal facets on the knuckles and the slender titanium bones beneath the translucent skin. That hand was such an important part of Cal, just as my disobedient legs are a part of me. Even though it was not his dominant hand when he was born, it was perfectly steady, so he always used it to write, pipette, and dissect.

An image of the hand leaping up and attacking Aryl comes to my mind, but it makes me imagine the rest of Cal waking up too. His eyes twinkling at me before he asks how my experiments are going and if I want to talk to him about anything . . .

Stop! I order myself. I focus on Aryl: "Why would that hand still move, when its power source—Cal's heartbeat—was gone?"

"Maybe, after Cal died, the hand activated some kind of defense mode so no one would tamper with it," Aryl says.

"Unlikely." Using my burner flexitab, I search the Neb for the keywords *malfunctioning artificial limb*. Old news articles appear, from fifty-some years ago, when smart limbs sometimes betrayed their owners. But manufacturers corrected the problem by replacing artificial intelligence algorithms with lab-grown neurons genetically identical to the wearer's. These were wired into the brain, the implanted cells communicating seamlessly with the preexisting ones. Cells turned out to be more trustworthy than code. Problem solved.

By the time Cal got his hand, mistakes had stopped happening. Which means . . .

I drop my head in my hands, fingers forming into fists. "We have to consider the possibility that someone tampered with Cal's hand. *Before* he died."

A moment of quiet passes between us. Aryl claps a hand over her mouth and whispers, "The angle of the injection, to the left side of his neck. It was his own hand, the artificial one!"

Her face is a mixture of horror and elation. I cannot believe we failed to think of this earlier. And how horrible Cal's last moments must have been! His body betrayed him.

"Kricket," Aryl says. "Could he have hacked into the hand and reprogrammed it?"

"Maybe," I say. "But only the manufacturer would know how someone might do this. Which company made the hand?"

Aryl looks at me, confused. "Cal didn't tell you?"

"I could not just ask our boss where he buys his body parts."

Aryl shrugs. "Out of everyone in our lab, you'd look the least weird if you did."

I glare at her.

"Sorry. I just meant . . . you were closest to him."

I sigh. "I *thought* I was." Staring again at the holo of Cal's hand, I tell Aryl, "Zoom closer."

Aryl increases the magnification and resolution. As the image glides over the artificial hand, I am struck by how *different* it is. Hairless. Smooth as the skin of a polished apple. Not human, with human imperfections.

"What is that on the inner wrist?" I point to a fold of translucent bioplastic at the joint, scrawled with what look like black squiggles. It is still blurry. Aryl zooms in more and I see a line of ten letters and digits. A serial number.

"Search for that," Aryl says.

I squint to see the characters. Carefully, I copy down the sequence on the burner flexitab and scour the Neb. Results pop up immediately.

"Hoverbikes," I say, disappointed. "Worker IDs. What are the chances . . . ?"

Throughout history, many numbers have been assigned to many people and things. There is always a chance of duplication.

Aryl leans over my shoulder. "There," she says, pointing to a serial number listed under a company called Paion Prostheses. "That one sounds like an artificial limb manufacturer."

I tap the company name. Images pop up on the screen: arms that resemble flower stems, tree-like legs, a calf and foot shaped like a lightning bolt. The limbs meld seamlessly with their human models, artifice flowing into flesh. Aiyo, how pretty! I try to imagine myself with a pair of long, flowing flower-legs, but something about it feels wrong.

"This could definitely be the company that made Cal's hand," Aryl says. "Though their style's gotten, uh, louder since Cal's day." She sucks in a breath through her teeth. "And these prices are astronomical. Who can afford parts like this? Half a million Feyncoins for a hand! And we heard so much about Cal's humble beginnings in the mountains."

The bitterness in her voice when she talks about Cal makes me uncomfortable. "He never lied," I say. "He told me his whole town pooled money to pay for his hand after the accident."

"He really made you feel like his confidante, didn't he?" Aryl says.

I sit back, looking at her. Perhaps she wanted Cal to like her. Over the past few days, I have doubted how much he liked *me*. He seemed to share so much of himself with me, but he did it with only one goal in mind. If my devotion to his science had wavered for a second, how would he have treated me?

Returning to the search results for "Paion Prostheses," I find body parts for sale from dozens of vendors. They range from steady fingers for dissection-weary scientists to super-muscular or super-slender legs for athletes or models. Top quality; buy brand-new, secondhand, in bulk. If your body parts are not to your liking, replace them. Just as you would a hovercar or a spaceship part.

But some crucial information is missing. There seems to be no homepage for the company itself. All their products are being sold through other distributors. I visit the Gui Moons Market page, where people with money buy and sell stocks. *Paion Prostheses*, I type in. Nothing. I search through the healthcare sector, where the company is sure to be listed. Still nothing! I look at the robotics sector. No results there either.

"Did a supermassive star eat this company? Why is there so little information about it?"

A crease forms between Aryl's eyebrows. A dent in molten bronze. "Yeah. It's weird."

I go back to our initial search results. One image catches my eye: a shining factory in what has to be the desert of G-Moon Three. The sunset-colored sands and the faint shimmer of the habitat dome in the background give it away. *Better than what you were born with!* is displayed in block letters above the pair of semicircular yellow doors on the large cubic building. Pipes protrude from the cube's sides, and a ring of metal towers surrounds it like the spikes of a crown.

The rock formations reflected in the towers' windows look vaguely familiar, like an image in a dream. But then again, so much of the desert landscape on Three looks the same. And the data associated with the image says nothing about location.

"Where is Paion based?"

Aryl drags her finger up and down to scroll through the search results but has no answer for me.

"Who is their executive?" I go on. "Why can I not buy their products directly from the manufacturer? If I search *Paion Prostheses factory*"—and I do—"why are there no results?"

Aryl sighs. "Does it matter? Ver, it's been twenty years since Cal got that hand. The company might've shut down or changed its name—who knows? Besides, how much could they tell us about the flaws of a bionic hand from decades ago?"

I look up at Aryl's exhausted face. "We have no other leads, and there is something odd about this company. How did it disappear?"

I return to the image of the factory, the mountains reflected in the shiny window, and project it in holographic mode from the flexitab, gradually increasing the resolution.

I see a tram stop in the distance, rusting and steely, just like the ones back home. *Could it be?* Honey Crater and its surrounding towns had those same pyramidal structures sprinkled along the tram routes!

"I am not sure, but . . . I think that is G-Moon Three." I remember something Jaha said after she was fired. "Jaha used to work in a medical factory on Three. There could be a connection."

Aryl chews on this information. "Well, too bad we don't know where Jaha is now, or how to get in touch with her in case she knows anything useful."

"If Paion had a factory on Three, then people there would remember it. I know how to talk to those people." I swallow the word *Ma*. In spite of myself, I want to see my mother again before I get locked up. I surely will not see her after.

I get to my feet and hold out a hand for Aryl, because I need courage for what must come next. She takes it. "We need to find that factory, or what is left of it."

Aryl stands, still holding my hand, without resting any of her weight on me. "Are you sure about this?"

"Yes. When I came here, I swore I would never go back. But I will, Aryl. For Cal's sake. And for our sake." I will breathe that dust into my lungs if it means erasing the black mark on our names.

Aryl nods. "Then I'm coming with you."

CHAPTER 37
Aryl

"I can't help you this time," Ford says. The projection of his head and shoulders slouches, silhouetted against the gray light in his room.

"Didn't you offer your services?" I say. The intention's to tease him, but it doesn't come out right. I sound half mocking and half desperate.

"I know you're going to hate me for this. Call me a million names if you want. But I can't go to Three."

Ver, who's sitting next to me, looks at him sternly. "Why?"

In the projection, Ford goes red with embarrassment. "My mom . . . if she finds out, I'm—"

"Enough about your mom," I say. "You told me you were going to start standing up to her."

Ford goes even redder. "Look, Two was one thing, but Three—it's terrifying, all right? I've grown up in this . . ." Ford gestures at the sculptures and the magnificent bay window behind him. "And I'd be worse than useless in the desert. What if I get kidnapped, held for ransom? My skin's worth giga money, and I'm not saying that to brag."

Ver's trying not to let pain cross her face. But I know how she's feeling. I know how it feels when the things people say about your moon are actually true.

"Ford, come on," I say. "We've got forty-some hours until Ver and I go on trial for *murder*, and unless you can help us, we're going to spend all of them trying to get to Three." If he says no, we're Sandbag meat.

Ford shakes his head. "The thought of going to Three makes me want to puke. You're brave, both of you. But I'm not. I can't do this."

I sigh. "I was starting to believe in you, but you really know how to disappoint a girl."

Ver speaks up, twisting her hands together in her lap. "Ford, no commercial spaceliners go to G-Moon Three's crater region. We would have to take a spaceliner from Lucent City, land at Phoenix Port, take a ten-hour vactrain, transfer to another train. The authorities would scrutinize our identities and search our belongings at every stop. We would never make it in time."

Ford massages his temples. "I know, I know. I'm sorry." A ray of Pangu's light flashes in through the window, temporarily blinding us. Before I can blink, Ford closes the curtains with the push of a button.

He can do so much from his desk, I realize. He doesn't need to be physically present for our trip. He didn't touch the *Mercenary*'s controls when we flew to G-Moon Two.

We don't need him. We just need the *Mercenary*.

"Ford," I say, "can your ship leave Celestine without you on it?"

"Theoretically, yeah," Ford says. "I can program in any destination and the AI pilot will calculate the best route." He looks at my hopeful face and says, "Scrap. I know what you're going to ask."

"Let the *Mercenary*'s AI pilot take us to Three," I say. "If you're going to tap out of looking for the killer, at least lend us your ride."

Ford chews on a nail. His face softens. "If you promise to look after this ship as if it were your own . . . I'll send the *Mercenary* to campus and input your iris scans to make sure you get access."

It's the bare minimum. But I'll take it.

"I'll get the ship ready for you right away," Ford says. "I just have to move the antichronowave detector. I've finished it, by the way."

"Already?" I try not to show how impressed I am. I'd known he was close to completing the project, but Ford always surprises me with his competence. "Well, at least *one* member of the lab has been productive."

"Yeah, and it seems to work, based on the tests I've done locally. Though, weirdly, it gives higher values when this side of One faces Gui, and lower values when it faces away."

"That lines up," Ver says. Her eyes take on a faraway expression and she seems to drift off into thought. What does she mean? I'll ask her later, in private.

"I'll move it to my room at home," Ford says. "If it breaks, I'm worse off than Kricket."

"You need to keep the detector on the ship," Ver says. I've never heard her sound so forceful.

Ford raises his eyebrows and starts laughing. "Ver. What? I just finished the thing! What do you want it for?"

"Please," Ver says. "Trust me. This is related to Cal. It might help us."

"Well, if it'll help keep you out of the Sandbag . . ." Ford trails off.

189

"It will," Ver says.

"Okay. I've got the schematics, so I guess I could make another one if the original gets damaged."

Ver looks stunned at having gotten her way so quickly. "Ford, for someone so scared, you are more generous than I thought."

"Or just not as smart as I should be," he says. "I'm giving you two my ship and my wave detector and my trust. Don't mess up, okay? Because if they catch you and put you away, I'll be the guy who helped two murderers dodge travel restrictions, and even my mom won't be able to protect me from that. I'll end up in the Sandbag with you."

CHAPTER 38

Ver

The happy pink suitcase, which Ma bought me secondhand as a goodbye present, follows me around my room. I toss an extra outfit and my twelve-chambered pill organizer into it.

Ma. Gou, I miss her! But not the Ma I have seen too often, who flies on Happy Patches and, when she comes down, screams at me for being useless. I miss the Ma who sat me down in the factory's employee breakroom with leftovers from her lunch so that I could concentrate on my homework.

I do not know which version of Ma I will see when I return home. For the past few years—since her hands started aching from overwork and she started using those patches—her personality at any given moment has been determined by an internal coin flip. True or false, kind or cruel. Impossible to predict.

"Going somewhere?" Charles asks.

"The beach," I say. G-Moon Three is covered in sand, but there is no water except for polar ice. Does that count?

The keycard for our apartment, which I could never bring myself to throw away, goes into my zippered pocket. Along with two capped syringes.

"Are the syringes for your medications?" Charles says.

Is it just me, or does his AI voice sound judgmental? Am I being paranoid?

"No," I say. "But I appreciate your concern."

I have never carried weapons before, not even when I lived on Three. Going straight from home to school and back before night fell meant that I avoided trouble. But something tells me my home moon will be more treacherous to me now that I have become a One resident. Rich, according to the stereotype. So I have taken some ketamine solution from the controlled substances cabinet. A milliliter will knock out a mouse during surgery. The amount I am taking with me can put a full-grown man on his back in less than a minute. I considered a more lethal chemical, like cyanide or sodium pentobarbital, but we keep those in such small amounts that anything missing would attract attention.

Before I go, I take one last look at the room where I have lived the best and worst days of my life. It was my first space with a door I could shut against the world. But I always knew it was only temporary. A place for the Three-er visitor to sleep until fate came for her.

Charles closes the door behind me as I step into the hallway. I straighten my back as much as I can and march toward my first home—and whatever it has in store for me.

CHAPTER 39
Aryl

The AI-piloted *Mercenary* picks us up at the airfield north of campus. Ver stares openmouthed at the interior, especially the workbench, microscope, and automated soldering irons.

Seconds after we've strapped in, side by side, the force of our acceleration pushes us down into our seats. We're jetting along an orbital path around One, the whole moon glittering beneath us. My heart races with the excitement of seeing another new place . . . and the fear of it. If we can't find the killer, we'll spend the rest of our lives there.

Three's linked to the early days of space colonization, with its hermetically sealed habitat domes and tightly regulated microclimates. But it feels more important as the moon that formed the girl sitting next to me, who's currently shaking.

"Hey," I say, turning to her, "you okay?"

"Scared," Ver says, her voice soft. "That, after all this, we will still be considered guilty."

"Is that all?" I ask jokingly, but she shakes her head in total earnestness. The ends of her hair swish over her pretty, round ears.

"You have asked me so many questions. And I have not answered any of them fully. Not yet."

I don't speak. I wait, hoping she'll let me understand more of her.

"If I do not tell you now, you will be fumbling in the dark to prove your innocence. Especially if something happens to me."

"Don't say that!" I say. "Nothing will happen to you."

"That is not up to us."

The history of her body pours out of her. Two years ago, her joints started to ache. After a fall during a discdisc game, she got tested and learned the cause: Rapid Cellular Degeneration. She cried and begged to be tested again, refusing to believe it, but the evidence didn't lie. It was a death sentence. Still is.

I've heard of RCD, but in the abstract. And I knew Ver's health was fragile, but I never imagined the wrenching details. *How could this happen to you?* I want to scream.

"I came to Cal's lab to save myself," Ver says. "And to help others like me."

"Is that what you and Cal were doing at those weird hours?"

Ver nods. "Experimenting on me. We never talked about it to anyone."

"How'd it start?"

Ver smiles, her eyes far away. "A week after I arrived on One, I noticed that I was feeling better. Or at least not worse. So I stayed in lab late. I wanted to see how degraded my cartilage proteins were. After a few nights of that, Cal walked in. He could have been angry that I was playing with his equipment, wasting funds. But he just asked, 'Hey, can I see?' I was so nervous, I nearly fainted! But I let him look into the scope." Ver pauses, whispers, "I will never forget the look on his face when I told him those cells were mine. That they looked *better* than the last samples I had taken on Three."

Ver's voice wavers. Tears gather in her eyes, and she turns her face toward the ceiling, toward the stars. Her body exudes love and regret and wishes for the impossible. "Then Cal burst out crying."

"Crying?" I say in disbelief. "Our Cal?"

Ver nods. "He said we should both go home, that he needed to rest so his mind could focus again. I spent the next day terrified he would kick me out of his lab. But that night, he said, 'Whatever is happening to you, Ver, it will happen whether we observe it or not. Let's see it all.' So we started experimenting, trying to figure out why I was maintaining my strength, even slowly improving."

"And did you? Figure it out?"

"We got closer. We believe it is related to the concentration of antichronowaves on One. But even if we had learned nothing, the process would have felt rewarding. I finally felt like someone cared about me."

Ver details their work, and I listen in awe. I thought *I* was strong—disciplining my body through force of will. But Ver's body obeys nothing and no one. She and Cal extracted samples, despite the pain of pushing needles and tubes into flesh that was already wounded. From her bone marrow, her muscles, even her digestive tract, all to probe her body's inner workings.

"Ver," I say, "do you think Cal saved the details of these experiments on his hand? And if we were able to extract the files, we'd find . . . you?"

Silence from Ver. Finally, a nod.

"For Pangu's sake," I say, reeling. "He should've known better." Saving data from secret, unapproved studies on a bionic hand was not Cal's best idea. "I wish you'd told me this sooner."

"Do *you* share your medical records with everyone you meet, especially if they are also murder suspects?"

"But it would've gotten us here so much faster!" I say. I feel heat rising in my chest, and my voice comes out fast and fiery. "If someone found out about your research, knew you were on to something big, and knew they could access it through Cal's hand, that's a reason to kill him! Maybe Kricket's accomplice was jealous of Cal and wanted to scoop you."

"But why not just publish our research in their name, then? Why kill him?"

I wave away her question. "I'm not saying I've figured it all out. All I'm saying is, Cal had a huge secret that I didn't know about and you did. Why'd you keep it from me? Do you think I would've judged you?"

The sorrow that takes over her face makes me want to reel my question back in.

Ver says quietly, "I have always wanted to impress you."

My heartbeat surges until I can feel it in my fingers and toes. I remember everything that used to irritate me about her: her drive and her logic, her stubbornness and her quiet brilliance. Now, I wouldn't have her any other way.

"Ver," I say, "I'm more than impressed."

She lets out a strange sound, a sigh of relief coupled with a sniffle, maybe a laugh. I smile down at her. Our hands find each other.

"But why put yourself through so much work and pain? Why risk getting you *and* Cal kicked out of the Institute? Why not just accept that you feel better on G-Moon One?"

"Because in all of this," Ver says, wiping her tears with her free hand, "there may be a treatment."

"Sounds like just being on One is the treatment."

"No—whatever is distinctive about One has slowed my decline, but it will not cure me. And the small improvements I have noticed will soon be neutralized by the aging process. We need a real cure."

My brain hits a wall. "I don't know much about RCD treatments. But aren't there already drugs that can help?"

"Only Telomar, the one ExSapiens put out two years ago," Ver says. "I could never afford it. And it is not as effective as other ExSapiens products. Although it is supposed to restore deformed proteins, it is only collagen mixed with painkillers: a cheap bandage for the musculoskeletal system. People who try it feel better for a short time, but on the molecular level, their bodies are still a mess."

"Why's the drug still on the market, if it's so useless?" I ask.

"Good marketing," Ver says. "But there must be a way to treat the *cause*, not just the symptoms."

Heartbreak is clouding my mind. I try to think about this like a scientist. "What are the causes?"

"No one knows," Ver says. "I am looking. Sometimes I feel like I am the only one who cares enough to look."

"Cal cared," I say softly.

Her face crumples. "He did."

Ver wasn't just some investigator's pet. She worked hard to gain precious time for herself and for others who share her condition. The blanks in my vision of her weren't full of misdeeds and sneakiness, as my mom warned. Hidden there was pain, bravery, and a heart capable of holding it all together.

"Come here," I say, extending my arms.

She unbuckles herself from her seat and floats over to me. Folds herself between my arms, as if she's done it her whole life, and holds on tight.

"I care too," I say into her hair. "If we both still have our freedom after this, we'll figure out RCD together."

Ver looks at me, her eyes shining. "I would love that."

Eventually she floats back to her seat, straps back in, and gazes out of the window at the stars—her face hidden, her hand over her mighty heart.

I wonder if there's a spot in there for me.

CHAPTER 40
Ver

Over the four and a half hours of the spaceship ride, repressed memories, fears, and hopes surge out of me. My mind is a crumbling old mansion overgrown with weeds. Together, Aryl and I clear out and explore the many rooms, one at a time—circling back to the ones with the strangest, loveliest things inside.

Aryl invites me into her mind too. Although she appears to be in optimal health, she tells me that she has sustained dozens of dance injuries. The click in her right shoulder needs laser surgery, which she cannot afford. She has dreamed of becoming a professional dancer all her life but has chosen to pursue science, a more reliable path—and learned that her two passions could intertwine. One takes place second by second. The other unfolds over months, even years. Both are subject to the forces of nature. Both occupy every corner of her heart.

I tell her about my mother. The woman who built friendships with our neighbors so we would have a place to hide when rival drug distributors came for my father. Who took on the burden of his scathing words to protect me and eventually banished him from our home. Who watched over my shoulder as I studied and took tests and studied again so I could escape Three.

The conversation meanders, stream-like. Swelling and waning, sometimes to a trickle. But it never dries.

By the time the yellow curve of G-Moon Three appears, I am thrilled to see it. Never mind that we are here in a hopeless push to clear our names. Never mind that I might get sicker with every kilometer we cross. Never mind that if we fail, we will be thrown in the freezing penal colonies clustered near the moon's icy poles.

I let myself believe that together, we can find the answers we have been hunting. And maybe walk away with our freedom.

(((

The *Mercenary* touches down behind a rocky outcropping a hundred meters from the Honey Crater residential bubble. According to the standard clock, it is early evening, but darkness shrouds this side of G-Moon Three. Typical for my home moon: no correlation between the time and whether it is light out.

I am used to shadows. Used to the walls of the crater casting them over the hermetically sealed town within. The sight is familiar, but it has never made me this sad before. Because I have seen so much more now.

Aryl and I board the *Mercenary*'s oblong hoverpod, detach from the ship, and pilot across the sandy yellow expanse to the nearest airlock, just over the lip of the crater on the west side of town. We go through the first door and scan in the *Mercenary*'s access code. I hold my breath, releasing it slowly as the second door opens. The Mercure vehicle is a licensed craft.

We step out into a town frozen in time. The triangular blocks of buildings are made of glued-together particles of the same yellow sand that covers the moon's surface.

Cheet! Cheet! A tram whistle blows. The tracks, traversed by dingy, rusting cars, carry people back from the looming factories on the outskirts of the residential bubble.

"Wonder which one of those belongs to Paion," I say. I speak to the hoverpod, calling the mothership's AI. "Hello, *Mercenary*."

"Your inquiries are welcome," says the sophisticated female-coded voice.

"Where is the Paion Prostheses factory? Can you take us there?"

"Searching now." After five long seconds, the AI emits a descending series of beeps. "There is no structure known as the Paion Prostheses factory."

"Did you check every database? Try different spellings."

The ceiling lights up with moving yellow dots as the AI ponders. "I'm coming up blank after searching fifteen regional and moonwide address databases."

Disappointment seeps into my belly, though I knew this was likely. "Thank you. Go back to sleep."

The AI logs off with a tinkling melody.

"You didn't expect it to be that easy, did you?" Aryl says.

Sighing, I let my head droop onto her shoulder. "It may not exist anymore," I say. "It could have moved or been buried by the sand. We will have to ask Ma. She has worked in so many factories during her life, met so many people. She must have heard of Paion."

Aryl's mouth twists. "Didn't you say your mom's always flying on something or other?"

"Not always," I say. "And just patches."

"Just patches," Aryl says, disbelieving. "Don't they affect her memory?"

I shake my head, swallowing the lump in my throat. "Not the long-term memories. She can remember conversations we had when I was five—things I forgot long ago—but she forgets what she ate for dinner last night. Even if she knows nothing about a Paion factory, though, she has older coworkers who might know. She can point us to them."

"Okay, let's go. I guess we can't take this shiny little pod—it'd be too obvious. Right?"

"We can walk," I agree, trying to keep my voice steady.

We abandon the pod near the airlock, camouflaging it behind a sparkling gray asteroid and activating the electrical security feature. Until we scan our irises and deactivate the shield, anyone who touches it—trying to rip off parts or steal the whole pod—will be electrocuted. An awful way to learn to keep your hands to yourself.

My memories steer us home. Each spot in the desert that surrounds the town is unique to me, marked by its own sand colors and dune shapes. In the windless habitat, the hills and valleys stay put. Footprints never fade—they only get trodden upon. I might have left small shoeprints of my own when I played here as a child, running and throwing sand, Ma looking on and smiling. But I don't go looking for the marks I made. They would remind me too sharply of a life I miss.

As we walk toward the nearest tram stop, we see a dozen of the oldest ladies in Honey Crater on a flat spread of sand, dancing silently. Not Aryl's sort of dancing, all agile leaps and turns. Here they sway, sway, step, step, each lady never straying from her spot in her row. Shiny black bonnets protect their faces from Pangu's weak rays. People here are afraid of their skin darkening—afraid of looking like the field laborers on Two.

"What's their dance about?" Aryl says.

I shrug. "This is their daily exercise. It means something different to each of them."

As we pass, Aryl smiles at the ladies, but they ignore us. I feel sad, looking at them. They are in their sixties and spend time together out of necessity. Most of their partners and other friends have died.

Side by side, Aryl and I cross the swinging footbridge across the deep gorge of Lightning Park, Aryl holding my cane while I use the handrails for support. I look down into the crack in the earth, marveling as I always have at the stripes of ferrous and ferric iron, which over time have painted the landscape's sediments orange, red, and brown. If I am hungry, the land reminds me of the inside of a peach. If I am hurt, it looks like blood in various stages of drying. But most often, it looks to me like fire.

Ahead of us looms the tram stop on the edge of town. I smell grease and chilies and fried canned meat from the row of food stands in front of the station. Few people are present. There is one family—three children, their black hair dusted with sand. Perhaps they were playing by the park, like I used to, but none of them are talking now. The children fearfully clutch their parents' legs.

A sense of danger sets in. This station is patrolled by drug ring members, laser guns flashing at their belts. I make out three older men as well as a young woman wearing high-heeled boots that come up to her thighs—all armed. Aryl stares, petrified.

"Do not look at them. We should be fine," I say.

Click chugga click click! An inbound cargo tram cruises through the station without stopping. Each car is blinding white—the bottom halves collecting dust—with *EXSAPIENS* printed in huge letters at their tops. And below that, the spinning DNA helices and the familiar motto: *Optimizing the human body, faster than evolution.*

"ExSapiens transports stuff through your town?" Aryl asks.

I squint, puzzled. I have never seen their freight trams here. "They do now, apparently."

An outbound passenger tram pulls in, grabbing our attention. Factory workers stumble out of the rust-colored cars, weighed down by heavy, falling-apart bags and soul-deep exhaustion. Beside them, the primary school students bounce home in their neon discdisc uniforms or off-white school clothes, the brightness faded from wash after wash. Seeing the children makes the adults smile. I am not sure how to react, since I am right in between.

"I dressed like that," I say, pointing to the students. "Just six months ago."

Aryl smiles and watches a group of three girls, maybe thirteen or fourteen years old. "They're holding hands," she says.

"People do that here," I say, thinking of my friends at school, who would thread their arms through mine as we walked. I thought nothing of it then, but on One, the first thing I noticed was the physical distance between people. Like everyone was worried they smelled bad or would catch some infection.

"It's sweet," Aryl says.

Without thinking, I grab her long fingers. Her hand spasms in mine, but she does not let go. Electricity courses up my arm. It is almost too much to take when she presses my palm to her cheek.

I go dizzy, overwhelmed that she feels something too.

"Ver . . ." she whispers, stepping closer. What does she want? What will she do?

Whoosh. The rumble of the tram as it leaves the station reminds me that we are here, in public, on Three. We need to be careful.

"Shh," I say, my whole body heating up. "Not now."

"Okay." Aryl lets our intertwined hands fall to our sides. We walk in silence, but her presence lends me bravery.

As we approach the apartment bloc, our feet stir up yellow dust clouds. I fix my eyes on the concrete buildings, whose small windows are made to keep the sand out. *Ma is at home in one of those buildings!* My heart reaches out for her.

There is the savory pancake vendor, Eli, just outside the gate. He has known my order since I was eight. Even though he is closing for the day, the air around his cart still smells of scallions and crispy, oily dough.

Tattooed young men, dressed in the signature black of the drug rings, are clustered around his stall. They must be burning their tongues on the hot pancakes, but they keep eating.

"They're less scary this way," Aryl whispers as we pass. Still, we trace a big loop around them.

We are here: the building in which I grew up. My eyes crawl across the checkerboard of windows until I find our unit. Fourth floor, second from the right. A hint of pale-yellow curtain makes my heart leap.

We approach the gated entrance, each step seeming to take a lifetime. I feel in my pocket for the keycard. Heart pounding, I lift it up to the reader outside the building. Go in. Resign myself to climbing the stairs, as there are no elevators. Walk up the concrete steps, Aryl's hand in mine. I run out of breath three times on the way, but I have more nervous energy circulating in me than ever.

Apartment 408.

When I enter, I still hold Aryl's hand for comfort. The room seems to have contracted, become even smaller than I remember. The window is shut. The lacy, pale-yellow curtains hang still. Our red foam couch is a mound on the floor. Two beds: at night, Ma and I slept stacked one on top of the other, me on the bottom bunk, her just a meter above. She has not thrown out my cot, even though it would give her extra space.

For privacy, a sliding plastic panel seals each bed off from the rest of the room. I used a razor to carve slender oval leaves on mine, to Ma's annoyance. But to me, the beauty was necessary amid the clutter. One wrong move could set off an avalanche of dirty clothing, plant bulbs, shoes with flapping soles that we had tried too many times to fix.

Across from my cot, a three-pronged metal stand is mounted on the wall. Because we had no home AI, I created this out of spare metal from shop class, used it to get dressed. Put the edges of my underwear on the bottom two prongs, stepped through, and pulled it up around my bum. Or I would raise the contraption, hang my shirt on it, tug down . . .

With a jolt, I hear the door open behind us. I turn to see the person who has made me feel the deepest joy and the fiercest pains.

My mother looks at me, at Aryl, at our entwined hands, at me again. After a long moment, a whirlwind carries Ma into my arms.

"Baobei," she says, her voice heavy with emotion. *Precious baby.* She does not let go of me. "Have you eaten?" She pauses, looks at my body, and corrects herself. "You're hungry. Let me steam some dumplings I made yesterday. If I'd known you were coming, I would've made them fresh."

"Ma, there is no need. Really," I say into her shoulder. She can be aggressive with her hospitality, especially if she wants forgiveness.

Ma sounds grounded now. Not far away, like when she is flying. But she is too thin. I watch her more carefully. Happy Patches suppress appetite. Since they adhere to the roof of the mouth, you cannot eat while using one.

Aryl lurks near the doorway, sheltering herself from Ma's burst of activity. She rolls one ankle in circles but is otherwise still. Watching, listening.

As Ma bustles about the kitchenette, she keeps curling and uncurling her fingers, which are always in pain. *Crick, crunch!* as she cracks her knuckles. Her torso bends at an angle to her legs—a postural problem from decades spent sitting at the textile factory looms. Patches of gray creep over her long black hair like an invasive species.

I wonder irrationally if I should have stayed for her. Even though for sixteen years, she was pushing me to go.

Because of pain, neither of us is completely functional alone. Together, we had a life. Just not the life we wanted.

"Tell me the real reason you came back home, Ver-xin," Ma says—*my heart*. She leans across the table on her elbows, her face propped in her hands. Like I do, sometimes. "Are you here to hide? To wait out the storm? Because I know you didn't cross two moons just to see your old mother."

"Well, no." I feel my face flush with guilt. "But it is good to see you, Ma."

Ma looks through her curtain of gray-black hair at Aryl. "Why did she come?"

Aryl's fingers curl into fists at her side.

My words get stuck in my throat. "Aryl is also . . . accused of—"

"Murder." Ma slaps a plate of boiled cabbage dumplings on the cluttered table. "I've been following the case. This girl's already here, though, so I suppose it's too late to take your mother's advice."

This is too familiar. Ma gave her opinion on each of my friends when I was in primary school: they had perfect grades or a parent with an addiction or a sister who did sex work, too much money or too little. To her, every person in my life was an example for me, good or bad. She expected me to imitate some and take warnings from others, to become the person she wanted me to be: smart enough to escape Three and strong enough to endure far from home.

How do I make Ma look long enough at someone—at Aryl—to see the person inside? To see what I see? To realize I do not want to *be* the girl that I brought here tonight; I just want *her*.

I have no appetite for the dumplings. I pass the plate to Aryl. Defiance burning in her eyes, she picks up two with her fingers and swallows them whole.

CHAPTER 41
Aryl

Ver's frozen up in front of her mother. So I jump to her aid, bringing out a crystal-cut One-er accent, because it's clear what Ver's mother thinks of people who look like me.

"The dumplings are delicious, Auntie," I say. They're too bland and fibrous for my taste, but I'm showing I can be polite.

"They're for my daughter." She's not pretending to like me.

"Listen," I say, pushing the plate away from me and toward Ver. "We don't need much from you. Just information. And then we'll—I'll—leave."

Ver's mother looks taken aback. Maybe she wasn't expecting me to be so articulate, or so calm. "Go on."

I say, "Do you know anything about the Paion Prostheses factory?"

"The what factory?" asks Ms. Yun.

"We thought you might have heard of it, Ma," Ver says.

"It's critical to proving our innocence," I say, and Ver nods.

Ms. Yun rests her chin on her hands. "What does it look like?"

Ver unrolls her burner flexitab and shows her mother the image we found. A building carved out of rock. The trapezoidal yellow plateaus Ver says she recognizes. Stormy, gaseous Gui and placid G-Moon One floating in the black sky above.

As Ms. Yun leans forward to take Ver's device, I notice that she smells of menthol. Mint-flavored patches is my guess. The sickly scent makes me hurt for Ver. She had a poor childhood, like me, but with a parent whom she could never rely on. For my parents, nothing came before Ester and me. It's hard to admit, but we're just as lucky as they're always telling us. My parents had options, like playing chess and finding a rich senator to hire them. Ver's mom? Staying out of the fray on this moon was the best she could've hoped for.

Ver's mother squints at the image. "Can you put this in 3D mode? I don't know how, with these newer models."

Ver nods, and a projection of the image materializes. With her fingers, she expands the edges so that the factory and plateaus take up the whole kitchen table. Ms. Yun switches off the light with a swipe of her finger. In the dark, the bright spots in the sand and stars of the holograph light up Ver's face. Her eyes, wide and full of hope, watch her mother.

Ms. Yun rises and walks around the edges of the holograph. I can almost picture her mind working, like her daughter's: image-sorting computer script, toggling around until she finds something she recognizes.

"They tore it down," she says.

My heart falls ten stories.

"If I remember correctly, this building was in the sixth ward, if you took the yellow tram line and walked westward from the Terralectric factory, perhaps half a kilometer . . . It's gone now, but when I was a child, we climbed over that fence. I remember the tightly woven links. We had magnetic shoes; we made them in sewing class. I don't know what we were looking for, but someone chased us out, called the authorities." There's a smile in her eyes. "One of our exciting days."

Ver shuts her eyes. "I cannot imagine you as a child, Ma." She gathers herself and adds, "Are you sure the factory was destroyed? Did they move operations to another location?"

"Ver-xin, it's gone. And listen to me: searching for it will end badly."

The tears spill out over Ver's cheeks. "How much worse of an ending is possible for us at this point?"

"Don't cry, yatou."

"So many things are gone," Ver whispers, so quietly that only I can hear. I put an arm around her, but when Ms. Yun's eyes flash at me, I drop it.

Awkwardness overwhelms me. I shouldn't have come here, shouldn't be witnessing this strained reunion between mother and daughter. "I'll go take a look outside, see if I can spot this rock formation," I say, standing up.

They barely notice I've moved. They're absorbed in each other as I hurry toward the door.

"I made many mistakes, Ver-xin," Ms. Yun is saying. Ver's head is bowed toward her clenched hands, and her mother is leaning close to her to speak. "I didn't want you to make the same ones. But now it looks like you may not even have the chance."

CHAPTER 42
Ver

Addiction leads to a physical change in our genetic material and the way our cells decode it. Not quite a mutation, but close enough that I know Ma cannot function without her fix.

Which does not make it any easier to watch.

As soon as Aryl steps out into the hallway and closes the door, Ma digs into her pocket and takes out a gum-sized piece of plastic. Peels away the wrapper, opens wide, and tacks it onto the blotchy red roof of her mouth, where I can see several open sores.

"Ma . . ." I murmur, but I give up before getting any further. Ma using patches is as inevitable as time. Still, I feel sick inside, and scared. She leaves me alone, even while we are together in the same room.

Come back, Ma. Be with me. Be with me. This may be the last time we see each other.

"My neck is full of needles," Ma says, massaging her shoulders with her bony fingers.

I know pain, and I hate seeing her in its grip. How can I begrudge her the relief the patches bring? I visualize the dancing hexagons of the chemicals' fused aromatic rings. They rotate laterally like boomerangs. Invading my mother's body, changing her from the inside out.

As the endorphins diffuse into the roof of her mouth, her body relaxes. Her eyes take on a faraway gaze, pupils dilating like black holes opening in the sky.

"You know what you should do?" Ma says.

I brace for what she will say.

"Don't trust that girl. Prove your innocence on your own. The fact that you haven't managed to show *she's* guilty yet is ridiculous, guniang." *Little girl*, she calls me. "They had no business accusing you in the first place. Look at you! You can't even walk. How could you have killed your investigator? That girl's guilty, don't you see? She's using you to set herself free. And you're letting her play you."

Her words tighten around my throat like claws. My feelings cannot form into thoughts, let alone words. I shake my head.

"Listen to me, Ver-xin. I've survived this moon. I survived your father. Proving you didn't kill that investigator? It's easy. Let that Two-er girl fend for herself. Let *her* rot in the Sandbag. You're like me. You've survived too much to let the rest of your life slip away."

"No," I whisper. More loudly, I say, "That might be how you survived, but that is not how I will live. Aryl is innocent."

"She's fooled you," Ma says, her eyes flashing. "Charmed you. You think you like girls now? For shame. You let her hold you like that, in my house."

She turns from me and reclines in her chair, sucking on the roof of her mouth, eyes closed. Floating away from consequences. She will say anything when she flies. The fallout is below her, on the ground, and she can barely see it. It hurts knowing that she thinks these things while sober too.

"Thank you for the food," I say, rising. "And the advice. But I will not take it."

I am seething. I want her to know it, to fear losing my love. So that she will take back what she has said and offer me the affection I long for.

Ma opens her eyes and blinks once, but she is focused on something far away from me.

"I have to do this the way I think is right," I say. "Goodbye, Ma."

She does not really hear. Her eyes are closing, her mouth curving into a smile. "I've only ever wanted you to be happy," she drawls. "Happy and free."

The words catch me off guard. *She still loves me.* I wish I could take that love and purify it to get rid of the parts that hurt. My chest is swelling with sobs that I trap inside. For what we both have lost, and for the little time we have left. *I miss you, Ma.*

As the sadness builds, I slip out the door as quietly as my body will let me. Behind me, my mother slips away too, off into the cluttered attic of her mind.

CHAPTER 43

Aryl

When Ver leaves the apartment building, there are tears in her eyes. I've been waiting for her, pacing heel-toe on the side of the road.

"Everything is fine, Aryl," Ver chokes out. "Ma is flying now. She is happy. She gave us the information we need, I think."

She wipes her eyes with her sleeve. Building residents are coming home, and they look us up and down, suspicion burning in their eyes. I wonder if they're staring at me because I'm an offworlder. But even if they're paying undue attention, it feels less pressing to me than whether Ver's okay.

I pull her against my chest. She starts shaking, and I feel the wetness of her tears soak through my thin shirt. I'm worried for her body if we set off looking for secrets in the middle of the desert. Her body, her heart.

"I can never do things right," she says in a small voice. "In her eyes, everything I do is wrong. *I* am wrong. She talks about the things I can't change, like the way I walk . . ."

One of my hands combs through her short, smooth hair. It's unbelievable that Ver's talking this way about herself, when everything about her that I can see and touch is perfection.

"Her life has been hell, Aryl. Mine was supposed to be ten times better. She devoted her whole existence to giving me every opportunity, and I came out like this. Broken. I might as well be a criminal."

Each word hurts my soul. I can't understand what Ver and her mother have experienced, even though I want to. I'm powerless to help. I'm infuriated with my own uselessness and ignorance, and overwhelmed by what Ver deals with every day. How could the universe let this happen—not only to her, but to the thousands of others on this moon whose bodies are breaking down?

"Ver, you're not—"

"Shh."

If she doesn't want to talk, I'll still try my best to comfort her. Remembering how wonderful it felt, I take her small, cold hand in mine. She squeezes gently back.

My eyes sweep over the desert, and I'm suddenly aware of how alone we are. Before I can say anything else, Ver winds her free arm around me and presses her face into my shoulder. I hold her lightly, cautiously, not wanting to hurt her.

The moment passes. We untangle ourselves and walk back to the ship's pod. Even though we're not touching anymore, my body is a lit firework—I'm shaking, wanting so badly to pull her close. Amazing that it took our boss getting killed to take us from scornful lab mates to uneasy allies to—I hope—something more.

"I have to check something," Ver says. "One last experiment. We can do it on board."

We fly the pod back to the *Mercenary*. Once we've docked, Ver hurries into the main compartment, where she begins to rummage through drawers and crates, examining Ford's stashes of instruments.

I glance at Ford's portable detector. "Hey, the antichronowave reading is really low here. Is that a mistake?"

"I expected that," Ver calls back. From the rear of the cabin, where the biology tools are stored, she retrieves a kit labeled *Dissection*. Out come sterilizable fitted gloves, smart forceps, a steady-hand surgical blade, polystyrene petri dishes. I help her arrange them on the workbench at the rear of the cabin. She perches on the tall stool. There's no second stool, so I hover next to her. Working this way, we're nearly the same height.

"This is for Cal," Ver says.

My brain snaps back to our conversation on our way to Three. I don't like what she's about to do. But I have to respect that she's choosing to do it.

"No, Ver," I say gently. "This is for you."

Ver nods and breathes deeply. Her muscles relax. "Yes. For me."

I take my own deep breaths, forcing my mind to treat this task like a typical lab procedure or first aid for a dance injury, both of which can be difficult to stomach.

We take a routine blood sample: disinfect, extract, quick-stain. With the quick-diffusing solution, it takes only a few minutes for the fluorescent probes to penetrate the tissues. Next we turn to the all-res microscope. My hands are sweating as I set the instrument, directing it to give us saturated holographic projections of the slides.

Ver's blood cells float in the air in front of our eyes.

So many of her red blood cells are elongated, thin, and a distinct maroon color, as opposed to the fat, healthy red discs of normal ones. Some of her platelets lack the fingerlike membrane projections that make them useful in blood clotting.

This is bad. Really bad. I'm speechless.

"And now we will see how well Ford set up electron tunneling mode," Ver says, fiddling with the magnification. Her voice is flat, as if she's dealing with a routine sample that has nothing to do with her.

When we zoom in thousands of times closer and play with the focus, we can see single-protein molecules. Hemoglobins are misfolded—instead of the characteristic four-leaf clover, we see blobs. Or the proteins are denatured, floating uselessly, no structure to them at all. No wonder Cal started sobbing when he first observed Ver's cells. On every scale, there's something wrong. Something to cause her pain, to threaten her life.

Again and again, I look away, chest heaving with the shock of it all, while Ver calmly takes pictures with the scope's camera. Microscopic chaos is happening inside the girl in front of me. I wish I could grab the hemoglobins with my hands and twist them back into shape. But they're so impossibly small, just as a galaxy is impossibly large. I have just as much hope of bending either to my will.

"Good job, Ford," Ver says sadly. I can hear her throat closing up. We're both struggling not to cry.

Even without running any numbers on the data, it's clear how vacked things have gotten inside her body. It's enough to know that a year in the Sandbag will kill her.

"Worse than the last set I took on One," Ver says.

And it's been less than a day since we left. I'm burning to hold her. To try and make it better, even though I know I can't.

"I am dying faster here on Three," Ver says. "And the antichronowave concentration here also is much lower, as Ford's detector shows. This supports our hypothesis. Of course, it still is not clear *how* the antichronowaves are connected to my RCD. We have correlation, not causation, and there are still many experiments left to do. But it is the beginning of an answer. With these results, someone else can continue the research even if I cannot."

Words swirl through my brain, all of them pathetic and useless. Eventually I say, "What can I do, Ver? What do you want me to do?"

Instead of answering, Ver leans her head on my shoulder, nuzzling her nose into my neck. I reach around her, near enough to smell the clean, sweet scent of her hair.

Ver shifts so that her face is level with my collarbone, tilting her head up to look at me. Her breath tickles. She reaches a warm hand around to cradle the nape of my neck.

Somehow, my lips cross the canyon of air between us to kiss her. I freeze there, worried that any more movement might shatter the fragile world we've created. What surprises me is how she tastes: sweet and a bit sour, like the kids' cough medicine I used to drink even when I was healthy because its flavor was so nice.

After a moment our mouths begin to move together like we've always been doing this. My heart's alight, the warmth radiating all the way to my fingertips. Maybe Ver's been imagining this moment too. Practicing the steps in her mind, just as I have.

Too soon, she ends it. I'm glad she's the logical one—there's no time to lose.

"Come on," Ver says. One of her hands lingers on my cheek. "We have to find what we are looking for."

CHAPTER 44
Ver

In the hot, dense guts of a star, atoms crush together until they combine into elements that are heavier and more complex than their individual parts. Push two fluorine atoms together until they fuse, and you will get argon, one of the most stable elements known. A noble gas.

Now that I have felt Aryl's lips on mine, I know *we* will be greater than *she* or *I* alone.

To avoid unwanted attention, we have left the spaceliner again and boarded the tram that goes to the western edge of town. Dark desert slides by outside the window. The tramcar's yellow lights are shining bright, though the inside is empty except for us. This route is barely used after 20:00. The car might as well be a star, and we, a couple of atoms. Small but violently reactive ones.

I spend the ride squeezed next to Aryl, our entwined hands hidden in the narrow space between our legs. My thumb traces the curve of each of her knuckles. Neither of us can let go of the other.

What set off this fusion reaction? The proximal cause: seeing my misshapen blood under the microscope pushed me over a hill of uncertainty and sent me careening down the other side. I am dying. Faster than before. And in less than two days, I face the possibility of spending the rest of my short life in a penal colony, paralysis creeping over my body and mind. I have no time to waste.

The ultimate cause? I am seeing Aryl, finally. Another layer of her. The surface was always beautiful. She shone in a hard, gilded way. But now I know her softness. There is comfort in her eyes and dignity in every step she takes. And I want to know her, day by day, for as long as I can.

At the last stop, perched at the top of a sandhill, Aryl and I exit the tram. Near the edges of Honey Crater's enormous habitat dome, I see the desert. On the outside of the dome, eddies of sand slam into the transparent walls.

"Your mom said to walk half a kilometer west," Aryl says. With the compass on her burner flexitab, she ensures we are moving in the right direction. We set off slowly on what is sure to be a difficult walk for me. My legs are weak. To conserve energy, I hold on to Aryl's arm and let her take some of my weight.

Factories dot the landscape, their ugly rusting towers curling toward the sky. A nearly vertical wall of sand, complete with a slight overhang, reaches up toward the edge of the habitat dome.

I make out a pair of rounded yellow doors, set into the base of a high sand dune, camouflaged by the surroundings. I recognize them from the image Aryl and I found online. The factory's central structure and ring of towers have been buried under tons of sand, it seems, but the doors remain visible, looking as if they are built into the dune itself.

We trudge across hills and valleys of sand. It trickles into my shoes and mixes with my sweat, gumming up my footsteps.

My heart pumps, thumps with fear. I cannot afford to fall. The injuries would set us back days. We do not have days.

Even Aryl is slipping, stumbling. When my cane becomes useless, she holds it in one hand and supports me around the waist with the other.

We are only thirty meters from the factory when the doors slide open and a woman's small silhouette dashes outside. She runs toward us, kicking up sand in her wake.

My temples pulse. I twist my head from side to side, searching for an escape. But it is too late to turn around. There is nowhere to hide. Running is out of the question. Next to me, Aryl's body goes rigid.

As the person approaches, I see that they are clutching their right arm to their chest. When they are ten meters away, I recognize their face, which is twisted in a grimace of pain. My panic undergoes a phase change, becoming confusion.

Jaha?

I am so shocked to cross paths with her here, near the border between vacuum and breathable air, that I cannot speak. My temples, my neck, my chest—everything is beating along with my panicked heart.

"What in the infinite galaxies are you girls doing here?" Jaha hisses when she reaches us. Her forehead is streaked with sweat, her eyes so wide they seem glued open.

"What are *you* doing here?" Aryl hurls back.

"What happened to your arm?" I demand at the same time.

Jaha's head twists. She urgently surveys our surroundings. Her voice drops to a whisper. "I used to work here. Back before they buried it under this artificial sand dune. Back when they only manufactured, before they started . . . spying."

Aryl gasps. *"What?"*

"So you know they made Cal's hand . . ." I say.

"Shh!" Jaha says. "Not here! We have to leave." Jaha is squeezing my hand, crushing it so hard I worry something will snap. "Let's get to a safe place. I've got a scooter waiting just over that hill—"

Aryl smacks Jaha's hand away from me. Jaha sucks air through her teeth.

"We will not go anywhere with you," I say. Maybe I was wrong to stop suspecting her. "Why should we trust you? Why are you even here?"

"I thought Paion might be connected to Cal's death. I came here to find out."

"Why didn't you tell us? Or the police?" Aryl says. She sounds like she feels betrayed. "We spent so much time chasing clues that led here."

"Why would I tell you and risk getting you involved? As for the police—you saw how interested they were in listening to you. If I'd told them a shuttered artificial-limb manufacturer helped kill my husband, they would've laughed in my face."

"So why should we stay out here," I say, "if our exoneration awaits in there?"

"I looked inside that buried factory, Ver, and I turned away. I'm not ready to give up my life, not even to find out what happened to my husband. I can't leave my daughter without a mother. And you two have to survive till your trial. You need a *chance*. You'll have none if you go in there."

"What's inside?" Aryl demands. "Tell us. What drove you away?"

Jaha goes deathly pale and shakes her head, repeating, "We need to leave." Watching her, my palms break out in a cold sweat. I want to comfort her, yet I want to run far away from her. I have learned too much about her, Cal, and myself to process.

"Gou, Jaha," I swear. "What did you see in there?"

Still shaking her head, Jaha starts walking in the direction of the tram stop. It is not like her to run out of words, or to retreat from a problem so close to a solution.

"Jaha!" Aryl shouts. "We can't turn back now." She looks at me for confirmation, and I nod. Between certain death in the Sandbag and potential death there, I will choose the factory.

Jaha turns and beckons to us, asking us to come with her, away from the danger.

We do not follow.

CHAPTER 45

Aryl

Ver and I press forward through the sand, toward the factory. I expect Jaha to call after us, to try again to convince us to come with her, but she doesn't.

"There might be a trap inside," Ver says under her breath. "If Jaha is not on our side, she could have set it. But then why did she tell us not to enter? Is she trying reverse psychology?"

I shake my head. The mental gymnastics are too much. "If she *is* on our side, then there's something Paion doesn't want her to find, and they scared her off."

Ver's hand is slick and sweaty in mine, and I worry about losing my grip on her. "Let me go first," I tell her. "You can use my body as a shield if anything happens.

"Aryl, I . . ." Ver begins, but stops. She knows it's better to be realistic than prideful.

With me walking ahead of her, we approach the door in the dune. Its color and texture help it blend in with its sandy surroundings. Nothing has confronted us yet. But I can't forget Jaha's panicked face. With every step we take, I want to turn back even more.

Though the factory's not supposed to be in use, the enormous four-meter-high doors yawn open as we approach. We lock eyes for a second before we walk inside. I return Ver's cane to her.

Cold air and icy-blue light envelop us. The walls and the checkered floor tiles are varying shades of white and gray. Everything's rounded, like in a planetarium—surfaces with no clear edges. There's no mark of who this empty place belongs to, no signs, no map to show us the building's layout.

All I see is another set of doors. Plain white, no handles. Like the first, they open for us. Immediately, we're sunk into near-total darkness. But when my eyes adjust, I stop in my tracks.

On the room's ceiling, depicted in shifting multicolored lights, is an enormous human form made of DNA strands—running, turning, jumping.

The cargo tram we saw earlier was coming from here.

"ExSapiens," Ver and I murmur together.

A chill runs through my body. We're facing an entity bigger and more powerful than almost any other. I remember Pauling Yuan in Jaha's apartment, handing the lab's funding over to her. Vouching for Ver's and my innocence. The way he hugged Jaha—like family. Covering for himself.

Beside me, Ver's eyes have fixed on something in front of us. "Aryl—look at the shelves."

Floor-to-ceiling shelving units cover the walls. The room is divided into three sections.

On the left, row after row of hands, wrists, and arms, from infant-sized to the diameter of a manhole cover. Every conceivable human skin color and beyond, to sparkling lavender and near-transparent limbs like Cal's. Some look like thorny vines that split into finger-tendrils.

On the right are lower-body appendages—thick legs modeled after ancient columns, thin ones like leafless branches.

Even unfinished models, naked wires wrapped around carbon-glass cores.

In the center: Everything else. Ears. Eyeballs that change color every few seconds. Rows of identical noses, all small and button-shaped. Bottom and top halves of faces. Slender torsos composed of interlocking steel rings, like they're covered in body armor.

Ver and I approach, her hand shaking inside mine. When we get to the center of the room, a bright blue-white light on the floor traces a circle around our bodies. That whole round section of floor we're standing on shifts—breaks away from the rest of the floor, and rises giga fast.

The ground floor retreats below. Ver heaves as if she'll throw up. I'm also queasy—I'm fine with heights, but there's nothing to keep us from falling.

"Don't look down," I tell Ver. But I'm struggling to obey my own directions.

We keep rising, toward the DNA human on the ceiling. About halfway up, I see a large, dim balcony interrupting the rows of shelving units. It's full of desks and computer monitors—and the first human beings we've seen since coming to this vacked place.

That's where the rising platform stops, and where the nightmare begins.

CHAPTER 46
Ver

A fundamental paradox of science states that observation may influence the behavior of the phenomenon being observed. We look and listen, but we stay as silent and invisible as possible. They cannot know we are here.

Aryl and I have rushed off the platform that brought us to this balcony, which has now descended back to the lower level. We huddle in a corner of this higher story, behind a semitransparent glass wall, clutching each other's hands and hoping no one notices us in the low light.

Fear bludgeons me from the inside. I grow lightheaded. How much more of this can my body take?

Seated figures stare at wraparound computer screens. Each screen displays everyday household scenes, but from strange perspectives: close to the ground as someone walks, a hand cooking vegetable soup. One worker scrolls through a document about a company's jewelry sales. All files that must be stored on smart limbs.

The seated figures doing this spying are unquestionably human, with the random tics and gestures of true biological entities. A bouncing knee, a runny nose. Bounce, wipe, scratch. Goggles cover their eyes and cheeks; gigantic headphones cover their ears. Watching, listening.

What kind of factory is this? Can it even be called one, if the workers are not making things, but observing feeds? Each person has a set of controls at their fingertips—but for what? Sometimes they press buttons, but the effects are a mystery.

One worker stands, facing a small table upon which a blue-skinned foot rests. With a touchpad, he causes each toe on the foot to rise and lower, then lifts all five at once. The foot simulates walking, heel to toe, across the table.

I take in the information and process it, haltingly.

In an artificial system, input code gets translated to a series of ones and zeroes. That binary code then gets translated again, into output. Commands, usually. Could be speech. Or motion.

The workers can control the artificial limbs.

"Aryl." My whisper barely makes it past my lips, but she hears. "Cal's hand was not malfunctioning when it hit you. Someone else was controlling it remotely."

She follows my gaze to the worker controlling the foot. Electricity seems to zap up her spine. "Then someone was also controlling it remotely when it—"

"—killed him," I finish. The irony is sickening. This company creates artificial body parts, machines meant to help people live so-called normal lives. Not to kill.

"But why would ExSapiens want him dead?" I ask, but the answer is obvious.

If they could control his hand, they already had access to the records stored on it.

Aryl's eyes open wide. She is thinking the same thing. "The research you two were doing. It could prove ExSapiens was off base with Telomar, make their signature product obsolete."

The only way to permanently stop that research from developing further, to guarantee that it would never go public, was to cut it off at the source.

A green light on the ceiling blinks twice. Half the watchers leave their stations—a shift change. The round platform from the ground floor returns, carrying new workers who switch places with the departing shift. The transition is seamless, except for one small, brown-skinned worker who trips on the leg of her desk, sits down hard, and adjusts her goggles.

As the new workers settle down, a shadow drifts over Aryl and me. Blood pounds in my head. *They have found us.*

We turn to face a figure standing near a side door, his face obscured by shadow. Fear suffuses my every cell. *Run, run, run!* my body screams. But I am frozen.

"Welcome, welcome." I have heard that voice before.

A headache stabs through my skull, even as my blood circulates faster and faster.

"Ver Yun, Aryl Fielding. I'm impressed that you've found us. All the media outlets say that the ExSapiens skyscrapers in Lucent City are our most impressive buildings. But this factory? Truly, this is the heart of our operation."

He steps out of the shadows and into the pale light from the monitors, wearing his orange knit cap. His smile reveals a flash of bluish-white teeth.

Behind him is a larger shadow with a bald, domed head— the bodyguard from Jaha's apartment. My pained legs freeze in place.

Pauling Yuan is here.

CHAPTER 47

Aryl

"You . . ." I stammer. "This is an ExSapiens factory."

"Very good, my dear. My company acquired Paion Prostheses five months ago," Yuan says. There's no trace of the warmth I remember from him in Jaha's apartment. "Around the time my old friend's nightly doings in lab became a mystery to us. The purchase aligned with our mission to improve the human body and its abilities millions of times faster than evolution alone could."

Ver steps in front of me. I grip her shoulder, silently warning her not to do anything that'll get her killed.

Can I grab Ver and make a dash for it? Yuan's people would catch us in seconds. But I have to do something. Maneuvering my free hand in Ver's shadow, I activate my burner flexitab and hold my finger down on the "record" feature.

"But mostly you bought Paion so you could control its products," I say, for the benefit of the recording. "Specifically, Cal's hand, which you hijacked remotely—"

"Cal left me no choice," Yuan says. "It wasn't easy for me." With shadows under his eyes and gray at the roots of his hair, he looks older than he did at Jaha's apartment, and far less polished than he does on the news. Did he rush here? His jacket is crinkled, his stubble a day old. Yes, he did. He probably chartered a shuttle as soon as he heard that Jaha, Ver, and I were no longer on Institute premises.

"Our experiments," Ver says through clenched teeth. "You were following them. Accessing the results Cal saved on his hand. What you saw was happening to *my* body! It was *my* illness. You had no right!"

The bodyguard, Osmio, steps closer to Ver. His electric-blue eyes rake over her, scanning for weakness. But she doesn't flinch.

"I understand your concern, dear," Yuan says, in the sort of pitying tone I know Ver hates. "But truly, you must think about someone other than yourself."

A shudder runs through Ver's body. "How can *you* say that?"

"I must protect the interests of ExSapiens," Yuan says. "You can't imagine the responsibility of having forty thousand employees. Of looking out for each of them."

"If they are so important to you, perhaps you should tell them what you did," Ver says. "They would be flattered that for their sakes, their boss spied on an innocent gi—"

"*Spied* is a strong word. I had every right to monitor what Cal was doing with the funds I funneled into his lab. And admittedly, I was curious. I'm a scientist by training, like you."

"Then you know, from reading those records, that my RCD was improving more than in anyone who has been given your useless drug," Ver says.

"Telomar," Yuan says through gritted teeth, "has benefited millions."

"It is a money grab," Ver says. "Our antichronowave research would have shown that. If Cal and I had completed our experiments, we could have connected RCD to something as simple as *location* and published the results for all the moons to see."

"And people would finally see you as the liar you are," I say to Yuan. "They would see that Telomar doesn't help anyone, and that what *does* help isn't something ExSapiens can monetize."

Osmio takes another step forward. This time, he's not scoping out my body—he's deciding how to break it. Yuan puts up a hand to stop his advance, as if to say, *They're not a threat. Yet.*

"Telomar is worth 15.7 billion Feyncoins to you," Ver says. "People living on Three can barely pay for it. But you do not care. Your company cannot afford to have it pulled from the market."

Yuan shakes his head. "The company, the company. Do you think that's all I care about? No, dear—you don't understand. This isn't just about ExSapiens. It's much bigger than that."

I shoot Yuan the most skeptical look I can muster. *Keep talking*, I think, hand tightening on my flexitab.

"It's about every human living in Pangu's light," Yuan says. "Who *hasn't* noticed the differences in lifespan across the moons? But what if you did uncover why Three-ers die young, why even Two-ers have no hope of living as long as we do on One? What if you found a reason for the discrepancy, one caused directly by the properties of each moon? What would happen when you broadcast that knowledge?" He heaves a dismayed sigh. "Mass migration. Economic collapse. Chaos. Two and Three would fall into depression and cease to function as societies. G-Moon One would be overrun by medical refugees."

"G-Moon One has enough space for everybody," I say.

"By many estimates, the lake district alone could support fifteen million more people," Ver rattles off.

"But if more of you migrated, then One-ers would lose our way of life, our culture." Yuan lifts his palms as if begging us to understand. "You would bring your drugs, your violence. You might live longer lives, yes, but *we* would pay the price. By welcoming you to One, we would lose everything that makes us the last advanced human civilization in the universe. I couldn't let that happen."

"So you killed Cal. Your old friend," I say, feeling every fine-tuned muscle in my body flex.

"He'd changed too much to be reasoned with," Yuan says. "His lab was becoming a migrant camp. Even if I'd destroyed Cal's research, he would've started over. If I'd gotten him fired or withheld funding, he could've told too many of *my* secrets. I had no other option."

Bright spots of red swim in my vision. Whatever Yuan says about the greater good, he killed Cal to protect his company's image and his own reputation. His own sense of superiority. "You killed him with your limb takeover and let us take the fall," I say. "Even me—I had nothing to do with the experiments."

"I'm sorry," Yuan says. There's sincerity in his voice. "Ver was supposed to have been alone with Cal. Then he would've been . . . removed, and she would've been arrested. Everyone who knew about the experiments—gone. I thought no one else would be in the lab that night. But you showed up. So I gave money to the police, not so they'd investigate other suspects but so they could manufacture evidence implicating you. I expected the forthcoming trial to find you both guilty. But then," Yuan says, sighing again, "the two of you trusted each other."

My heartbeat pounds through every capillary. Adrenaline surges into my limbs—not anger this time, or even the thrill of learning the truth we've been chasing, but fear.

Reaching under my sleeve to touch the burner flexitab, I end the audio recording.

CHAPTER 48

Ver

Up on the shelves where the artificial limbs are stacked, crawling and rustling begins. Transparent fingers unfurl, covered with microchips. Disproportionately long, rainbow-toned legs stretch artificial tendons. A reflective, glassy torso vibrates, then shimmies to life.

Aiyo, please let this not be real.

Sticky sounds emanate from the artificial limbs as they clasp onto one another. Limbs that are better—by Yuan's twisted standards—than what anyone was born with. *Clap, squelch!* They form conglomerates of barely recognizable hands, arms, legs, abdomens. Like bacteria making biofilms. Glomming together, sticking to a surface, and multiplying all over it. Burying it.

In this case, the surfaces will be Aryl and me.

Some of the masses the artificial limbs form are six-sided, like snowflakes. Others are two legs that walk, like real human legs, with two hands attached to them. Hands ready to strike, to grab. Fingers ready to dig into flesh like claws. I wish the homunculi had heads to give them some semblance of humanity. They barrel toward us, guided by the movements of the expressionless human workers still fixated on their monitors.

Terror floods every cell in my body, red and violent. My headache scorches my skull from the inside. Beside me, Aryl curls her fingers into fists. I test out my cane in my hands, knowing it will be useless against the onslaught.

Yuan watches his creations with pride. Beside him, Osmio opens the side door that he and his employer must have used to reach the balcony.

"This will be such an unfortunate accident," Yuan says.

He turns his back on us and walks away, too weak to watch us die.

CHAPTER 49
Aryl

They come for me first. A hand larger than my head catapults itself into the air. Gnarled fingers thick as bananas tangle themselves in my hair and pin my head to the wall behind me, nearly snapping my neck. Terror washes through my body, bringing with it the spine-tingling reminder of Cal's hand in the medical repository.

Ver lunges toward me, cane swatting feebly at the artificial flesh attacking her.

"Ver, no!" I shout, even as the limbs move closer. An arm bulging with silver muscle twists my hands behind my back, and I feel ligaments snapping in my shoulders.

A fuchsia leg as long and slim as a gazelle's kicks me in the stomach with shocking strength.

Pain obliterates everything but the need to survive. I've never wanted anything more than, in this moment, I want life.

Please, I beg every star that's watching, *let me live. Let me dance again.*

Shouting with the effort, I wrest one arm free, throwing the muscled artificial limb away. It lands with a crash on an approaching set of metallic legs.

Using my free arm, I pry the enormous hand out of my

hair. My scalp burns as it rips out a hunk of my curls. Tears blur my vision. Blood flows from the left portion of my scalp, but I dash the trail of it out of my eye and shout, "VER!" Her small form and the glint of her cane are nowhere in sight.

As desperate as I am to live, I want life for *her* more. She's fought harder than I ever have for what I've always taken for granted. Besides, losing her and living on might hurt more in the long run than a quick death.

My legs drag with exhaustion. My fists hurl themselves at the body parts assaulting me. All brutish, flailing movements. A punch lands on my eye, and it swells shut—my legs tangle in a sea of hands—a kick to the head—a firestorm of pain.

I see nothing but black sky.

CHAPTER 50

Ver

Before I can reach Aryl, a pale brown hand with long white fingers capped like mushrooms latches on to my own, tangles around it, and pins it to a wall.

Who would want this fungal limb attached to their body? The sticky material is so cold! I can feel each individual hair on each stem. I shut my eyes, shut out the horror.

Now my brain is conjuring an image of Cal wearing that hand, pinning me down. His eyes are soulless blanks. Yuan controls all of him now.

I open my eyes again. A forelimb with razor claws flies at my face. I duck as low as my back will let me. Pain plucks my spine. I stay crouched, bracing for impact—

Everything within two meters of me drops to the floor. A rain of body parts: silicone, metal. Pattering to rest. Suddenly harmless.

I exhale. Beyond the stalled limbs, more terrors edge in. But for the next few seconds, I am safe. How? Who has bought me this precious time? I look around wildly but see no sign of an intruder.

The workers keep staring at their computer screens, furiously manipulating their controls. All of them are concentrating, but their eyes are blank. They do not care about the outcome of this brawl. They are simply protecting their employer.

Among them, though, one woman's mouth is screwed up in a scowl. The shape of her nose is familiar, as well as the angle of her mouth.

Jaha! She has sneaked in disguised as a worker, likely during the shift change we just saw—morphed briefly into the employee she used to be. She must have severed the connections between some of the limbs and the workers controlling them.

A lion's paw on the ground before me trembles. The screen on its palm lights up with a message.

Control room. Up three flights of stairs on your right. You'll need a worker's iris scan to get in. Hit emergency alarm. Up to you now, Ver-hai.

I would recognize Jaha's tone anywhere. She believes in me—so much that she once felt threatened by my talent. Now, she is counting on me to save us all.

I have not moved faster than a brisk walk in two years. But now is the time to ignore the resistance of my body. I *run.*

Sparks shoot down the outsides of my legs, and cramps rocket through my abdomen as I cross the room. Inhale, exhale, push forward. I propel myself with two weak legs and my cane, which by some miracle is still in my hand. It seems to weigh a ton.

By the time I cross the barrier into the rows of cubicles, the workers have noticed that something is amiss—that none of the artificial limbs can touch me.

Their eyes fall on Jaha, the only person still typing. One of them approaches and rips off her goggles, revealing her face for all to see.

"*Go!*" she shouts at me as workers surround her, pulling her out of her chair and bending her arms behind her back.

If only I were as strong as Aryl, I would turn back and help her. But I am not, so I must trust that she will manage on her own. Jaha is from this moon. Survival is in her blood.

I can survive too. *I want to.* I want to live.

I want to see Pangu rise again.

The stairwell is a black echo chamber. Each of my footfalls sets off a thousand more sounds, bouncing off the walls. I am falling, hauling myself up the stairs. Pulling myself up the rail with one hand. My cane flails in the other, trying to make up for my tired and wobbly legs. Sparks of pain zip from my hips to my feet. My vision fades to a muddy haze.

But somehow I climb. One flight, two. Three flights, turn the corner—

A shadowy silhouette. Weaponless, except for the blade of a smile and eyes that burn electric blue. Behind him, the larger shadow of his protector, and the door labeled *CONTROL ROOM*. Above him, on the ceiling, the retinal scanner that will grant access to that room.

Pauling Yuan and his bodyguard stand between me and my last hope.

"Who would have thought *you'd* be the last one standing?" Yuan says. "Pity. If you'd taken one of those sets of legs back there, you'd be out by now, running across the desert. But alas."

I feel around in my back pocket for the loaded syringe and peel off the cap.

"What's that you've got there?" Yuan says, chuckling, even as he steps aside to stand in a corner. "Acid spray? A pocket knife? Well, Osmio brought something too."

The bodyguard lunges, fists raised.

I block the first punch, aimed at my neck, with my cane. Osmio sees it coming and brushes it aside. The impact rattles through my arms, wringing each joint. I cannot do that again. But I will have to let him get close to inject him. I need to jab one of his veins . . .

Osmio aims his fist at my chest this time. I twist painfully, as far as my spine will allow, to dodge the blow.

I shuffle toward the corner where Yuan stands, hoping that Osmio will moderate the strength of his blows if Yuan is within striking distance.

The next hit is meant for my groin, an area I cannot defend. But Osmio lowers his head just enough—

I jam the needle into the purple vein on the side of his thick neck and push the plunger.

At the same time, the pain hits me. Blunt and explosive, spreading from my ribs, where his fist has dug into me, through my abdomen. Bones splinter. There is no air left in my lungs to scream. *Please* . . .

Ketamine does not work immediately. Even a large dose takes twenty, thirty seconds to circulate through the body. That is why I have chosen a thick vein in Osmio's neck, so that every microliter from the syringe will be carried directly to his heart.

Osmio punches me again, in my abdomen. My broken ribs shift inside my chest. The pain is blinding, deafening, numbing. I can barely sense anything else.

But his movements are becoming slower, less precise. The ketamine is plugging up his NMDA receptors, inhibiting his nervous system from communicating with itself. If he is hallucinating, I hope his visions are hideous.

Now Osmio cannot lift his arms. His fists unfurl. He

rocks backward and forward, as if deciding where to fall. Yuan shrinks farther back into his corner, eyes darting from side to side. He leaps—but not soon enough.

Osmio crumples, crashing into his boss. Yuan topples with his bodyguard, pinned on the floor beneath Osmio's powerful body, his face showing the first signs of fear.

I fight to stay conscious. To live. I hold my abdomen in a futile effort to stop the internal bleeding. Is my lung punctured?

I limp toward the fallen men. With one shoulder I brace myself against the wall for support. One hand protects my ribs. The other clutches my wavering cane. *I do not need this now*, I think and toss it to the side.

My fingers curl around the second syringe. I lift it, trembling, and hold it to the murderer's neck. The silver tip trembles against Yuan's stubbled skin.

"This is sodium pentobarbital." The lie slips between my teeth. "You will die painlessly. Just like Osmio. But you will die. Or you can scan me in."

Yuan's eyes are wide. With his bodyguard still lying on top of him, he cannot maneuver enough to either escape me or overpower me. He lifts his head, looking toward the sensor on the ceiling. It beeps green, granting access. The door swings open.

I lurch into the narrow control room, fighting the blackness encroaching on the edges of my vision. Beeping buttons and switches and levers are everywhere. *Where is it?*

The big red button is on a control panel off to the side. *EMERGENCY ONLY*, a sign cautions.

If this is not an emergency, I do not know what is. My body is breaking—muscles failing to contract, blood rushing outward, lungs depleted of oxygen. I collapse forward, using the last of my strength to aim my palm at the button.

CHAPTER 51

Aryl

When the first thoughts come, I know my mind is still here. I try to keep it from straying to my body, from trying to quantify the damage. From learning that what was once strong and carefully honed has been destroyed. There's pain, yes, but I don't want to know any more than that.

To distract myself, I list the things I know for sure:

That Pauling Yuan killed Cal Eppi from a distance.

That his workers set their creations loose on us.

That I failed to protect myself.

That my family's still locked in their apartment.

That the last thing I remember is not being able to find Ver.

I'm alive, but what about her?

CHAPTER 52
Ver

My body has become pain. Someone is holding a torch to my skin and twisting all two hundred and six of my bones out of their joints.

I am used to a dull, incessant background ache—not this. This pain drills deep into my mind. It leaves no room to think about anything else. Stabbing, swelling, metastasizing.

If you know the half-life of a radioactive element, you know how long it will take for half of the atoms in a mole of the element to decay. But you cannot predict when or if any single atom will emit some particle and morph into something else.

Just as there is no way for me to know when I will decay into a corpse. Or if I will continue on as a lesser form of my past self.

Lying here in the Paion Prostheses factory, I want life. More than anything, I want to know what the next days, months, and years will bring. I want life—but not a life like this.

CHAPTER 53

Aryl

I learn from the doctor, a woman with a kind but careworn face, that I've been out for three days. Three whole days. I'm back on One, at the Institute Hospital.

"Where's Ver?" I croak, lifting my head to look for her and wincing at the pain.

"She's here too, recovering," the doctor replies, and my head settles back on the pillow.

She tells me Ver set off the emergency alarm in the factory, shutting down the power and drawing the attention of the authorities. They got me out before I sustained further injuries. As it is, the ones I have nearly killed me.

Every muscle group in my lower body will be useless for weeks: quads, hamstrings, adductors, abductors, gluteals. I'll have to stay still. I wish I could do a slow, unfurling dance of despair.

When I venture a look in a mirror, I see the collage of scratches and cuts covering my face. Impact wounds tattoo my skin, from the blue-and-green patch over my right eye to the violet smudges crawling along my legs. Not even stage makeup can hide this mess.

When the artificial hand ripped out a chunk of my hair,

skin came with it. That explains the gauze patches on my scalp. The hospital staff have grafted on new tissue cultured from my cells. The hair will grow back to its full length in two years or so, but the seam where new skin meets old will always be there.

Aside from that, there's no permanent damage—except for the new accusations scarring my legal record. The trial's been postponed, but only so that the Lucent City Police can add to the charges against Ver and me.

Ford's the first to come see me when I'm allowed to have visitors. The staff have to stop him from hugging me, as it might hurt my bruised ribs. But we can talk all we want, as long as we keep the door open so the nurses can check on me.

"You're not afraid to be seen with me?" I ask him, half joking. My dance friends won't be showing up with get-well-soon gifts.

"Come on, Aryl. I'm trying to start fresh. I made sure you and Ver won't get charged with spaceship theft; I told the police I loaned you the *Mercenary*."

"Oh, thank Pangu," I say dryly. "A criminal charge like that would've really weighed on my mind." Still, I appreciate that he stepped up and told the truth. I can only imagine how that went over with his mom.

"I broke up with Rhea yesterday."

"Yeah? Good for you." Maybe he's finally growing a spine. Rhea might retaliate, using her money or popularity to vack his life. But any consequences for Ford will be short-lived. As soon as she finds another high-status boyfriend, it'll be like their relationship never happened.

"I'm going to miss her, but it's for the best. I didn't like who I became around her."

I know what he means. I miss the feeling of belonging that

Rhea gave me. The way people wanted to be near me so they could be near her. And I'll miss the dancing. But I won't miss the mask I had to wear, onstage and off.

"So enough about me." He forces a sardonic smile. "What's new with *you*?"

The story pours out in a hoarse whisper, and as I go on, his face changes from shock to terror to relief.

"Pauling Yuan," he says. "They were going to name a star after him! Oh, this is going to mean big changes—if you can prove what you're saying."

I tell him about the recording I made in the factory.

Ford laughs, tears in his eyes. "Your dad will be so proud you thought of that. That reminds me—I talked to my mom about your parents. I haven't convinced her to lift their house arrest yet, but I'll keep trying."

Speaking of my parents, there's an incoming holo-call to the room. I accept it and my family's faces appear. Dad looks like he hasn't slept in years. Exhaustion has imprinted dark blue seashells under his eyes. Mom's gained weight, her flesh heavy on her neck, and I know it's because she eats everyone's leftovers when she's stressed. As for Ester, her shoulders are slumped under an invisible mass that's never been there before—and there's disappointment in her eyes.

Wasn't I supposed to be an example for her? Didn't my parents give me all their strength so that I could pave the way for my baby sister?

I did this to you, I think, guilt rising up like bile inside me.

Or did I? I could've been the perfect apprentice, the perfect citizen, but as long as I was a Two-er, this moon would've chewed me up for *something*. It would've treated me as a threat no matter what I did.

As I watch, Mom begins to cry. Dad puts a hand on her shoulder. Ester just looks scared. Mom usually covers her sadness with annoyance or anger. She never wants us to see her looking weak.

"We've only ever wanted the best for you," Mom says.

"What we want doesn't matter," I say. And nobody disagrees.

CHAPTER 54
Ver

The moment I am off the opioid drip, the police arrange a conversation with Aryl, me, and several others.

They question us in a hospital boardroom. Medical diagrams plaster the walls. Before, I might have studied the posters of the lymphatic system and the bones of the foot with interest. Today I recoil at the images of hollowed-out humans. The room flickers before my eyes.

Hands, arms, legs . . . They flew at me! Grabbing, punching, kicking.

I wait for the memories to subside. I open my eyes, cautiously. The boardroom is full. The people here are also a nightmare reborn.

First, Pauling Yuan, dressed in an impeccable black suit. True to his executive status, he sits at the head of the table. If he is relishing our impending downfall, he does not show it: his narrow face is solemn, sorrowful. Maybe guilty. But even if he shows remorse, I will never forgive him.

Polished-looking people who must be ExSapiens employees surround him, all with equally grave expressions. They dress like him. They straighten their spines like him. Looking at the ExSapiens crowd, I almost think I see clones

251

protecting their creator. Genetic cloning of human individuals is illegal, but duplicating your DNA and injecting it into an egg cell is not the only way to copy yourself. Yuan makes that obvious here.

Ford reclines in his chair, looking bored. But the rhythmic tap-tap-tapping of his foot betrays his anxiety. He probably never thought he would have to face the law like this.

Kricket sits across the table from Ford, his habitual smirk giving nothing away. But he twirls a strand of hair from his ponytail around his finger—a sure indication that he is thinking hard.

Jaha sits farther down the table, looking at no one in particular. There are bruises on her face and an unhealthy blue tint to her skin. Otherwise, she seems to be unhurt.

Nurses have wheeled Aryl and me in and left our chairs parked close together. Close enough that I can take her hand if I need to.

"Where do I start?" says Detective Xenon, who is sitting next to Detective Card at the table's far end. "If I were to split up the charges against Ver Yun and Aryl Fielding and assign them to separate people, they could fill a whole prison bloc in the Sandbag."

Aiyo, this man! His tone is as smug as ever.

"For both of you: evasion of justice, aggravated assault, controlled-substances theft, trespassing on no fewer than three pieces of private property," Xenon reads off his flexitab. "And the one we're all here to discuss: premeditated murder."

I do simple addition in my head. The non-murder charges alone will land me in prison for at least ten years. More than long enough for RCD to kill me, if the other inmates do not get to me first.

"Do you have anything to say for yourselves?" Xenon asks, his satisfaction palpable. "Or shall I just—"

"We do," Aryl says. "Give me my flexitab back. The burner. I know you have it."

Xenon snorts. "According to protocol, we can't return personal devices to suspects until they're cleared of crimes."

"What protocol are you reading?" Detective Card says. When Xenon frowns at her, she adds, "The protocol allows supervised access to personal devices when they may contain evidence." She turns to me and Aryl, saying, "We have our AIs independently review personal-device contents and lock them so that nothing can be added or deleted. *We* try to be as objective as possible, you see. Not let *donations* from suspects bias us."

Xenon looks as if he wants to smack her. "Miranda—"

"Yes, Roderick, I know about the direct deposit into your account from an unnamed benefactor," Card snaps as the room breaks into whispers. She must be referring to the "donation" that was supposed to fund Cal's autopsy!

Pauling Yuan's eyes flash. "Careful there," he says softly.

Staring down Yuan, Card reaches into her nylon bag and retrieves both of our burner flexitabs. Our original ones too. She slides mine across the table and tosses Aryl's to her.

Why is she helping us? I remember when she said, *I swear on all our lives, justice will be done.* Apparently she meant it.

Her face grim, Aryl swipes on her flexitab's screen. She holds the device at arm's length as Yuan's recorded voice emanates from it.

. . . I had every right to monitor what Cal was doing with the funds I funneled into his lab. And admittedly, I was curious . . .

To think these could have been the last words I ever heard!

Detective Xenon pinches the bridge of his nose and scrolls through files on his own flexitab, ignoring the recording as best he can. Detective Card listens closely, her right eyebrow twitching.

Yuan's face is a mask, his expression giving nothing away. His associates' eyes dart between the police and Yuan, waiting for instructions from their boss.

I give Aryl a huge, adoring smile. *Genius!* With the tap of a finger back in the factory, she has saved us both.

When the recording ends, Detective Card tucks her green hair behind one ear and leans forward, eyes fixed on Yuan. "This is quite a turn," she says softly. "What do you have to say, sir?"

"It's doctored," Yuan says, shrugging. "I never said those things. Do you know how easily one can fake a voice? The sound quality is terrible—how can anyone be sure it's me?"

"My flexitab was hidden under my sleeve," Aryl says.

Yuan laughs. "My dear, this isn't the first time someone has impersonated me. It's more common than you think. I commend your efforts, though."

Detective Xenon looks down at the table. As if it has become his whole world. Jaha studies her hands, jaw clenched. Ford's knuckles are white as he digs one fist into the table. And Kricket . . . Kricket is shivering, his foot jerking about on the floor.

"I've been falsely accused, yet again, of a crime I did not commit." Yuan sounds bored. "My business has faced false accusations of fraud, lacing our medicines with illegal substances, and worker abuse. I'm not surprised to be slandered again. I'm only sad that these two girls have stooped so low as to claim I would want to take the life of Calyx Eppi, a promising scientist and one of my close friends."

"We wouldn't have picked *you* to accuse if it weren't true," Aryl says. "Considering how likely it is that we'd lose."

Detective Card drums her fingers on the table as Detective Xenon watches her, scowling. "How do you explain the injuries sustained by these two apprentices in your factory?" she asks Yuan.

"Trespassing in a manufacturing center and playing with dangerous equipment has consequences," Yuan says. "They should have the sense to know that."

His words are smooth, but beads of sweat drip down his forehead in vertical lines. His skin looks like a barcode: wet, dry, wet, dry.

"They hacked into our system and found out when I would be inspecting the factory, then attacked me there. Miss Yun injected my bodyguard with ketamine when he tried to stop her from attacking my employees. You have to understand, she's not as weak as she wants us to think."

A hot blue flame ignites inside me. I nearly stand up, wanting to fight back, but Aryl clutches my hand: *Don't.*

"If what you say is true, then Yun and Fielding went through a lot to frame you," Detective Card says. "Their injuries were nearly fatal. Moreover, you had a reason to want Calyx Eppi gone and the resources to kill him. I think you tried to frame these two girls, and you nearly succeeded."

"Don't let your emotions interfere with your judgment," Yuan says.

But across the table, Kricket is shaking his head. Yuan shoots him a warning glance, but Kricket speaks anyway. "I see two ways this could end for me," he says, "and I prefer the version where I tell the truth and get a lighter sentence."

"Go on," Card says, leaning in, her flexitab and stylus at the ready.

Kricket clasps his hands together. When he speaks, his voice is flat and steady.

"Pauling Yuan murdered Calyx Eppi. And he asked me to help."

CHAPTER 55
Aryl

The room bursts into chaos, the ExSapiens crowd losing their cool all at once.

"Quiet!" shouts Detective Xenon, cutting through the protests of Yuan's associates. "Mr. Kepler, tell us more."

"Yuan promised me the funding to start my own lab as soon as I completed my apprenticeship," Kricket says. "And I accepted. All I had to do was create a distraction. Did Yuan tell me why he needed the alarm to go off? No. Did I suspect that Cal would be targeted? Again, no."

Detective Card is furiously scrawling on her flexitab.

"You're lying," I say. Kricket's too calculating to do whatever's asked of him without at least wondering why. "Claiming ignorance to protect yourself."

"Shut your mouth, Fielding," Kricket says.

I laugh, throwing my shoulders back, even though it hurts. "Ohhh, I've made you angry. I'm so scared."

"Quiet, both of you," says Detective Card. "Mr. Kepler, how did you create the distraction?"

"Benzoyl peroxide," Ver says. She mimics an explosion with her hands. *Always the first one with the answer*, I think, my heart warming.

There's no guilt in Kricket's expression—if anything, he seems proud of his biggest, final trick. "I altered the code of one of the custodial robots. A little after midnight, it slammed into the chemicals cart with the BP on it. Earlier, I'd swiped Ford's DNA from his lab coat, and I copied it, smeared it inside a glove, and left it near the explosion site so that his genetic material would be found there. My small contribution to make things even between us, Ford."

Ford glares at Kricket. "You tried to take all of us down in one go."

"It nearly worked," Kricket says, breezy as ever.

I lean over the table, and Kricket shrinks back. "You ruined our lives. Took Cal's from him. And for what? Money? You worked next to us for years, and still you sold us out."

Kricket holds up his hands. "I didn't mean for you or Ver to get hurt."

I lean back in my hoverchair. "If I were like you, Kricket, I'd want to kill you for this. But I don't. I hope you live for a long time and think about what you did every single day."

"Enough. This is all we need for now," Card says, putting her flexitab on her wrist. "Krick Kepler, you're under arrest. Pauling Yuan, do you confirm or deny Kepler's testimony that you were responsible for the murder of Calyx Eppi?"

All eyes turn to Yuan. I can see his mind flipping through so many useless words.

One of his lackeys tries to answer for him. "Excuse me, my employer does not—"

"I'm sorry," Yuan interrupts her. "I'm sorry it's come to this. I'm even sorrier that despite my greatest efforts, these moons will devolve into chaos and One will be overrun by offworlders. I was only trying to protect the order that makes life here so precious."

"At least you won't be around to see things break down," I say dryly.

Next to me, Ver laughs. My arms reach out to hold her, but our chairs aren't angled properly for a hug.

"Pauling Yuan, you're under arrest," declares Detective Card. "And we'll be dropping the charges against Ver Yun and Aryl Fielding."

Ver's face is slick with tears of relief. I start crying too. For the first time in a week, I can breathe. My family will be free. I'm free. I'm going to do science and dance and live. My future is truly mine.

And Ver! She's been released from a death sentence, and now we have so many days together to look forward to.

As for Pauling Yuan, Cal's killer—it's clear that he's convinced himself he did the right thing.

Everyone thinks they know what's best for the moons. Schoolkids, senators, farmers, factory workers. But so many of them disagree in their answer to one question: Who's human, to you?

Pauling Yuan can't accept that people from one moon are just as important as others. And with that in mind, I now understand everyone in my life—Rhea, Senator Mercure, Yuan—who's hurt me the most.

CHAPTER 56
Ver

Yuan has gone death-still. Observing him, disgust and disappointment percolating inside me, I can barely believe that all humans are made of the same elemental material. Sixty percent oxygen, eighteen percent carbon, ten percent hydrogen, and so on. How can people as different as Aryl Fielding and Pauling Yuan be identical if you zoom in close enough?

Yuan has the sense not to speak further. Instead, the middle-aged, suited-up woman on his right says, "Any further discussion regarding Pauling Yuan will take place between me, his vice executive, and the police."

Ford rushes to Aryl and me, pushing our hoverchairs together so we can hug. He wraps his arms around both of us. "It's okay," he says over and over as if he can't quite believe it.

Jaha comes to stand beside us as well. "To find the people who killed my husband, you both took risks I was unable to take," she says, resting her hand on my shoulder. "Thank you."

Kricket is sweating uncontrollably, his palms squeezed between his shaking legs. I can only imagine that his heart feels like a star-storm. I begin to feel sorry for him, until I remember what he did.

Let him burn. Let them both burn from the inside out.

CHAPTER 57
Aryl

When I'm released from the Institute hospital a week later, I'm three kilograms lighter and light-years away from dancing condition. But I'm alive, and I know I can climb to that peak of physical fitness again. All I need is patience and time.

I'm not supposed to move my arms while the soft tissue heals, and aside from walking—slowly—I'm not allowed to use my legs. It'll be excruciating, but it's better than never dancing again.

Ford escorts me back to my dorm. He walks in front of me along the lush green path, carrying my backpack, buffering me against collisions with people and bots. Above us, Pangu shines through a clear sky, blissfully ignorant of every catastrophe that's happened in the last few days.

As soon as the police dropped the charges, Ford's mom released my family from house arrest. But she refused to rehire my parents, so they've been living on what's left of their meager savings.

"I know some families who might need security and housekeeping help, and would pay well for it," Ford muses as we walk. "But they're all in Lucent City." No one in Celestine, which is more or less Mercure Town, would hire Titania's castoffs and risk upsetting her.

"Great," I say sarcastically. "Mom can ship them her food by vactrain."

"Hey, why not? As long as they pay a fair price," Ford replies.

It's early evening, and hungry apprentices are heading to dinner. A lot of them stare. Maybe it's because Ford and I are together, without a dozen friends to serve as social cushioning between us. Or maybe it's because Aryl Fielding has seemingly gone from dancing to murdering to limping over the course of a week.

"Fielding!" a man's voice calls. I hear the light pad of footsteps running toward us. It's Kandel, looking nervous—with *her*.

When I see Rhea's apologetic face, I'm hit with every feeling there is. Nostalgia lands first, for the friendship we used to share, followed by grief for its death. I'm also seething about the way she made me feel like scrap.

"I can't believe what happened to you, Aryl," Rhea says. "Everyone's talking about it—how Pauling Yuan framed you and nearly killed you."

Ford stiffens by my side, and I see Rhea glancing at him while pretending to ignore him.

"Is it true that he had a whole human made of artificial parts try to chase you down?" Kandel sounds too interested in the story—as if he's forgotten it actually *happened*. To me.

"What do you care?" I say. "Ford, let's go."

Before we can take three steps, Rhea calls, "We made a mistake, Aryl. Come back. Please."

I blink at her.

"Come dance again. It's been awful without you." She holds out her arms and rises on tiptoe, as if expecting me to fall into step with her.

Even now, I feel the old temptation—whatever Rhea wants, I'll give. But that would be an insult to everything I've gone through. How can she ask me to dance, after flaming me and my family? *You know what you are.*

Now, I'm the center of attention, the girl who's clawed her way back against all odds. I'm useful to her again.

Ford grips my shoulder. I know he agrees: they don't deserve me.

I put on my softest, most gracious voice. "Rhea. Kandel. Thank you. But I won't be dancing with you."

Kandel clears his throat. "Fielding, you're the strongest person we have. We haven't found a replacement, and we probably won't." I can tell it's killing him to admit this, and I'm filled with smug pride.

His words give me an idea too, one that warms me from the inside out. "Since I'm so valuable, I think I'll audition for real dance companies. Professional ones that tour all over One."

Rhea scoffs, the façade slipping. "You? Oh, they wouldn't even consider *you*. You can't pay for the retraining you'll need after those injuries—"

"I'll find a way," I say.

Still leaning on Ford, I straighten my back for the first time in what feels like months and stride away on legs that can only get stronger from here.

In my room, Ford helps me lower myself into a sitting position on my bed, then scoops up my legs and guides me until I'm reclining on a stack of pillows.

"Will you be okay without me?" he asks.

I nod, not wanting to burden him—though I should probably work on getting used to leaning on people from time to time. "Thanks, Ford. I mean it."

"Well, I'm off then. I have to straighten out some things in Celestine. Take care of yourself."

With a wave, he exits, leaving me alone to think about what my old—new?—friend has said.

Take care of myself? That means dancing. That means channeling everything I'm feeling through my body, in whatever way I can. If no one will dance with me, I'll dance alone.

I look at my hands, which sport only light cuts now, scabbed over. I play some mid-paced symphonic synthesizer music on the speakers my room's AI installed on my ceiling. I flex my wrists, rotating them in their sockets, forming my fingers into different shapes: a tree, a wolf, a star, changing with the phrases in the music.

This is movement and magic. Who can tell me that I'm not dancing?

When the song ends, my hands are tired, but my heart is light. I've given all I can. It'll have to be enough.

CHAPTER 58
Ver

My body heals more slowly than Aryl's, so I have spent more time in the hospital than she did. Pain lingers in my abdomen and limbs, but not to the extent that I need to escape from it into unconsciousness. An autonomous campus security vehicle picks me up and transports me from the hospital to the first-year dorm. Back in my room, I am greeted by Charles, who was bored out of his artificial mind while I was away.

"I've been reborn!" he exclaims. "I feel like I was just released from the factory."

I chuckle. "Aiyo, do not remind me of factories!"

Jaha has rented a cheap hotel room that smells like mold and perspiration. The curtains are drawn, and the one purple LED lamp flickers like a dying mouse's heartbeat. She has been evicted from her Institute-owned apartment and is staying here until she can find a new one.

She, Ford, Aryl, and I can barely fit together on the floor, especially with Dimmi's crib set up near the small circular window. Aryl chews nervously on a day-old açai croissant that the hotel's AI included in our breakfast. No one is talking. We focus on the live holo of the trial.

Trials proceed the same way every time. Evidence for the defendant's innocence or guilt is presented. The judicial computer cluster, programmed by the government to be "neutral," processes the evidence. It also accounts for the occupations, criminal histories, and "contributions to society" of the parties involved, then spits out a verdict. A five-member human jury also votes. Most of the time, the jury and the cluster agree. When they do not, more evidence is collected and the process repeats. The cluster decides the punishment based on everything it knows about the guilty party; likelihood of committing another crime, lost productivity, and family members are three major factors.

We have already seen the recorded testimony from Jaha, Devon, Ver, and me, as well as from several of Yuan's associates. In my statement, I alluded to Cal's and my research—to the possibility that spending time on G-Moon One may mitigate the symptoms of RCD. Judging by the news coverage and Neb chatter on my flexitab feed, this has made an impression on the public.

While we wait for the trial's results, we watch Yuan fidgeting inside a balloon-shaped holding pod at the police station. Hulking Osmio is at his side. Krick Kepler sits across from them. I touch the brace over my ribcage, remembering the devastating punches the bodyguard threw.

A banner slides across the bottom of the projection: *Detective Roderick Xenon retires with distinction from LCPD.* So that is his only punishment for taking a bribe. How ridiculous!

Osmio's verdict comes first. For assault, the computer delivers a guilty verdict, and the humans vote four to one in agreement. The computer promptly calculates Osmio's sentence: six years in prison.

I blink. To my disbelief, the number does not change.

Comprehension washes over me like a freezing ice bath. Six years is much shorter than I expected. My ribs might never be the same.

Kricket's face appears next. The computer calculates: guilty, and four of the five human jurors concur. The computer gives him three years in prison. And not the Sandbag—the Lucent City jail.

My eyes go wide, unblinking. There is a *crick click* as Aryl cracks her knuckles.

Three years, with parole after one. Kricket likely expected to lose his entire youth to a penal colony, but now he will have many years left after he is out. Decades to become something, still.

Finally, it is Yuan's turn. I stop fuming long enough to listen to the crimes he is accused of: manslaughter, accessory to manslaughter, invasion of privacy, bribery. I blink. Why has he not been charged with murder?

The human jury votes three-to-two: Yuan is guilty of . . . *accessory to manslaughter*? The computer cluster renders the same verdict. My stomach churns.

The cluster takes the next 6.7 seconds to decide on a sentence.

When I see the numbers flash in front of us, they take a moment to sink in.

I press my still-healing hands together and feel tears leave my eyes.

Five years in Lucent City Prison. Possibility of retrial and release after two years.

Case closed.

CHAPTER 59
Aryl

On the projection, a slow smile spreads across Pauling Yuan's face. In spite of myself, I burst out laughing. Even though I'd been prepared for a lowball figure, this is a joke.

Five years. Doesn't the cluster mean fifty-five? Five hundred fifty-five? For murdering a man, spying on countless people, conspiring to hide potentially life-saving research, and trying to kill Ver and me, you'd think Pauling Yuan would spend the rest of his life behind carbonglass. But the computer cluster never lies. It knows everything about Yuan's life, from his birthplace to his giga accomplishments. It's decided that Yuan is too important to put away for any significant amount of time.

My heartbeat speeds up, and my tense shoulders roll forward as if preparing for a fistfight. Ver's face is buried in her hands.

As if on cue, baby Dimmi starts to bawl—a stark reminder of what Yuan has taken from the universe. Not just a scientist and mentor. A man, a father, who for all his flaws should've had the chance to see his child grow up.

It's Jaha who breaks my heart. She's hunched over her crying daughter, letting their tears mix. They deserve better than this. A longer sentence for Yuan wouldn't have made up

for what they've lost, but knowing Yuan will face nano consequences makes me feel rotten inside. For all our trying, Ver and
I couldn't get justice done. This system wasn't meant to bring
us justice.

"Oh, my baby," Jaha murmurs softly. Almost like a lul-
laby. "Baby, I'm glad you learn it so young. That it's not fair.
It's not fair . . ."

$$\smile \smile \smile$$

We stay for another hour in the hotel. I try to console a crying
Dimmi with a knit blanket while the others huddle together,
checking the Neb on their flexitabs as fallout from the trial
pours in. My own flexitab lies by my feet, and it beeps with
messages, full of my parents' relief and my former teammates'
shock that Pauling Yuan—not me or Ver—killed Cal.

"I'm coming back to the Institute," Jaha says, glancing up
from her device. "My colleagues sent the message just now."

"They let you back?" I say.

"They'd be errorcodes not to," Jaha says.

All of us, the remaining members of the lab, sigh with relief.
No moving, or applying for new jobs, or going even longer without pay. Not that it'll be easy for Jaha to work among the people
who kicked her out—but that's her problem, not ours.

Jaha feeds Dimmi a bite of goopy orange baby food, and
Dimmi gurgles. "Since I signed that sponsorship deal with
ExSapiens, the company is obligated to give me four million
Feyncoins over the next two years. Now that my name's clear,
the Institute can't say no. I'm basically free money."

I pick up my flexitab and check my own messages. The
Institute has reactivated my contract, and likely Ver's too.

Maybe they knew it would look bad if they didn't take us back, but I can't help hoping they also believe in us—if not as the decent human beings we are, then at least as promising scientists. In any case, I'm not surprised that they waited to contact us until after the verdicts. As far as they were concerned, we were on trial today too.

"Does anyone know who the new head of ExSapiens will be?" Ver asks.

"The board will duke it out among themselves," Ford says. "In business and politics, these power vacuums always get filled the same way. Nepotism and negotiation. But whoever steps up to lead them, ExSapiens will probably pull Telomar from the market. The Senate's probing their business practices as we speak, and Mom's leading a vote for tighter regulation of the medical industry."

At the mention of Senator Mercure, my hands start to tremble, and so does my voice when I turn to Ford. "Ford, your mom . . . my family . . ."

A smile spreads across Ford's face. "Forget my mom. I bought your family tickets to Lucent City so they can celebrate your exoneration with you. And I've set up some job interviews for your parents here. The best prep schools are also taking an interest in Ester. If my glowing recommendations are well received, they could all live here while you finish your apprenticeship."

I grin at him, nerves thrumming with joy. I'm not sure which is making me happier: my family finding brighter futures in Lucent City, or Ford doing good deeds without worrying about the consequences. "You mean—?"

"I mean, you should check the hotel lobby. Right about"—he glances at his flexitab—"now."

My heart pounds as Ford helps Ver and me to the elevator. We ride down to the tiny lobby, which is decorated in shimmering metallic fractal patterns that swirl enough to make you dizzy.

Standing by the entrance are my parents and sister, their million reflections sparkling. Ester looks disoriented. Dad's swallowing tears. Mom is full-on weeping.

"Sweetgum!" Dad calls out. "My baby."

I let out a wordless joyful shout. Despite the fact that I'm still healing from my injuries, they wrap me in all six of their arms, pulling me closer until we don't know whose tears are falling on whose face.

For weeks, I've feared losing them. But now, enveloped by these three, with Ford and Ver looking on, I'm more than relieved. I haven't lost anyone. My family has only grown.

Ver

The night our antichronowave study is published, the stars dance, and so do we.

On the top floor of BioLabs, twenty stories high, we hover above most of Lucent City's light pollution. Jaha arranged for our lab to relocate here, and her funding will more than pay for the ongoing renovations to adapt the space to our needs. It made no sense to return to work in the old lab, where we were all traumatized.

The quarter-sphere, floor-to-ceiling window reveals the wonders of the sky to anyone patient enough to stand here and watch. A trio of ice-covered blue comets, the Snow Sisters, is racing past G-Moon One tonight on its lasso of a path around Pangu. I imagine it zipping, whistling by. Leaving fragments of other worlds in its wake.

Tonight's sky is so clear, I can see Sol. Burning yellow somewhere behind a brighter neighbor. Releasing photons that have traveled billions of kilometers to bless my eyes.

But the brightest, nearest lights come from approaching spaceships from Two and Three. Ships filled with people riding on a last hope.

Some people do not welcome them, but they do not

understand history. Even before there were humans on these moons to build spaceships, chunks of G-Moons One, Two, and Three would break off and smash into the others. Those collisions built and shaped the magnificent landscapes on each moon. Exchange of material is inevitable in a planetary system due to the high velocities involved in a multitude of objects orbiting other objects.

Billions of years ago, all of these moons formed from the same material, spat out by a young Pangu. More recently, all the humans living on the Gui Moons originated from the same Earth. With that history in mind, I think as I watch the skies, anyone should be free to fly where they want.

Jaha's new lab space is a work in progress, but I approve of these windows—and of the walls, painted in a celebration of the visible spectrum. One is hot pink, another lilac, yet another the soft blue of Lake Celestine. The nursery Jaha has made in a corner of her office is pale green, which seems to be Dimmi's favorite color. Cal would have approved.

From my workstation, I can see G-Moon Three rising. Only one other station, Aryl's, is occupied. Ford has been cleared to finish his apprenticeship thanks to the antichronowave detector he built. Strange to think I will be showing new apprentices around soon. Stranger still to imagine Ford jumping into politics. He will start as a local official in Celestine and work his way to the top, hoping to eventually take his mother's place. And I hope—I know—that he will be fairer and kinder to the moons than she has been. Based on priors, Ford will do just fine.

"You're done for today, Ver," Aryl says, dancing up to my workstation. Swish, glide, *whoosh*. Her rehabilitation therapies have done her wonders. She has started stretching and turning again, with jumps to come.

I have been tracking the views and comments on our newly published article, in which we detailed how antichronowaves are densest near One and fade out at Three, how my body reacted to being on each of these moons, and how blasting cells with antichronowaves in a lab setting slows their aging and decay. *Blasphemous claims*, people are writing. Some of those people are investigators at the Institute, older and more highly regarded than we. The harshest critics even accuse us of fabricating the data, though it has passed rigorous review.

Journalists have picked up the story, speculating about a "medical migration" to One. But that is already happening, inspired by the evidence we submitted for Yuan's trial. A meteor shower of passenger ships is falling to this moon. I have viewed multiple holograms of sick people testing out their legs on One's soil. A pair of ten-year-old twins with RCD gazing up in wonder at Lucent City's tallest buildings was the image that struck my heart the hardest.

"We've done all we can for now," Aryl says—that soft rustle of her vocal cords, vibrating air molecules cajoling the hairs on my neck to stand at attention. "Will you dance with me?"

I twist around and slowly rise. Put my hand in Aryl's. My body still aches when I wake up every morning, but thanks to the sub-cellular injections of actin, myosin, collagen, and other structural proteins the doctors gave me to heal my injuries, I am managing. The antichronowave barrage on G-Moon One helps too.

And so does the peace I am finally starting to feel.

I put on one of the new songs Charles played for me recently. It streams from the surround-sound audio system Ford built for the new lab. The music is simple: human voices ranging across different pitches, layering notes into different sonic colors. Melancholy, at times, but always resolving into sweetness.

Our movements constitute more of a slow shuffle than a dance. We sway from side to side and turn in circles, tracing an undefined shape over the open portion of the lab. Above us, more ships full of offworlders streak toward us, their taillights creating a blaze in the sky.

Tomorrow and after, we will find ways to help the people inside those ships, many of whom have come here based on our word.

Tomorrow, we will meet them. But tonight, it is enough to watch them shine.

Author's Note

When I started writing this book, I'd just entered a PhD program to earn the highest qualification for an aspiring scientist. I'd spent my life mucking around in nature and in labs, thinking that hard work and love for discovery would carry me through grad school.

I was quickly proven wrong.

A chronic back injury caused stabbing pains in my legs, and it naturally impacted my studies. For two years, I walked with a cane, could not sit comfortably, and consulted every medical specialist around. I needed accommodations in class and lab, encountering bewilderment and often cruelty from the people around me. Even though I slowly recovered mobility thanks to Chinese medicine and physical therapy, I couldn't forget how chronic pain had made me feel. In this book, I wanted to depict complexity in how Ver navigates the world: her disability doesn't mean she's any less of a person, it doesn't define her, and yet she has the right to search for ways to ease her own existence and that of others with her condition.

As I continued in my science career, I learned that to some people, what was in my brain didn't matter as much as how I looked. Neuroscience is a male-dominated field. On top of being a woman, I was also Chinese American. It felt like no professor wanted me in his lab. When I was bullied or excluded because of my gender and skin color, the university did nothing. After a year and a half of searching for a scientific home, I joined a lab that gave me a chance to do exciting science on mosquito brains, tracing the neurons and synapses that enable them to sense human prey. But I will always empathize with many of the challenges faced by scientists with identities outside the "norm."

Science must include everyone. Science is *better* when everyone participates, as Ver and Aryl show with their investigations. Soon, I hope, people of all identities will be welcome to illuminate our world without questioning whether they're the "right" kind of person. We are a long way from that ideal. Maybe things will get better.

Maybe people like you are going to make it better.

Acknowledgments

This book was my "science feelings" book. Writing it helped me work through the intersection of doing neuroscience with all of my identities: Chinese, female, second-generation immigrant, queer, and more. It would not exist without the efforts and support of so many people.

Veronica Park took on, edited, and championed this story, all while making me laugh on every phone call. Tricia Skinner continues to go above and beyond as my agent, encouraging me to write the things I'm scared to write. I'm tempted to send cookies to everyone at Fuse Literary for their excellence in everything they do. At Lerner/Carolrhoda, Amy Fitzgerald's magic touch and deep connection to the story turned our shared vision into a real book. Thanks also to cover designer Viet Chu and the rest of the Lerner team, including creative director Danielle Carnito, production editor Erica Johnson, copyeditor Heidi Mann, and publicist Megan Ciskowski.

This manuscript went through countless drafts and is readable thanks to the superhumans who suffered through the early ones: Genevieve Gagne-Hawes, Romina Garber, Laura Rueckert, Karuna Riazi, Mia Council, Julia Byers, and Jess Creaden. Ryan La Sala, Ryan Dalton, Shveta Thakrar,

Gabe Cole Novoa, Kemi Ashing-Giwa, and Dahlia Adler came in strong with the publishing advice and generosity that I needed. I deeply appreciate the friendship of authors Rona Wang, Angela Paolini, Nivair Gabriel, Diana Pinguicha, Kylie Lee Baker, and Birukti Tsige. Kim McDonald, your illustration of Ver and Aryl is breathtaking!

Applause to booksellers, librarians, and teachers for bringing stories to readers, especially those who hunger to see themselves and their friends in literature. (Special shoutout to Cody Roecker for their boundless knowledge and energy!) I'm so grateful to bloggers, BookTokers, podcasters, and reviewers, who spread the word far and wide, and who've made the online book community a wonderful place to hang out and find my next read.

I'm indebted to the friends and family who looked out for me during this time. Even as I saw doctors and went through treatment for chronic pain, a global pandemic and challenges in my day job made it tough to keep on writing. But thanks to you, I did. Thank you all for being there.

Finally, to readers: Thank you for giving my words a chance. Thank you for sharing my world.

Questions for Discussion

1. What assumptions do Ver and Aryl initially make about each other? When do those assumptions first seem to shift for each of them?

2. Why has Ver become so attached to Cal? In what ways has Cal exploited her and acted inappropriately?

3. How does Aryl feel about being a child of immigrants? How do these feelings drive her actions?

4. What do Aryl and Ver come to admire about each other? What makes them a good team?

5. How is the justice system of the Gui Moons different from and similar to the justice system of the United States?

6. Aryl reflects, "I think it's crass to *buy* superhuman strength and install it onto your body instead of working to build it naturally like I have." Do you agree? Why or why not?

7. In what ways do Ver's experiences with her fictional condition, RCD—and with other people's reactions to it— echo experiences that people may have in the real world?

8. Why did Aryl's friendship with Ford collapse? How do they begin to repair it?

9. Why has Jaha been jealous of Ver? Why does Jaha's attitude toward Ver change?

10. Were you surprised by the identity of Cal's murderer? Why or why not?

About the Author

Karen Jialu Bao does science in the lab, then goes home and writes about it. A PhD candidate at Harvard University, she studies mosquito brains by blasting them with an electron beam. Her favorite activities include cooking, tending her plants, singing, and playing her violin. She is the author of the Dove Chronicles sci-fi trilogy and a contributor to the YA mental health anthology *Ab(solutely) Normal*.